Galahad's Fool

ALSO BY BISHOP & FULLER

Realists (a novel)
Co-Creation: Fifty Years in the Making (a memoir)
Mythic Plays: from Inanna to Frankenstein
Rash Acts: 35 Snapshots for the Stage
Frankenstein (DVD)
The Tempest (DVD)
King Lear (DVD)
Descent of the Goddess Inanna (DVD)

Available at
www.DamnedFool.com

Bishop & Fuller

Galahad's Fool
— a novel —

WordWorkers Press
Sebastopol, CA

Galahad's Fool

© 2018 Conrad Bishop & Elizabeth Fuller

All rights reserved.

This work is fully protected under the copyright laws of the United States of America and all other countries of the Copyright Union.

No part of this publication may be reproduced in any form without prior permission of the copyright owners.

For information:

Bishop & Fuller
eye@independenteye.org

For purchase:

www.DamnedFool.com

ISBN 978-0-9997287-0-3
LCCN 2017919736

Cover design; Nessgraphica

CONTENTS

I

Of the Puppetmaster Albert and of his lost Lady

With puppets, the soul is in the eyes. That's what a critic wrote about the Fisher Folks' *Orpheus* twenty years ago. Now, shivering in an April cold snap, Albert Fisher sat at his workbench, groping for a soul.

He finished painting the white of an eye, turned the glass glob between his thumb and forefinger, picked up its mate, and met their gaze: a steely glint of cruelty. He sighed and thumbed the paint off the back of the glass. He'd try again after lunch.

Never, in all these years, had he started with the eyes. Normally he would glop clay onto the armature, knead it to a vaguely humanoid shape, then follow the clues that its bumps and hollows gave him. Sometimes the face might resemble his charcoal sketches. More often, the clay guided his fingers, teasing an odd bulge into a beetle brow or a doorknob chin. Macbeth had wound up with the pointy face of a weasel aspiring to lionhood. Caliban evolved into a baby-faced Algerian with a harelip, a more disturbing blemish than the gross deformity Albert had envisioned. Those features lay in the clay, and he was only the midwife, not the dad.

But Sir Galahad was no clay-bound mortal. He was the well-scrubbed hero whose soul, if he had one, would shine in the eyes—firm jawbone soon to follow. Fellow puppeteers had always admired Albert's eyes: simple hobby-store glass globs, one side flat, one curved. On the flat side, he painted the pupil, then iris, then white. The frontal curvature caught the light like a natural eye, and the soul would be coaxed in like a feral cat, as Albert once joked to an interviewer. It was touchy work: a minute shift in the pupil might glitch its DNA, begetting a sensualist, a saint, a serial killer, or the blithering idiot that Albert saw on his driver's license. After two or three scratchings-out, he'd usually get it right. "Thanks be to the thumbnail of evolution," his wife Lainie used to joke.

Now, every nuance eluded him. The eyes glared back, implacably cruel. Yesterday, in a fit of exasperation, he'd given Galahad the wall-eyed ogle of the Mad Hatter from their staging of *Alice Underground* that a reviewer had called "the Muppets on acid." Whatever he did, these eyes seemed to threaten: *Right now I'm too tired to focus, but when I do I'll kill you dead.*

Albert tossed the globs back into their plastic cup, brushed the paint crumbs off his shirt, and switched off the radio perched on a shelf among wire, gaff tape, and thermoplastic above his table—then realized it was already off. He swiveled to face the open space of the disheveled studio.

In the outbuilding adjoining their house, he and Lainie had worked for weeks installing a sprung floor and insulation, painting the walls dark maroon, and piecing together beige carpet scraps to define a rehearsal area. After decades of scrounging for work space, they could now build, rehearse and light a whole show right in their own digs, commuting a distance of fifteen yards to work. They couldn't put in a toilet or heater without some goddamned license from the county, but it was only a few steps to the house to piss or to thaw or to come in for dinner. In the far corner was Albert's workbench with its pegboard, its shelves, its racks. Lainie had rewired the building for heavier amperage and replaced their ancient tour dimmers with DMX—ready for the next decade of theatrical triumph. It had felt so permanent.

Now he surveyed a junkyard. Soon he'd have to root out the gnarl: repack storage bins, shelve spotlights, sort boxes of props and bags of upchucked fabric. He felt the clutter moving in on him like crabgrass, but there was no time to deal with it now. As Lainie used to say in mock horror, he was pregnant again.

Why? He had no monetary need for a new project. Social Security and savings from their fat years paid the bills, plus royalties from a couple of plays he'd written that were still being produced by people, as he joked, who didn't know any better. No new story was burning to be told. But the anniversary was coming up—May 10th—so it must be that he needed the distraction. Anniversaries could be lethal.

Flicking off the light, he pulled the door shut to keep out the feral cats, walked across the yard to the house, grabbed his jacket from the hook. Weather for the past six months had been as screwball as his dreams. Global warming, he feared, was less the result of CO_2 than of a worldwide updraft of rage from the human race. No, dammit, he thought, stop stewing over planetary doom. Walk to town, have a cup of coffee, get your ass out of the meat grinder and your head out of the swamp.

He walked down the driveway, leaving the Honda to snooze away the morning. At least he'd remembered to set out the garbage can for pick-up. Keeping up with the chores was progress. He was worming his way out of a year's frigid numbness just in time to feel springtime stab him in the face.

The springs he recalled from his youth were incurably Midwestern, advancing one careful step at a time, so he was still startled by Northern California's frenzy of blossoming. He took the back road down past the Valenzuelas' house and the dog-trainer's field. Flowers in profusion: lilacs and wisteria drizzling extravagant fertility, a stand of pampas grass ten feet high, a tiny lemon tree poking forth buds for another flirtation with bees, a red maple afire with morning sun.

He used to loved walking here. Along the left side of the road, an aqua-blue fence shielded the yard of a mysterious soul who didn't want to be seen. On the right, he passed a hairy eucalyptus grove, plum trees covered with lichen, and a tangle of manzanita that stirred Boy Scout memories of trying to tie a sheet-bend. Through the bare studs of a ruined barn, he glimpsed an orgasm of bushes all in pink and apple trees in opulent blossom: bridesmaids lined up in their finest array.

Why had he walked this way? It was all a flood of life. He didn't need floods of life right now. He needed anesthesia.

In town, he went into Friendly Joe's, not his favorite coffee shop but closer than the others. He ordered an Americano and a chocolate chip cookie, which came to $4.91. The barista said to forget the penny, but he insisted he was trying to get rid of pennies, then had to root in his pocket to find one. Was this coffee actually better than when it cost a quarter?

He found a table along a wall with large gawky paintings of naked ladies, not quite naked enough, and looked around to see if any other old guys were there with their gray ponytails, doggy eyes, and dingy workshirts. None today: he was the only one. He uncrinkled a loose page of the Arthurian story he'd tried to write five years ago and read the start of his comic riff:

Friends, do you know what you're looking for? A new
Mercedes, a trip to Cancun? Sweet wife, two kids
and a dog, and a hot babe on the side?
But if you think you'll be happy with that, you're so
fulla shit. You know what you're really looking for?
You are looking for the Grail.

"Are there different kinds of asparagus or just one?" one
of the baristas asked the other. Albert had an urge to log onto
Wi-Fi and check that out, but he resisted.

The what? Well, the Grail, the Holy Grail, the Sangreal.
For Christians, this was the mug from the Last
Supper. For the Celts, it held healing waters. For
Muslims, some kinda wash basin, maybe.
But they all agreed it would bring us joy and rapture,
and somebody must have left it someplace—but
nobody's got a clue.

A kid got up, put on his backpack, said goodbye to his
friends, mentioned a concert he wasn't going to. Neither were
they, they said. A portly man was talking politics with a slicked-
back older woman; both agreed that life on Earth was doomed
but the weather was nice today. A black girl, crouched in the
corner, had a laptop exactly like his, though hers was covered
with stickers.

For the Knights of the Table Round, this was their big
thing. They'd sit round the Table Round, boozing,
ho-ho-ing, and every now and again somebody gets
off his butt, yells, "Tally-ho for the Holy Grail!"
Week or so, he comes back dented. "Well, did you find
it?" "No, man, it's a pisser."

A couple of tables down, a skinny man in a stocking cap,
pine-needle hair shooting out the sides, was spinning a yarn to
his girlfriend about the proper technique for gelding swine. It
was hard to concentrate on Camelot when the world held such
richness.

And then there was Sir Galahad: the noblest and deadli-
est bore of them all. He's out there really shagging
ass for the Holy Grail. Swatting guys off horses,
whacking the black knight, whacking the blue knight,
he's on a roll, and he swears by all that's holy, "I'm
gonna find! that! Grail!"

Cute, Al, but it's a one-trick monkey. You're like that guy
rambling on about pigs' balls. What's the story? Finding the

unfindable? Story of some old fart with a frantic need to be telling a story? Lainie had never responded to that old Galahad riff, so he'd let it drop. For him, writing was like lovemaking: if your partner didn't react, what was the point? After those teen years when sex was basically an excretory function—*O blessed relief!*—lovemaking was about bonding, sharing the flow with this creature who was shaped so peculiarly. Storymaking was no different. If it didn't spur the cry, the moan, the chortle from your beloved, why bother? Galahad roused no chortle.

You know the problem, Al: you don't give a shit about Sir Galahad. You've just picked an old whim out of the Miscellaneous folder because it might be an easy spoof, like the Monty Python movie. Maybe a half-hour piece for library shows and a raunchy version for the puppet-slam fringe. But why Galahad? Why not *Cinderella* from the pumpkin's point of view? *Goldilocks* as a fable of Western imperialism? A kiddie version of *Medea*? There were loads of half-baked ideas filed under Miscellaneous. Elevator music to mute the blaring silence.

"What's happ'nin', Al?" A short, bubbly fireplug of a man waved from the counter, lofting his carry-out.

Albert knew that he knew him, but couldn't think how. The problem with performing: they know you, or think they do, but you don't have a clue. Dave something, or maybe Rudy? Riley? Randy? "Hi, how you doing?"

"I'm good, I'm good," said the little man. "How's your lady?"

How's Lainie? Doesn't the whole world know? Lainie is stark, stone, cold-butt, icy-boob dead.

Albert took a slow breath and mumbled a line from one of his plays: "She's peaceful." Rudy, Randy, whoever, waved and went out the door.

She had died quietly in a coma, early morning as the light began. He had drifted off in the hospice armchair, woke to an irregularity in her breathing. A few moments later, the breathing stopped. There was a slight jerk in her chest. He looked toward the window as if expecting to see her there but saw only the silhouette of flowers against the dawn. Then he looked back to her face, knowing that she was gone. He felt nothing. No white-water rush, no shock. He felt what she felt: absence. They were too closely attuned.

It was coming up on a year now, early May. He recalled the rainy spring weather, odd for the season, during the weeks after the death. He thought of it only as *the death*, like *the wedding* or *the birth*. Mara had come to be with him then. He'd been grateful for his daughter's help, cooking meals and juggling the logistics of disposal, but it was torture being the object of concern while knowing the depth of Mara's own pain and having not one damned word, of the hundreds of thousands he'd written, that could touch it. He couldn't even find his own grief: he'd misplaced it somehow. His heart was a dead shopping mall, an acre of concrete, old signage for K-Mart and Target standing like snaggly teeth in ravaged gums.

Time to get home. He folded the Galahad page and made a little rip in the fold. Eyes glued to the road, he walked back. Tonight he should struggle with the tax forms, though he'd filed for an extension. Last year he'd still had Lainie to coach him through the accounting. They'd both laughed at the oddity of his taking instructions from a woman with tubes in her nose. And now he felt a familiar twinge of preposterous, infantile rage at Lainie for being dead.

He sat to check email. Junk, junk, junk, and what was this? An inquiry about *Orpheus* from a festival in Italy. Ye gods, *Orpheus*! How long could you be haunted by success? Their one piece that really took off: rave reviews, touring all over the States and to festivals in Scotland, France, and Brazil. A beautiful piece, he had to admit, and remarkable in telling a story about song with no music whatever. Orpheus' voice was simply a moving hand.

> *Dear Festival Director,*
> *Very sorry, but it's out of repertoire. Grateful for your*
>   *interest.*
> *Sincerely, Albert Fisher.*

He felt a rising in his throat. Tears never flowed in him, only a strangled yawning. He might choke out a ridiculous sneeze of grief, nothing more. Those five months, from her first symptoms to the end, had been the proverbial actor's nightmare: you don't know the lines or even the name of the play, you try to improvise, but it all falls into a hideous mess. Though you couldn't really call it a nightmare: you always woke from nightmares.

When in doubt, work. Out to the studio for a while. On the way, he glanced at the garden—what had been the garden, now only weeds. Every year Lainie had expanded the planting, arguing sustainability but just plain loving to plunge her fingers into the dirt. This year it had tried to seed itself, sprouting haggard collards, frazzled fennel, a vagrant squash vine, and raspberries running riot—the last remnants of the garden that was Lainie.

Albert sat at the work table, scooped up a lump of clay, and slabbed it onto the armature. With an in-draw of breath, he reached out to the place where the eyes would be and dug in his thumbs.

II

Of Sir Galahad's true History and of a straying Child

Here's the twist. Young Galahad burns with lust for the Holy Grail. When he finds it, he'll be raptured to Heaven, his ashes floating down like fairy dust on a bleeding world. But in fact he never does. Sure, the legends give him angel choirs and ticker-tape parades, but if he had actually found the Grail, it'd be perched in the Louvre or in some Vegas casino.

Instead, Galahad gets older, tires of horsing around, marries, settles down. He's got this ranch-style castle out in the suburbs where he sits on the patio with his beautiful wife and grows a belly. Sir Bors and Sir Percival drop in for a poker night. No TV back then, so they just flip on a minstrel, toss a pork rib at him to change the channel, and he sings of his boss's glorious deeds, just as he's paid to do.

Albert sat at Lainie's desk and wrote whatever came into his head. He gazed out at the scraggly yard, watching the two feral cats in their choreography of status at the food bowl. Last night he had dug into his sack of clay—he preferred the texture of water-base to plasticene—hoping it might be dried out so it'd take a few days to soak before coming to a usable consistency. But it was ready to go; he wasn't. What was he thinking? He never started sculpting until he had a script, and right now he didn't have even a stammer.

So Galahad settles in, drinks more than he should. He defends the Faith, sponsors a hot-shot painter to paint the Nativity, with Magi shoving for front-row seats while he and his wife kneel in their Sunday best. His Lady loves him. She still seems to see the young knight with the blinding vision, his eyes clear as amber. But Galahad, gazing on the chapel crucifix, has to admit that even the dying Savior was in better shape than he is. He hates his belly.

He still thinks about the Grail, but it's on the back burner, like that trip to Disney World. Bards can't even agree what to call it: the Grail, the Holy Grail, the Graal, the Sangreal—an endless game of name-that-goblet. More pressing are his duties to his family, his vassal knights, his clergy, his yeomen, his servants, and his peasants.

Peasants. Those damned peasants. Cheating on their taxes, poaching deer, beating their wives, starving their kids, living like pigs. Hard to believe they're even human: humans couldn't stand to live like that. When he sees a skeletal child, he can't help feeling its pain. Yet he knows that poverty and disease are the judgments of God upon their intractable sloth. These creatures work sluggishly from dawn to dusk, while his own cares stretch deep in the night.

Dead end. Albert was rambling on, scribbling to no purpose. He saw this riff drifting into politics, and whenever he let that happen, depression started an intractable munch on his head. He could have fun with Galahad if he didn't get serious. Maybe he needed to frame the story differently, see it through other eyes—some little kid who'd read about King Arthur, made a stick sword, and chased the dog around the house. Maybe a family of tourists at some English castle, and the kid wanders off—

That could work. The kid's naïve vision would be a bridge to the story. The family could be touring Tintagel— No, Tintagel had been the digs of King Arthur's mom, and it was in ruins now. This was a job for Google. Albert searched *English castles*. Lindisfame, Pevensey, Warwick— Yes, Warwick might do it. Built in 1068, it saw lots of pillage and slaughter, then was purchased in 1968 by Madame Tussaud's. *Britain's Ultimate Castle*, they called it, the perfect tourist trap for Mr. and Mrs. Armbruster and their little son Bobby or Jimmy or Tim, destined to wander through time in a puppet show. Not a deathless concept, but it would serve, at least for library shows.

Albert envisioned the family in a small tour group led by a uniformed guide, crossing the cobblestone courtyard toward a crenelated tower, and caught snatches of conversation.

"I'd just like to get back to our room before it gets late."

"We spend this much for admission and then run off?"

"Well, you were the one that wanted—"

"I just said a castle would be educational, and this one had the best website."

"Weird to pick a castle for its website."

Albert caught himself. He was pumping out a few cheap laughs. He and Lainie had had countless quarrels during their travels, but they'd never sounded that stupid. Or had they? Memory was as slippery as soap in the shower. Keep it light, but make it real. Say the couple were in their late thirties when Bobby came along—a total surprise—just as she was going back to school and he was changing jobs. The guy edited technical manuals, maybe, and she worked in a realtor's office. Bobby was one more ball to juggle. They always felt imperfect as parents, rattling too fast through the bedtime story or forgetting that Bobby could hear all the explosions and screams on the evening news. Light but real. Lightly real.

§

Bobby ran to catch up with his parents. His dad was fiddling with the camera, his mom jabbering as she pointed at one of the dials. The clutch of tourists walked toward the tower.

"Mommy? Is this where King Arthur lived?"

"Well, he might have. You liked that story, huh?"

His father interrupted. "No, Bobby, I told you. That was Glastonbury or Cadbury and those are a long way away, but this one is just the same. Actually it's in much better shape and there's a snack bar."

"What about Sir Galahad?"

"He didn't live anywhere. He was like a superhero, he traveled around and searched for the Holy Grail."

"What's that?"

"It's a gold cup or something. Nobody knows."

"It was the cup that Jesus passed around at the Last Supper," said Mom, "but only the bravest knight could find it, and that was Sir Galahad."

"What about Jesus?"

"He wasn't a knight," Dad said. "He was dead. We need to catch up."

The group went through the archway into the tower. Bobby followed, but just as he reached the archway a shadow fell across the stones. He turned, expecting to see a giant looming in front of the sun.

It was Sir Galahad. He was wearing armor with a cross on the breastplate, so it must be Sir Galahad. The boy stood stock still, his own shadow shrinking. The storybook Galahad was young and blond and smiled all the time. This one looked older and redder, more like Daddy when Mommy told him he'd had enough wine.

"Damned peasants," mumbled the Knight in Shining Armor.

There were soldiers. They held a skinny man in dirty clothes, like the people that Mommy called "homeless" and Daddy called "bums." Bobby thought of his friend Ralph, when the teacher caught him taking an extra cookie. Maybe the man's name was Ralph, because his friend Ralph's pants had holes in the knees and this man was raggedy too. Or in the King Arthur story there was a funny dumb guy named Rolf, and the kids all teased Ralph and called him Rolf, so maybe this was Rolf.

"Thy name?" Galahad's voice was low and flat, like the janitor at school. No telling if he was happy or sad.

"Rolf," the skinny man said. Maybe he was Ralph's grandpa, because this was back in the Old Days.

They'd caught Rolf poaching rabbits, brought him to Sir Galahad after beating him up. Bobby didn't know what poaching was, but it seemed a mean thing to do to rabbits. He turned to ask Mommy, but she wasn't there. Suddenly he was scared.

Galahad spoke. "Art thou a good Christian, Rolf?" The man didn't say. "Thou art, surely," said the Knight, "and so thou knowest God's justice." They all stood there. Bobby remembered when his class was laughing and the principal came in the door and said, "Well, children?" and then just stood there. They had to put their heads down on their desks and be ashamed for ten minutes. Rolf didn't look ashamed. "The law, Rolf: hands that steal must be lost."

A little round man in a cassock—a priest?—popped out from behind Sir Galahad. "If thine eye offend thee, pluck it out!" said Father Olyver and popped back out of sight.

The ragged man stared Galahad in the face. Like Bobby's friend Ralph: he'd never say "I'm sorry" to the teacher, he'd just stand there and stare. He knew he was bad, but he wasn't sorry about it. Now Rolf stood there, looking Galahad straight in the eye. A soldier poked him to talk.

"How should I live without hands?" he said. "How pay taxes, feed my children? The rabbits were gifts from God."

The little round Priest popped out again. "Devil's words!"

Rolf turned toward the Priest, as far as the soldiers let him. "Reverend Father, a hundred men would say it if they dared. We do our work, we pay our taxes, our tithes, and our children starve. How does it serve God that His little ones starve?"

"Ungrateful wretch! Thy duty is only to labor, to feed, then sleep. Who looks to the future? Who wrestles the demons pervading the world that would do thee harm? Who is appointed by God to dispense the justice of God?"

"Those who pay you to tell me that."

"My son," said Father Olyver in a tone of deep compassion, "mercy is the province of God. For thy master to offer mercy would be to usurp the role of God."

Galahad cringed at the fatuous words. He hated the role he'd been cast in: landholder, liege lord, judge and jury. Killing in warfare was something else. Those he killed were full participants in the kill. You thrust, and when it went to the heart you felt an agreement. The wild boar, the king stag, the ax-wielding Saxon, the recreant knight—they accepted that thrust like a brother. But killing a weaponless creature—Galahad choked down bile.

The peasant was trembling to the core. His breath was shallow and his eyes wide at the punishment to come. He had seen it twice before and knew he might spare himself the worst. Yet Galahad, in his warrior's heart, saw that he faced a fearless man.

"Hear me!" Rolf shouted, and his words burned into Galahad like the brand to the breast of a whore. "May God bring to you what you bring to me! Let you go begging on bended knee! Let your dearest creature die! Drink your own tears!"

The curse reverberated in the hollow skull of an elderly puppeteer.

Let you go begging on bended knee.

Let your dearest creature die.

Drink your own tears.

Bobby knew you shouldn't talk to grown-ups like that. Galahad gave the orders and strode away. The soldiers threw the peasant onto the cobblestones to start the long, sweaty job they had to do, and Bobby's mother asked her husband, "Where's Bobby?"

§

Albert stopped dead. All this for a puppet show? Turn off the freeway onto two-lane asphalt, veer onto a dirt track, and finally wind up in a scruffy trailer yard with a derelict fridge and a snarling mutt. This magnum opus would involve at least five puppeteers, three dozen puppets, a year of building, and who would ever want to see it? In one scribble he had a lost child, a corpulent hero, and a peasant getting his hands chopped off. What would he do for the kiddie version, just dock the ears?

He needed Lainie to tell him this was a lousy idea or else to licence him to commit them to another loony bin. After a lifetime of birthing shows, being slammed with postpartum depression, then hopping buck naked into the next impregnation, he just goddamn needed his partner in crime. The results over the years were one daughter and thirty-odd shows, spawned from their writhing DNA. Now the daughter lived in Spain, the puppets were packed into bins, and Lainie was ashes in a pot.

Ashes. Not long after they'd met and ignited, they took an overnight camping trip to Salt Point, a state park on the ocean just off Highway 1. He made a campfire, and she brewed a magical minestrone. As she poured it, he looked at her and laughed. Her nose was white with ash. She retaliated for the mirth, they fell into a fit of hysterical parry and smudge. At last, two ashen-faced ghosts dived into the tent, stripped, and made wondrous love. That's how they made their best work: funny or tragic, but always intense. Albert Fisher had never tried smudging his nose alone. Afterward, he recalled, they warmed up the soup and ate themselves silly.

Ashes now. When the fog of depression rolled in, his instinct was to focus on minutiae. If you're falling into the pit, one slurp away from the cyanide, then it's time to catalogue your CDs. Watching the sea go red and the mountains burn? Fix supper.

Spaghetti again? He heated the water, remembering for once to bring it to a boil before putting in the spaghetti sticks. He minced the garlic and onion, tweaked chorizo into spiky clots and started it browning, poured a glass of wine, and envisioned Galahad's wife watching in the courtyard.

With her lady-in-waiting, she stood in the chapel entry. Diminutive, fine-featured, fair hair done up in Celtic knotwork, she watched in silence. Could she hear what was being said? Would Galahad fear she'd think him cruel? No, the Knight would see only that she was present. He would turn away from the prisoner to show that he was pure as Pontius Pilate.

Concentrate on the cooking, dammit. Was it time to add the tomato sauce? He poured in the last jar that Lainie had canned.

Stir the sauce, turn down the burner, add some oregano, or was it thyme? No. Yes. He needed Lainie there to tell him what tasted good. "Know thyself," said the sage, but *himself,* Albert felt, was a pretty boring guy. Try the oregano, what the hell.

The sauce congealed, the spaghetti buckled under, and soon he was sitting at the kitchen table cranking the slithery strands on his fork. Not bad. He sipped a second glass of wine as Mrs. Armbruster cried out.

The parents dashed around the spruced-up ruins of Albert's brain searching for their son, though there was hardly anywhere to search. At Tintagel there would have been rubble to delve, and Bobby might have been found behind a crumbling wall. But here the grounds were manicured to 21st century sterility, leaving no trace of the disappeared. They rushed to alert the tour guide. They hadn't seen Bobby watching the peasant flung to the ground. They hadn't seen the throng of stone-faced villagers or the gaunt, hook-nosed woman, children clutching her skirts, whose eyes were fixed on a husband sprawled on the cobbles.

Albert took a full gulp of wine. Why this layering of realities, story within story? It was already tangled like spaghetti glopped with too much sauce. With a dry chuckle, Albert pictured the reaction of Mom and Dad if they knew their whole lives—their work, their failings, their fate—were the whim of an old puppeteer who'd drunk too much wine.

And who, he mused, was creating *his* story? Who was rendering him lovable, despicable, or pathetic—a tipsy dude on the verge of a trip he hadn't packed for? No bags, no maps, and his passport had expired. The peasant's wife cried to the soldiers to kill her man instead of doing what they'd been charged to do, and as soon as they started their day's work, Albert knew that the Quest would begin. He wasn't ready to make this trip.

He lured the last strands of spaghetti onto his fork, realizing that he hadn't actually tasted the food he'd eaten. Thyme? Oregano? Some gray-green fluff that brought to mind Lainie's comment one early spring as they were driving down the coast from Oregon. "Here, all around us, the hills are green," she said, "but the hills in the distance are this deep gray-blue. When we get there, they'll be green. So is the color what they are now, or what they'll be?" He was sure he'd said something funny in reply, but he couldn't remember what.

Albert never wept. Almost never. Well, his mom had given him a birthday party when he was five. There were games, and he should have won pin-the-tail-on-the-donkey because it was his birthday, after all. But he didn't, and he'd wept at the injustice of life. In quarrels with Lainie, he'd sometimes howled with impotence, almost to the point of tears, at her irrefutable quirks. Now, slurping up the last of her tomato sauce, hearing her words in his hollows, he felt his face crumple into a twisted grimace and his breath shorten to gasps. A reasonable facsimile of weeping.

III

The Death of a Villain, the Birth of a Fool

Galahad's Fool. That was the name of it. It came to him as the first conscious glimmer in his flickering head, ten minutes before the alarm. He often had little waking tweets of inspiration, his subconscious belching up a bonus from the muses: a new way to string a marionette, some crazy image of a dragon's teeth made of spark plugs, or a punch line that had eluded him for weeks. Then for ten minutes, till the alarm beeped and he recalled who he was, he felt like a fucking genius.

Albert was grateful for those tiny gifts, but he resented them. They didn't feel earned. Whenever he actually used one of his dawn inspirations, he felt as if he was handing in someone else's homework. But the new show's title, clearly, was *Galahad's Fool.* In the remaining minutes before the snooze alarm dumped him into another day, his idiot muse told him the full life history of Sammy the Fool.

§

His name was Samuel, after the Biblical prophet. To his parents as much as to Albert, he'd been a surprise. Born the youngest of nine, long after his mother thought it possible, he was another mouth to feed, but she and her man welcomed the odd little soul as a sign that God had a sense of humor.

It was a hard breech birth. The baby's skull was pulled askew, effecting an odd sideways tilt to his face, as if he were turning left without the rest of him following. He was very fair, almost albino—white hair, white eyebrows—yet instead of pink rabbit eyes, the lashes were dark, the eyes as black as a Moor's. His mother feared the neighbors would think him the Devil's child, but the next harvest was abundant, so he was counted as a good luck charm. Weather made all the difference.

His mother would have loved him even if he'd been a hedgehog, but she fretted how her husband would react. No need to fear: the bearded smithy saw the child as a miracle, a fairy's gift, a whisper of God in his ear. Of course the good man never knew that the real father was a puppeteer, who'd sired him early one spring morning, a minute before the alarm went off.

As Samuel grew, he achieved no Biblical stature. Thin, wispy, not much above five feet tall, piquant face, hands like delicate flowers, he seemed made of paper. When he had achieved a feeble adolescence, he sprouted a sparse chin beard with just a twist of lemon, but it was clear he'd never be a blacksmith. His parents spent long hours fretting over his future. The Church might have been an employer of last resort, but these were hard times, with a vast oversupply of monks, priests, and other assorted freeloaders. Feeding nine kids, the father had few coins for an apprenticeship fee until one of Sir Galahad's men, bringing a horse for shoeing, said, "Talk to Old Horny."

Old Horny was Sir Galahad's court fool. A dwarf getting on in years, he had a hearty repertoire of songs, jokes, juggling routines, and even poetry, but he nurtured a twisted acerbity and a legendary lewdness. Galahad had accepted him as a gift from Launcelot, who never acknowledged himself as the Sacred Knight's natural father but would appear at intervals with guilt-spurred gifts. Once he brought a pair of boots many sizes too small, once a lame horse, and then, some years ago, this wrinkled, filthy-mouthed fool.

Yes, Sammy could be a fool. He was funny-looking, no question, with a shy simplicity that masked an oddball cleverness. His mother worried he might suffer abuse—there was no predicting the moods of a bevy of drunken knights—but his father pointed out that he'd always be well fed at a nobleman's table. What more could you wish for your son?

Negotiating an apprentice fee was easier than they'd expected. Old Horny was glad to have a few extra coins and seemed charmed by the boy. Sammy bade a sad farewell to his parents, to his brothers who'd protected him, to his sisters who loved him as they would a pet mouse, and he took up abode in the castle. One factor made Old Horny less inclined to haggle over money. The first night at the castle, he taught his newly acquired apprentice to suck him off.

"Do I do it to everybody?" Sammy asked.

"No," said Horny, "only me."

There were other lessons to be learned, but Old Horny was less demanding than in his younger days when during banquets he'd hump the table leg, to the boisterous cheers of the knights. Such antics passed for high art in those golden days of Camelot. With the apprentice fee and what he saved from no longer paying Angelica the village whore, Old Horny looked to acquire a small plot of land, a few goats, and in two or three years to retire from the entertainment industry. His protégé could take over the task of making grim men laugh.

Sammy worked hard to please, honing the varied skills required for aristocrats' diversions. He learned to sing, to recite an encyclopedic range of couplets, puns, and lyrical flights, and to intrude gracefully into the discourse of his betters at just the right moment to amuse, startle, or enthrall. He learned the license of the fool and the judicious restraint of that license. From his virginal lips Old Horny's dick jokes, pussy jokes, and jerking-off jokes were hilariously incongruent. He was too weak for handstands or cartwheels, but he could do a girlish ballet that was silly beyond measure and sweet beyond words, like a butterfly with hiccups.

Every fool needed a specialty—a tag line, theme song, or riff—that his audience would call for again and again. Old Horny was no comic genius, but sometimes his muse would break wind. One morning he woke with a jubilant croak: "Samuel!" Sammy, still groggy, came running. The old dwarf grabbed him by the collar. "Yell this out, loud as you can: *Hear me, O Israel!*" In his piping voice, Sammy obliged. The dwarf went into convulsions of laughter, beating himself on the head, sputtering at both ends.

Horny had to clear it with the little round Priest, and the Priest had to read out the precise words for Sammy to learn. Master prepared apprentice for his debut. Finally, at the Midsummer banquet, Old Horny hopped onto the table astride the roast pig and hooted, "By special arrangement with His Holiness the Pope, we bring you the Prophet Samuel!" From the end of the hall, two servants shouldered a bier on which Sammy stood, in nightshirt and mistletoe crown, clutching a broom as a prophet's staff. He waved his cornhusk hand in a prophetic flutter and intoned:

"Thus saith the Lord of Hosts, now go and smite Amalek, and utterly destroy and spare them not, but slay both man and woman, infant and suckling, camel and ass—"

He never quite made it to *suckling*. The company erupted in laughter: a cacophony of guffaws, shrieks, snorts, fits, spasms, and seizures that lasted a full ten minutes, with aftershocks into the night. One elderly nobleman was found under the table paralyzed by stroke, his mouth wide with a beatific smile and a half-chewed leg of lamb. To an objective critic, it wouldn't have been that funny, but objective critics in Arthurian Cornwall were few and far between. Somehow it spoke to these men perpetually torn between jollies and judgment. It made Sammy's fortune.

And wrecked Old Horny's. Two days later, on an impulse, Sir Galahad invoked his manorial rights, announced that Sammy's apprenticeship was complete, and presented him as a gift to Sir Mordred, his Lady's father—the good Sir Mordred, not the bad Sir Mordred who later made headlines. For Horny, disaster. No more free blow jobs, no plot of land with goats, and he'd have to pay Angelica what he owed her before she'd let him climb aboard. He took sick and died as winter came on. His legacy died with him, though for years afterward an older knight might chuckle, reach down, and rub the table leg.

But show biz was unpredictable, and soon Sammy was back with Galahad. The good Sir Mordred, in a momentary fit of badness, led a revolt against the king and was quickly crushed. Soldiers were dispatched to slaughter all Mordred's creatures— man and woman, suckling, camel and ass. They moved with professional economy through the servants' quarters, slitting throats as they went, working their way at last toward the feathery, epicene freak aquiver in the scullery. The red eye of Death was upon him. With perfect timing, as the squad neared, he rose, flung wide his arms, proclaimed in a piercing falsetto, *"Thus saith the Lord, smite Amalek!"* and shat his pants.

The soldiers told it for decades, into their dying years. As with Henry on St. Crispin's Day, they might say, *"We few, we happy few, we band of brothers . . ."* Everything in those men— their savagery, their loneliness, their nausea, their terror, their tears—all was released in the feculence that burst from Sammy. Every man stood suspended in silence, like an insect in amber, as the Fool put his fingers to his nose and whispered, "Peee-uw!"

They laughed until they sobbed uncontrollably.

When he heard the soldiers' story, King Arthur guffawed. He granted the Fool a full pardon for having served a traitor and sent him back to Sir Galahad laden with gifts. The Fool returned with a nickname that spread far and wide: *Sammy Shit-pants.*

§

What the hell was Albert going to do with all that? Now he had a stinky freak, a lost child, a condemned peasant, and a yakkity priest. It was one of those curlicue freeway ramps that never gets you onto the freeway. Even if he cut out the Fool right now, the stench would endure.

Albert put water onto the stove for coffee, and his mind started to boil. He saw soldiers dragging Rolf to the grounds outside the wall. Galahad's wife was no longer there, but the Fool surely was. It was his privilege to be anywhere. He could be in the room when the council met, or as Galahad sat on the chamber pot, or at the foot of the Lady's bed as she woke to the song of a lark. It might have been stretching privilege to watch them make love, but now he stood present at a deeper intimacy.

Villagers and peasants began to arrive, and even the beggars. Folks took diversion where they could find it. The killing ground had been left filthy with encrustations of usage—blood, feces, petrified vomit—to awe new clients with the leavings of their forebears. Raptors circled overhead. A dry wind rose, a hush came over the crowd, and the phone rang.

Albert had forgotten. It was Mara, of course. She always rang when he'd forgotten to call at the settled time of the week.

"Hello?"

"Hi, Papa."

"Hi there." It was late morning, and that would make it six p.m. in Madrid. Come on, Al, try to listen, it's your daughter, for chrissake. He treasured her presence, but right now he was distracted, seeing the peasant dragged over the cobbles to the gibbet. He needed his coffee.

Mara was saying something about her boyfriend. Albert had met Alejandro about a year and a half ago, just before Lainie's diagnosis. He'd liked him "despite the fact that we're both named Al," he'd joked.

"Well, sweetie, that's good," he said, in response to the story he'd half-heard Mara tell. "Your previous guys all seemed humor-challenged. I can't imagine a relationship can hold unless you both acknowledge that at times you have to fart."

"We don't fart, Papa," she replied in a matter-of-fact voice. "We're college graduates." Mara knew how to deliver a punch line.

After Bryn Mawr, she'd tried the New York grind but burned out and moved to Spain ten years ago. He saw her only a few days every year, brief visits where he wanted to say so much but said it mostly in silence. Since the death, they'd talked by phone every week, and he'd started to open up a bit, though he felt—and felt she knew—that he was working a little too hard to convince her that he was fine, just fine, really fine.

"Papa, are you listening?"

"What?" Damn, what had he missed? "Sorry, my brain is on hold. To leave a message, wait for the beep."

She giggled. Thin humor, but it worked. She was talking about the apartment she and Alejandro were looking at. They felt it was time to risk moving in together. His dog and her cat had compatibility issues, but they'd have to work it out. Albert suggested they find a vet who did couples therapy. That earned another giggle. Strange: when he and Lainie ignited, it took them about ten minutes to shack up forever. Or relatively forever.

"Sorry, honey, I was thinking. Nasty habit."

"You must have a project going," said Mara.

"No, I'm kinda swimming through oatmeal. I don't have the need to make a lotta bucks, and literally for the first time since Cub Scouts I don't have deadlines. I could just sit here and turn into a lump of lard."

"I don't think that's the best idea."

"I concur." Silence. "Anyway . . ."

"Anyway?"

"Anyway, all my life I've driven myself with obligation. Make the show because we've got a grant, or we've got bookings for something I haven't even written, or choose your rationalization. I don't have that now. None of it. So my brain is running rampant."

The water was boiling. He turned it off. He wanted his coffee.

"Is this a hard time for you?" She meant that it was two weeks till the anniversary.

"Not this week. Try me next."

He glanced at the note on the phone pad: Jeanette something, with a phone number—a costumer some colleague had recommended. If he did this damned show, he'd need a costumer. Good reason not to do it.

"So how's work?" he asked.

"Same old. I like it, as magazines go. Their politics aren't totally disgusting, and they like the soft-serve stuff that I write. And I'm getting a raise, which helps."

"Ah blessed soft-serve."

Mara laughed, then changed the subject to unemployment rates in Spain and her volunteer work at a community center that was being closed down and the eternal whiff of Franco that was still in the air—after forty years—on humid nights. Albert heard every word, but his mind kept veering into the oncoming lane.

The Fool followed the soldiers out to the killing ground. He noticed a strange little boy standing by the Virgin's shrine where the high road began.

"Who's that?" asked the Fool.

Mara: "Who's what?"

"What?"

"You said *Who's that?*"

"My God, I'm sorry, sweetie," Albert said. "My mind was somewhere else. I'm thinking about this show. *Who's that?* I guess lots of people would qualify." No response. "No, I've got this stuff running in my head. Maybe I should take it seriously. Why don't you tell me maybe I should?"

"Maybe you should. And maybe you shouldn't try to multitask." A stiff silence. "Is this a kids' show?"

Albert saw Rolf tied fast to the gibbet, his back bared for flogging. "Probably not," he said.

She softened. "I guess my all-time favorite was *The Velveteen Rabbit*. I was a sucker for that."

For three decades the children's shows had paid the bills. Exhausting work, sometimes two or three shows a day. It was always a tough balance to do a *Snow Queen* that wasn't "too upsetting" or to buck the clamor for shows that taught a lesson. The Giant must learn that bullying is mean or the Big Bad Wolf improve his dental hygiene—though it was never a problem for sponsors if *Cinderella* taught little girls that if only they were cute enough they could marry the rich guy.

"Funny, you let me see *Orpheus* when I was eight," Mara said. "I cried for a week. And I was so glad I did."

They talked a while longer. He promised to call next Monday and be more coherent.

"Love you."

"Love you."

"Bye."

He went back to the stove, turned up the flame under the coffee water, opened his notepad on the counter, and watched what they did to Rolf.

§

They dragged him there. They stripped him naked. They tied him face to the gibbet. A throng of thirty or forty souls—peasants, villagers, artisans, kids—formed a wide, inscrutable circle. The man's wife, a scrawny woman with a hook nose and a wen on her lip, stood with their children and watched.

Torture was an expressive art that took as much practice as playing the violin. Some had a knack for it, but mastery took longer. The four soldiers had some training from a pro, and as beginners they tried to do their best. Each in turn took the braided leather whip and gave Rolf five stripes, more or less, arithmetic being a challenge. At each cut of the lash, the man grunted. His wife began to keen, and one of the soldiers yelled, "Hold the applause!" The beadle and a knacker laughed, but the peasants were silent. Sammy the Fool watched the strange little boy who'd appeared out of nowhere.

It was time for the hands. They untied Rolf, walked him staggering to a wide flat stump and gestured for him to kneel. Sammy noticed that they weren't rough with him the way soldiers usually were. They seemed awestruck, like newborn babies the moment they opened their eyes to the enormity of life.

The irons had been heating over charcoal. Father Olyver prompted the squad as needed. Rolf's face was impassive as he knelt at the stump, but two of the soldiers went pale. The third scowled at the Priest, and the fourth howled boisterously, "Hooo-ey!" but nobody laughed. A soldier struggled to tie cords to hold the wrists for the ax, but he kept getting tangled. The Priest tried to offer counsel, but the younger soldier barked, "Fuck off!" and turned aside to retch. The other kept fumbling with the knots while the rest held the peasant down, though his strength was drained. At last they were ready.

Sammy prepared to entertain. Sad shows required comic relief. The spectators needed to laugh. Laughter was like breathing: there weren't good laughs or bad laughs, there was just the primal need. The moment the ax fell, he'd yell "Ouch!" in a tone of childish wonder. It was all in the timing.

The burliest soldier, a woodcutter who had to join the army when they enclosed the woodland commons, hefted the ax. He raised it, aiming to sever both wrists with one deft whack. The ax came down—and missed. He jerked it out of the stump, raised it and hacked again, cleaving one palm. Abashed, he jerked and chopped, jerked and chopped in a frenzy of rage until the peasant's hands lay piecemeal about the stump. The young soldier gave Rolf a feeble kick in the side, and Sammy missed the moment for "Ouch!"

The victim was mute. His mouth gaped wide and he gasped. At last, when the blundering spasms were done and they seared the stumps with the white-hot irons, he began to cry. Not from pain: he cried for his hands. Sammy thought it might be funny to sing "The Rain It Raineth," but his mouth wouldn't work.

They dragged the peasant back to the gibbet. He tried to walk, but his knees buckled under him. His lips moved as if in apology to the soldiers who dragged him. Then a shaking took him: no way to stop it, the spasms of the reptile spine, the fierce, ancient yearning for life. The Fool felt someone holding his hand: the strange little boy. No one had held Sammy's hand for many years. He knew the child's name was Bobby, that Bobby saw in the eyes of the knavish Rolf the doomed stare of Ragsie when they took her off the last time to the vet. He tugged the Fool's hand, and Sammy bent to hear.

"Are they actors?"

The Fool nodded yes.

The Priest proclaimed that the amputation was for the poaching. The next judgment was retribution for cursing the master.

They hung Rolf upside down by his feet with heavy cords. Upright flayings were a better spectacle—easier to see the face—but a downward flow of blood to the head kept the victim conscious longer. "If you're doing all that work," the soldiers' mentor had said, "you want your guy to appreciate it."

Albert knew the face from a painting he'd seen—where, Madrid?—of St. Bartholomew. Torturers were doing their job on the saint, who lay twisted on his back, glaring straight at us—the breath before the lightning strike. *This is happening to me*, he seemed to be saying, and the viewer could only answer, *Yes it is*.

Now the soldiers were more workmanlike, awkward at times, but past the crude slapstick at the start. They went about their routine. How simple it was to let your eyes glaze over and just do your job—a testament to human adaptability. Torture was nothing personal.

As their mentor instructed: small blades, but sharp. Start with the feet. The feeling is in the skin, so don't cut deep or they lose too much blood. Best to slit as if skinning a rabbit, pulling it off in sheets. The same sensation as being burned alive, but you control the timing. When the pain gets too crazy, something kicks in and he doesn't feel it: the more it cranks up, the less effect. So ride the edge. Let it sear him to the soul, but bring him back. Then the riptide again, and he knows the waves will crash over him again and again for hours past counting, more hours than it took to birth him.

That's what they did. From the feet, they worked their way down toward the head, and at last the man started to scream— a basso scream from the spine, like a bull's mindless bellow, big with alfalfa bloat. The braying was loud enough, Sammy thought, to be heard in the castle. He murmured a prayer for Galahad's lady not to hear. When they got to the groin, he covered the little boy's eyes.

The soldiers took breaks. By the time they came to Rolf's chest, they were pretty drunk. At one clean jerk a huge swath of skin came away from belly to throat. Then they pulled off his face.

Normally, death would come before the flaying was done, but the witless gristle still panted and twitched as they cut it down from the gibbet. They left it all day in the sun, then poured oil and set it afire. The spectators dispersed. Another squad had burned the family's hovel and put his scrawny, hook-nosed wife and litter out on the road. A storm was blowing up. The exiles trekked into thunder.

The burly soldier reported to his sergeant; the sergeant rousted the Priest, now tipsy in the chapel; and the Priest informed Galahad that all was done. The Knight was sorrowful. It was torture to pass judgment, but one did what one must do. His Lady looked troubled, so he called for the Fool.

Sammy had stayed at the killing ground until they cut the glistening red carcass down from the gibbet. He didn't like seeing it, but the little boy wanted to watch. Afterward, he took the child to the servant quarters where he had his own tiny room. He made a nest in one corner, brought the child bread and soup from the kitchen, and sat there as he ate. Sammy asked no questions of the strange little boy. For him there were no questions to ask: life just went on, wafting you wherever. Eating, sleeping, doing whatever came next—that sufficed. Bobby said thanks for the soup. He knew to say thanks, whenever. Then Sammy was called to his master. He tucked in the little boy, found Galahad and his Lady at the hearth, and sang gentle songs late into the night.

§

Albert glanced over what he'd written. He could never avoid planting barbs and thistles in his stuff, but nothing remotely as loathsome as this. What point did he think he was making? Big news: the human race was vile. Dystopian visions should be futuristic, not retroactive.

He stared at the lump of clay on the armature before him, fed up with scrying its bulges to find its soul. Why offer the public two hours of torture? He'd been carried away by unmarketable obsessions too often. The point of getting back to work was just getting back to work, not launching Pickett's Charge. The rest of the day was shot.

His professional life had spanned forty-some years, but how could he still call himself a professional when he was making what nobody wanted—not even himself? Wasn't he now just a hobbyist whose hobby was cleaning septic tanks? Why not obsess over something more pleasant? Trips to the ocean. Astronomy, maybe. Attending every pancake breakfast or wine festival in the county. What mad aesthetic charley horse drove him to flay peasants and make little Bobby watch it?

Enough. Despair, like a trip to the fridge, was just another way of avoiding work. Tomorrow he should call this costumer, Joann or whatever. His puppets would need costumes, and the director at the Rep said this person was reliable. Even more, he had to make it real. Get himself back to a show that might really happen, something simple, funny, mindless. Get rid of the little boy, get rid of Rolf, stick to the Fool—the Fool could be a hoot. Yes, he needed distraction, but that needn't mean flaying his peasant and his audience and himself.

He began to work the clay into a rough head shape, about three-quarters lifesize, and gave it a crude jaw line and chin. Where to start? The mouth. The mouth that spoke the judgment.

IV

A Nightmare

In Albert's first moments of wakefulness, Galahad's dream began to arrive. Intestinal odors. Lines at the tents of the whores. The washing of bloody hands.

The alarm beeped. As Albert stumbled to the bathroom, he shook the fleas out of his head, but they hopped back to make his brain itch. Okay: the peasant's torment would live on in the noggin of the sedentary Knight, sprouting dreams that spurred him to a new quest. Horses, the clatter of armor, hanged men twisting, fire in the sky. The doomed man's curse: *Let you go begging . . .*

The dreams could be done with shadows.

Albert sat at the kitchen table with toast and coffee, reviewing his notes. He had started sculpting the model for Galahad without even deciding what sort of puppets he was building. Maybe his big guys for the major players—Knight, Lady, Fool, the scummy little Priest—but those were no good for two-person scenes without a second puppeteer.

Rod puppets? No. Marionettes, hand puppets? No. Shadows? He might work with shadows from rear-projected video for the liquid feel of reality's insubstantial onion rings. Easy with shadows to create a cast of thousands, plus major atrocities. Or maybe toy theater: little miniature sets with cut-out figures sliding back and forth, the storyteller himself looming like Jehovah over the microcosm. No, there had to be realistic faces. He couldn't give up on those eyes.

The flaying? Maybe the peasant is Mr. Potatohead, and the soldiers wield a peeler? Or he's a Ken doll with a skin of gauze and liquid latex. Or the little kid sees it on TV: a close-up of fingers peeling a chicken skin. Or the tourists are watching a puppet show and try to drag the child away when it gets too violent, but then he jumps into the show and he's lost—

But why the kid? How many layers could a story wear before it started to suffocate? Albert thought of shaking Bobby awake and telling him to bundle his little tail out of the show, but Bobby would only huddle more deeply into his troubled dreams. The child was sure that the torture and killing weren't real, but how did they do the special effects? Was the man they were hurting supposed to be one of the good guys or one of the bad? Why weren't there any commercials?

Albert realized that his lost boy had become the Lost Boy. The kid would have to stay.

§

Next evening, Galahad and his Lady sat in the great hall, opposite one another at the hearth. She was embroidering a floral design on the lappet of a cap for the young daughter of a neighboring lord. He gazed at a small silver crucifix he held in his palm, a childhood gift from the abbess of the nunnery where he was nurtured.

Galahad's Lady spoke. "What did they do to the man?"

"I regret that thou—"

At this point, Albert changed his mind about using *thee* and *thou*.

"I regret that you heard the cries," said the Knight.

Their words were never profuse. Their bond was in their gaze. But there were times when words were needed.

"You were weeping in your sleep," he said. "I woke you."

"May God bless your kindness, my love." A pause. "What did they do?"

He lowered his eyes to the hearth. She reached across and put her hand to his brow. She felt his shudder. She withdrew back to her embroidery.

"When my father turned traitor," said the Lady, "he was justly put to death." Her words choked. She continued, tensing against a tremor. "So too were my brothers, my sister, servants, my nurse Martha. They spared only the Fool, who made them laugh, and myself, here, your wife. Their distress, my fortune."

Galahad touched the tiny writhing figure on the crucifix, then raised his fingers toward her, as if to touch her heart across the distance.

"I accepted the King's act as a deterrent to treason," she continued, "yet I heard their cries across many leagues. I hear them still."

"We must pray that God shows mercy to all suffering." His words rang hollow to him, and he saw her face go pale as she fought her tremor.

"I asked what they did to the man."

"My judgment was carried out."

"How?"

Galahad's eyes flashed. "My care is for the welfare of my people, all. For the peasants, yeomen, servants, nobility, every soul. I hate the death of a fellow man. I spared knights in combat if they asked it, however much I bled. I feel grievous pain in punishing the poor, whose sufferings are deep." She saw in his eyes that he spoke the truth. "But I must do it. The man who says otherwise has never been forced to judge. I heard those cries, and it cut me to the heart, but death was the sacred necessity."

Her silence forced him on.

"An execution is a horrid act. Horrid not only for the transgressor but for judge, for priest, for the soldiers whose daily trade is death. One of those, the youngest, hanged himself in the night. A terrible sin, but a crime that God will charge, I hope, not to the poor young man but to the felon who compelled him to it."

The words struck Albert as overblown. The only characters who talked that way were comic-book heroes or political hacks. This guy would have to start sounding halfway human.

The Lady broke off her stitchery halfway through a rambling tendril and stretched chilly fingers toward the fire. The Knight rose from his chair, lumbered to her, and stood stroking the flaxen hair that had been his first taste of joy. She let the silence lie between them: silence often brought its own reply. She reached to press his hand to her temple. *In all seasons,* she had vowed. The weather was fickle, yet the sun rose each day.

She raised her face to him. "In all seasons," she murmured.

The Knight could say only, "Mara."

§

Mara? Albert rose abruptly, strode out to the porch, muttering obscenities. Mara was his daughter, not a puppet. He was sick of characters popping up, naming themselves, then hanging in there like a tumor you couldn't cut out and you couldn't kill and you couldn't wish away. Why not call her Lainie and be honest? Why not make it really hurt?

Mara was Hebrew for *bitter* and in Celtic had to do with the sea. It suited his daughter—a whip-smart cynic, a dark one, though when her joy peeped out, she was luminous as crystal. In fact the name might suit the Lady, might give him a stronger emotional stake, though he had no idea where that character was headed. He'd often used old memories of friends or foes as grist for the mill.

But why this sudden burst of rage? Very simple: he didn't want a stronger emotional stake. He wanted to get through this thing and get it out of his head. At the castle it was night, but for him it was an hour till noon. He took a deep breath of California air. Not a big issue, he told himself, only a working name. Call the wife *Mara* for now.

§

Albert had intended to phone the costumer right after lunch, but he stumped outdoors to weed the garden instead. After an hour he came back and sat at the phone. *Jeanette Wald.* He pictured a gray seamstress who'd say, "Oh, puppets! That would be fun!" A phrase ran in his head: *The world will little note nor long remember* . . . Right: the less said, the less remembered, the better. Forget it. Make the call tomorrow.

Back to the eyes. The Lady, looking into those eyes, had to see the torment. By dinnertime he gave it up, scraped off the layers of paint, went into the kitchen and poured his first glass of wine. By the time he went up to bed, he was stumbling drunk. He rarely got to that point, hated it when he did, but at least it would render him dreamless. He lay in bed, ran his hands over his dormant balls, thankfully numb. He flipped off the light, fell back into his wadded pillow, and saw the eyes he'd been try-ing to paint. A haunted slant, a plea, an odd glimmer of hope: eyes that looked outward to a blood-ridden world and inward to his own soul's hell. That night, a dreamless Albert dreamed Galahad's dream.

Dust rose from the plain. A line of tiny silhouettes advanced, a swarm of ants crossing a land forsaken by God, their line five thousand years long. The ants stretched into sprawling grotesques against the vast flat screen of the sky. They marched past a wind chime in the shape of a dangling man, tinkling a sol-dier's song. The sky emitted a hideous squawk, and Albert woke.

For a moment. A faint image crossed his vision like a bird in the blackness, then he drifted back into the shallows of sleep. He peered through the glass of Galahad's eyes and saw what

Galahad saw. Three snared rabbits. Taut lip with a wen. Severed hands curling in puzzlement. Clouds of blowflies enfolding a skinless torso. *Let your dearest creature . . .*

§

Galahad's eyes came open, a drowning man breaking the surface for a gasp. He rolled out of bed, fumbled into his robe, and shuffled his way to the great hall where the fireplace was kept aglow by an old woman who slept sitting up, popping awake at intervals to add a log. Trembling, he woke the serving boy and told him to fetch the Fool.

He was fond of Sammy, a soul who played his role with simple dignity. His vassal knights loved the creature, though at feasts they'd pelt him with food and hoot at his sweet girly face. Their behavior irked Galahad, but knights were knights and fools were fools. A fool's calling was to entertain, and audiences had varied tastes. He felt that to Sammy a gesture of charity would be a humiliation.

The odd little fellow came into the hall, groggy with sleep, carrying his lute. He had put on his doublet inside out. Galahad didn't know if he'd done it by accident or to raise a late-night chuckle, but he laughed to please Sammy. The Fool sat on a low stool at his feet, strummed the lute, and sang a soft ballad. Galahad found little comfort in the music, but as long as he sat with the Fool he would stay awake, and as long as he stayed awake he wouldn't dream.

"Do you dream, Sammy?" Galahad startled himself with the question.

"Dreams, I don't know if I do'em or if they just come through the window, but they better not make a mess." Sammy was doing his simpleton act.

"Sammy, I'm asking truly."

"Questions, oh boy. My mommy asked a question once, and the answer was me. But was I the right answer? That's the puzzler."

He could go on like this forever, but Galahad was in no mood for banter. "Answer my question, if you will."

Sammy paused. "Okay," he said, but fell silent.

Galahad was sorry he'd asked. One must never withdraw an order to a reluctant servant, but the Fool was out of his depth. He was about to ask for another song when Sammy spoke.

"Once I dreamed about birds. I wanted a bird, so I dreamed about'em all aflutter. I asked my priest if that was a sin. He said just to be safe let's call it a sin and I'll forgive it. So he did." Sammy shrugged, as if to ask whether that was enough of a dream.

"Where do dreams come from, Sammy?"

"Maybe God sticks 'em in our ears."

"Oh? And why does Our Heavenly Father do that?"

"To stop our noggins leaking."

"Of course. And where does He get these dreams?"

"I think little birds eat 'em and poop 'em out. Did you dream bird poop, nuncle?"

Galahad laughed. "So you're saying that God shoves bird poop into our brains? The Priest will be angry, Sammy!" The Knight knew that Sammy loved it when he played fellow fool.

"If it's touched by Our Heavenly Father, then it won't be stinky, and the Priest will want bird poop too."

§

Albert squinted at the alarm: four a.m. He wrestled himself out of bed, walked naked to the bathroom, pissed, got a drink of water, and crawled back under the covers. Galahad's nightmare had faded, but the cold fear clung. Albert saw Mara—his daughter Mara—two years old and terrified of sleep. They would read to her, cajole her, but she knew the nightmare was waiting with its yellowed incisors. She'd rage and fight till she was exhausted, then at last fall into the chasm. He had felt he was sending their child into the darkness to see what was lurking there.

As a small boy, he had learned to kill his dreams. When he felt the monster's claws on his neck he made a little hop, like a car hitting a pothole, and bounced out of his dream. He did it several more times and, amazingly, never had nightmares after that. The monster had gotten the message, gone off to other feeding grounds. But word went around to the rest of his dreams as they lined up to fill his years—flying, sports stardom, wild sex—and they too abandoned him. Now his dreams were housebroken, neutered. He wandered through huge rambling buildings or conducted rehearsals of nameless plays with half the cast missing. His dreaming mind had migrated to full daylight, where monstrosities could be edited and rehearsed.

But this time the nightmare had come unbidden, like Lainie's feral cats, and still crouched ready to feed. Was it Galahad's dream or his? Smoke rolled in and smothered him. He lay on a landscape from Dali or Goya, a barren plain of broken things, shards of bone or half-buried plastic toys. He lay awaiting death. He was long past all pain, but the simplest discomforts were agonizing. His dry lips cracked. The sun pierced his tight-clenched lids, and the hook-nosed woman was there: plain, gaunt, with a wen like a bloated tick on the upper edge of her lip. She held out a cup. Surely, at last, the Grail. His mouth was ash. He took the cup, saw his own haunted face in the liquid, drank, and gagged on blood.

"I'm lost."

Albert heard himself say it. At the far end of the hall he saw the Fool and Sir Galahad dozing by the fire.

"I'm lost."

Galahad jerked awake to see the child in his nightshirt standing in the archway.

"I'm lost," the Lost Boy repeated.

"I too," said Galahad.

V

Of the Questing Beast

Albert woke late morning, feeling like leftovers in the back of the fridge. After fitful attempts at sleep, he had stumbled out to the living-room sofa. It was comforting somehow, the snooze of a drunk in the gutter who no longer fears hitting bottom because he's already there. He was chilled and his nose was stuffy. With luck, he might descend into bronchitis, allowing a week's respite from working or grousing about his godforsaken Knight of the Table Round. Without excuses, he'd have to settle down to practical stuff: start looking at spaces to open the show, call the damned costumer, call her first thing, tangle his ass in commitments like a fly in the spider's web.

Or better after May 10th. What was it now, the third? Maybe the anniversary was flustering him without his being aware. Next week would come, then pass. Or he could dump the whole thing right now: cancel his ticket for the flight to Camelot.

He shuffled back to the bedroom, dragged himself into yesterday's clothes. A whiff of nightmare hung in the air like a dead rat under the house. Looking into the bathroom mirror, he wasn't enchanted by what he saw. His square-jawed Germanic face carried its aging well, except for the baggy eyes, but he hadn't shaved for three days, and now the razor would rip off his chin unless he changed the blade. But his grandpa came from peasant stock, and Albert had the genes of a tightwad: he'd sooner set fire to his stubble than use a blade for less than two weeks.

He took the back road downtown. Two dogs lay sunning in the dirt. The little yapper yapped, but the older mutt, who used to snarl and trot a nip away from his heels, had deeper things on his mind these days, like death. He'd get up for trucks but not for puppeteers.

The third of May. Blossoms were fervent with lust, crying out to the bees. He crossed the cemetery. Before Lainie's death, he often walked that way. Afterward, he avoided it. There were still Easter decorations. Resurrection, renewal, rebirth—the taste of the candy you lacked the nickels for. And the anniversary in a week. He crossed the grass, treading on the feet of the deceased, not on their faces.

One weird cloud in the sky. Could it be clouding up? Clouds always made him think of his trip to Big Lake, age eleven, that disastrous bicycle hike in the mud. It was a time when he had no goal, no Grail to be grabbed from the fingers of dawn, but it had something to do with desire. What brought that to mind? Yes, clouds.

Soon, he sat at the sidewalk table with his Americano, cherry muffin, and notepad, staring at a menacing blank page. All the way into town he hadn't thought of the show. Strange to call it *the show*. The show was always a bread-and-butter affair. Now, for the first time ever, he wasn't doing it for money. In his own head he might dramatize himself as a lone suffering widower and truly believe it, but the majority of his seven billion fellow Earthlings would define suffering in a vastly different way. He could munch his organic muffin and drink his fair-trade coffee under California skies. He wasn't lying there skinless in the dust.

Tonight, he had to remember, he was giving a talk to a puppetry guild in Oakland, so he'd go through the bins, pull out a few of the guys from *Orpheus* or *Frankenstein* for a small exhibit, and talk about his work. The life of an artist: stand up, sit down, do stuff. No, better to talk about how he painted the eyes.

"Hello, Albert." He looked up: Mitchell, a sweet, rumpled man of indeterminate age, smiled and held out a flyer. "Here's a new one."

"Oh. Thanks." Albert took it, nodded. Mitchell seemed to be more saint than crank, quite intelligent the few times they'd spoken. The flyer would be three pungent paragraphs about Truth and Soul. What moved this man to compose his weekly gospel, handing it to whomever would give it a glance before tossing it? Albert folded the flyer into his shoulder bag and took a sip of coffee. Mitchell walked on, his smile lingering in the air like the grin of the Cheshire Cat.

"Quest." Albert said it out loud, just to push it out of his head. In the Arthurian legends, Sir Palomides seeks the Questing Beast. Head of a snake, a leopard's torso, hooves of a deer and a lion's butt, with a pack of hounds baying in its belly. Not a beast that's questing, but a beast that draws men into quests. They send out vast armies to claim the Grail but wind up chasing the Beast. Mitchell's quest? His own? Galahad's? Did Mitchell hope that a flyer on Truth and Soul might plant a seed to reforest the boundless desert? Albert's Galahad had no true faith in a Grail: the Knight had long abandoned that childish whim. He sought only to escape the peasant's unearthly cry.

He got back to the house a little before noon and lay down on the couch to rejuvenate himself. After ten minutes of agitation, he rose. He had to make the phone call, and his mind was running full tilt inventing ways to avoid it—as absurd as the three days it took him to call Corleen to ask her to the senior prom. At last he heaved himself to the phone table, shuffled through papers to find the slip that said *Jeanette Wald*. He punched the number.

"Yes?"

"Jeanette Wald?"

"Speaking."

In one long riff, he introduced himself, described the project, the challenges of puppetry, the timetable—which he didn't know he knew—and asked if they might talk.

"Um. Sure." Her voice was flat as linoleum. The prospect of work with the renowned Albert Fisher—renowned to himself at any rate—did not arouse ecstasy. Albert felt suddenly anonymous.

They set a meeting for the following Tuesday. He suggested she come to the studio so she could see the types of puppets he used. And he acknowledged frankly that it was strange for him to hire so early in the process of a show but said she'd be paid no matter what, which seemed to soften the mood.

"Here's the deal. I'm talking to you at this point as a strategy for stepping into the quicksand. Bad metaphor, I guess. I was just remembering, I was a kid in Boy Scouts, we did a bicycle hike to this lake— Big Lake was the name of it. Yeah, Big Lake. No, well, that doesn't really pertain, I guess—"

"Sorry, what?"

"I guess a better example— First show I ever did with my partner, my wife, she's deceased, she's— First show we ever did, we gave it a title, wrote a press release, booked a stage before we had the slightest idea what we were going to do. And it was a hit. My point being—"

"Point being?"

"Point being that if I get sufficiently entangled, I can rely on my pathological sense of responsibility to make it happen, no matter whether— Yeah." He had made an utter fool of himself and waited for the click and buzz.

Silence on the end of the line. Then, "I can identify."

§

At his work table, he stared at the wad of terracotta that yearned to become a hero. He stuck two glass globs into the eye sockets to check the positioning. Staring into the face, he felt like the little boy standing in the archway, watching the hunched Knight sitting at the end of the hall. "Who are you?" he heard the Knight ask.

"Me."

"Who are your parents?"

"Mommy and Daddy."

"Where are they?" Galahad asked.

"In my fucking head, you pathetic prick!" Albert heard himself shouting out loud at the lump of clay. The knightly lump was not impressed. It sat on its armature glassy-eyed, dumb as dough.

Albert jerked himself out of his daydream. He could never manage a midday nap, but he could dither hours away. He glanced at his watch: past time to get ready for the evening gig, so he assembled a cluster of puppets from the dozens of bins, stashed them in the car trunk along with display stands and a few DVDs, on the chance there might be some purchasers. He'd made notes and would talk half an hour. Thank God he didn't have to perform. The notion of bringing something to life right now would be unbearable.

He grabbed some crackers and peanut butter—he'd have a late supper, maybe—then drove an hour to the East Bay, listening to some guy on KPFA predicting the death of the planet. Found the place, set up the puppets, and gave his talk to several dozen folks who seemed to enjoy it. One even bought a DVD. He had a glass of wine and a bunch of corn chips, packed up, drove home. These little freebie gigs were nice, made him feel he was still alive. Maybe he should be thankful that his current life had no consequence. His puppet show could be brilliant or putrid, and the world would not turn a hair. Hamlet asked, "To be or not to be," as if the decision mattered. His own response would be, "Whatever."

He could look at a sunset and see its beauty, as he could look at Lainie's death and see the grief. Feeling it: that was another matter. Lainie had been his channel to deep emotion. Through her, he could feel the beauty, the pain, the joy. Beside her, he could feel the heat of the bonfire, the eros of clouds, the frivolity of surf. If only a bit of Lainie were still alive to help him feel her death.

He passed the third Petaluma exit, getting close to home. Better to think about the show. Arthurian legend with finger puppets, maybe: he could play two characters or a whole ten-digit army. But Galahad needed a face of his own and so did the Lady and so did Sammy the Fool. That freak's soft wild eyes had to draw us in, and he needed one live hand at least to do his tricks. Above all, the Fool needed to sleep. Instead, he was summoned to attend Sir Galahad.

§

Shuffling past the tiny chapel, he saw the Lady Mara on the bench before the altar. She wasn't praying, she was just sitting there, as if waiting for Jesus to come down from the cross so they could leave the playground and go home for lunch. Sammy stopped at the door. She turned to him. He didn't know what to say, so he did a dance. A slow, sad dance, a simple shuffle back and forth, his hands as if in prayer. Then he stopped.

"Sammy, why are you sad?"

"Cause you look all rainy-face," he said at last.

She looked at him as she would look at an annoying sister, then smiled a slow, pained smile.

"Yes. Perhaps because it's clouding up," she said. "As a girl I loved the rain. One time it began to rain and my nurse came to fetch me out of the rain, but I ran from her and fell full face in the mud."

"The rain it raineth," said Sammy, not quite sure what he meant by that.

She stared at the altar. "Yes, the rain it raineth." She tried to brighten her eyes. "Have you ever been in love, Sammy?"

"No, my Lady. I watch where I step, so I don't fall in."

A flicker of amusement, then her face darkened. "It's not to fall into, although they sing of that. It's something slowly woven, day by day, between two souls who join in the promise."

"But I bet when Mama and Papa made me, they did it

fast." He caught himself: was it too ribald for her ears? He was relieved to see her smile.

"Well, I have no child, which I grieve. Though I shall if God wills."

"Or maybe I could, if God said I had to. Cause he's God, so I do what He says."

She was silent. His timing was off. No, in her face he saw that she felt she had spoken too freely. He had caught a glimpse of her soul.

"Never mind me. Go to your master." Sammy waved goodnight, and Albert drove on.

§

He turned into the driveway and parked, left the puppets to be unpacked in the morning. They might enjoy the night air, camping in the car outside their bins. He had probably consumed enough corn chips to qualify as supper, but he still felt hungry. He set about cooking an omelet, exploring the subconscious corners of the fridge to see what might be lurking. Tag-end of a sausage, a slice of jicama, cheese rind: bring it on. A chunk of semi-sweet chocolate? Probably not. He broke three eggs, chopped stuff, turned on the burner. The moment he poured the concoction into the skillet, he realized he'd forgotten to check the phone machine. He popped into the office and saw the red light blinking. He pushed PLAY. Mara's voice. His daughter Mara.

"Papa, hi. So I got your email from yesterday, but then I had to— So it's early morning here, we're going out looking for apartments, which is— Anyway, so I thought I'd call."

His daughter was sounding as incoherent as himself. For him, talking to a computer chip was like talking to a locomotive bearing down.

"Anyway, you just sounded— I mean I'm sorry you're not sleeping, but it's interesting that you're both having nightmares. I mean you and Galahad." She rambled on about the despair of looking for apartments, then said she'd be there a while and to call if he liked. "Bye, Papa. Love you."

No, he couldn't manage a call. He would sound as incoherent as she did. But he started an email. The dream, he wrote, was intended to spur the quest—

I mean Galahad's quest, not mine. I should call it the Quest, capital Q. And, hey, you're in Spain, so you've got the Knight of the Doleful Countenance.

> *But journeys change you, yes? Moses, Mohammed,*
> *Dante, Columbus, Goldilocks, the Three Little Pigs:*
> *they all hit the road to seek their fortunes. If nobody*
> *went out slamming the door, we'd have no stories.*
> *Of course, the ones who got et by the wolf—*

And as he revved up his wit, he smelled his smoking dinner.

"Ah, life!" he proclaimed aloud as he scraped the blackened detritus into the garbage. Too depressed to start over, he looked in the fridge, considered the leftover spaghetti but opted for a hunk of provolone with a double shot of vodka. He finished his supper, puttered about, then went to bed.

A gentler dream: he was at a party in an old Victorian house with people he didn't know. They'd asked him to perform a short sketch, but no one was in charge to gather people or to introduce him. The party thinned out, he wandered around, finally plopping down on the rumpsprung couch that his mom had found at a second-hand store for their house on Silver Street when he was very small. He stretched his legs to know he was still alive and dreamed that he fell asleep.

VI

A Vessel of Grace

May 10th. *Something terrible will happen today. No, it already has.* Albert hit SNOOZE and dozed off.

§

Far into the night, Bobby's parents sat on a heavy wooden bench at the police station. Whenever someone passed in the corridor or spoke to the night-duty officer, the father put his hand on his wife's knee as if to prepare her for the news, but there was never any news. She urged that they go out and search the streets, but he assured her that the police were doing that already, perhaps with dogs, helicopters, radar, drones.

Around midnight, he needed to relieve himself but feared being absent when the news came, so he held out until two a.m. when he had to ask directions to the loo. It seemed to mock their torment to urinate at such a time. When he returned, his wife rose abruptly and said, "Let's go." He was surprised but amenable. The desk officer took the name of their B&B and assured them they'd be notified promptly when their son was found.

In their room, the father sat on one of the twin beds, the mother on the fold-out cot where Bobby had slept. Time stopped. Each knew they ought to sleep, but neither could suggest it for fear of what the other might think. They rarely knew what each other thought, so they feared the worst. Each felt, privately, that they were cartoon outlines with the faces left blank, or movie extras—told where to stand, when to cheer—without knowing the movie's title or who was starring in it. The father knew that he'd promised to call his office, but his mind was blank. Where did he work? He would remember in a minute: someplace where he sat at a desk with lots of papers, and if people asked for something he told them no. He knew his son's name was Bobby. He knew that much. He was dead certain of that. He felt a cold, wet dread creeping up his ankles. What if it reached his bowels?

Somewhere an old man—or god—was dreaming him. A god who might strip him naked or whisk away his child. A god who had granted him a desk in Personnel but had not furnished him a soul. A god as half-formed as he. The dread hit his bowels. He excused himself and shuffled, weeping, to the toilet.

The mother knew she was sitting on the edge of a cot in a Wiltshire bed-and-breakfast at three a.m., but she too imagined herself held in some god's cold hands. She heard the doctor's voice murmur, "He's starting to crown!" She tried to remember what the baby's name would be, but she could only see the day when he first began to crawl, and when he began to crawl away.

§

The old god Albert slept till mid-morning, fingering the crumbs of his dreams. He imagined the Lost Boy asking for a hot dog and a Coke from the snack bar, trying to explain to his Arthurian babysitter what a snack bar was, and the Fool nodding, enchanted by the notion of magical instant food. Bobby was starting to think that the Fool was a fool, but it wasn't the first time he'd had a fool for a babysitter.

At last, the old god hauled himself out of bed. It wasn't till he was mixing his granola and yogurt, chopping nuts to sprinkle on top and dipping into the jar of dried apples he'd spent three days straight with Lainie peeling and preserving, that it struck him: it was May 10th.

When she'd died, on this day a year ago, his mind was a desert. Barren, frigid: no tears, no pain, no jackrabbits, no tumbleweeds. He sat like a pillar of salt, with the makings of tears but not the flow. He had discerned in Lainie, more or less, the classic five stages of death—denial, anger, bargaining, despair, acceptance—and he'd thought there must be some equivalent for survivors. But his own five stages seemed to be in gridlock at an unmarked intersection, too clogged even for the furious drivers to blare their horns.

"Honey," she'd said the day before, "your eyebrows are shoving each other back and forth. I don't want a bar fight here." He did a silly dance with his hands. It made her laugh.

Nothing had changed in the ensuing year. Surely, on some arbitrary Tuesday, his pain would come screeching at him like an eighteen-wheeler running a red light, but it hadn't happened yet. Now it was May 10th. The dried apples were still crisp and tart. Last summer, he had let the fruit fall and rot. Now, if he was going to have dried apples, he'd have to face the task himself.

He took his breakfast to the computer desk, deleted the spam, checked the calendar. Impossible: the costumer, Jeanette whatever, was coming early afternoon. "Next Tuesday," he'd said without thinking. How could he have made the appointment for this day of all days? He'd have to call to postpone. But why? So he could sit alone through one more numb afternoon? No, go ahead with it. Carry on the pretense of being alive.

She had been recommended by a theater in San Francisco where they'd played *Frankenstein*. She lived in Novato, close at hand. He would look at the woman's portfolio, explain the challenges of costuming puppets, and describe the workload as comparable to that of his *Tempest*, a huge production with thirty puppets, so that if he whittled it down she couldn't object. He would propose a fee, then kick himself for offering so much. He would say that he was also talking to somebody else and would get back to her in a week or so, just to give himself wiggle room.

§

Lady Mara summoned the Fool to her private garden— shrub, lichen, tendril, and blossom—enclosed by low stone walls. Galahad had ordered it built for his wife as a wedding gift, though he himself was leery of gardens: to him they were small angry bits of wilderness held captive. But he knew that Mara loved gardens. To Galahad, Mara's smile was his sole beam of light.

For Sammy, Mara's garden also held deep fascination, but he never came there unbidden. The flowers were beautiful, but they snarled at him, simpered, or beckoned like harlots. Once he dreamed they had started to eat him. Adam and Eve must have felt great relief at their banishment from Eden—all those vines and suckers and stickums.

But Sammy answered the Lady's call. She was seated on a stone bench, touching a lily's stem as if to feel its pulse. He waited at the gate, watching her eyes, so much like his own in their startling darkness. Sometimes she would ask for a song, but often, like Galahad, she wanted only a presence, some companion more responsive than a parakeet but no more intrusive. He loved those times. He could look at her and dream. If she saw his wide eyes upon her, she didn't mind. He was only a fool.

He did in fact have sinful thoughts of the Lady Mara, but his imagination was limited by experience. He had known the pleasures of the flesh only once, not counting Old Horny. Three drunken soldiers had carted him off to the brothel, where they paid an old whore called Fatty Dumpling to teach him the ways of womankind. As they stripped Sammy down to his chicken skin and hoisted him atop her, she couldn't stop giggling. She heaved from side to side, and he kept rolling off. Finally, she held him in place with a fierce bear hug, and he felt her guide him into some sort of slippery wherever. A violent shiver shook him, and it was done with. The soldiers lofted him onto their shoulders, carried him out in triumph, and tossed him into the horse trough. So that was the mystery of love.

It would surely be different with Lady Mara. It would be bliss simply to see her breasts or, like a cat, to hop onto her lap and dissolve. Of course he never confessed his thoughts to the Priest: he was a fool but he wasn't nuts.

Now she sat on a bench, touching the lip of the lily. Sammy stood as servants do, as if he were planted there. At last Lady Mara looked up.

"Who would you like to be," she asked, "if you weren't the fool Samuel?"

"I could be a big fat fool named Bellybump." He puffed himself out.

"Answer my question, if you please." She was asking for the truth, the way his master had asked for the truth, but Sammy didn't know what the truth was supposed to be.

"That flower there," he said. The lily she touched.

"But it only lives for the summer," she said, "and then it dies away."

"Well then, in winter it could be me. Wool stockings would be funny on a flower, and Sir Galahad would laugh." He did a few hops and capers, but she didn't laugh. He clapped his hand on top of his head as if to contain himself.

"But what if no one laughed? What if they fed you to a goat?"

Now she was joking. Now he could play the fool. "Better than someday I get fed to the worms. They tickle! Yi! Yi!" He shivered and pretended to brush off a thousand wriggling worms.

Lady Mara frowned. Sammy froze: comics of every millennium know when they're bombing. What answer did she want? If it were a real question, she would ask the Priest. Instead she had asked a fool, but she didn't want a fool's answer. He stood confused among the smirking flowers. At last, she beckoned toward the bench opposite her. He approached and sat.

The Lady Mara spoke to him in a voice he only heard when she spoke to his master. "We resemble each other, you know? We do. Same delicate face, though it's funny on a boy, or I guess you must be a man. And our eyes are the same. It makes me wonder if I look as strange as you, or if I shall when my hair turns white." She brushed back the flaxen hair that she wore unbound in the garden.

Sammy sat frozen, afraid to speak.

"Did you know I had a twin sister?" the Lady went on. "I did. She died. Of course I can't remember, we were infants. But I never look in my mirror without seeing her. We two, the two of us, could be sisters, Sammy. Could we?" Mara lowered her eyes to the lily. Again she touched its petals. "Sammy, I have the Priest to confess my sins, but to whom do I confess my heart? God hears me, I know, but God is so huge."

Sammy made an expansive gesture, pretending to measure God. A feeble try for a laugh, but she didn't mind. He was listening. Someone listened to her.

"I love your master, my husband. I love this man to the depth of my soul. But we speak few words. Our love is in our breath, our eyes. I have no one to hear my words."

The Fool knew that the kindness of masters was to be valued but never courted. Safety lay in never meeting their eyes or presuming a bond. His was a species apart: a fool. Yet now his eyes met hers. Breathless, he cried out, a queer, muffled yelp. From that moment until his death off the sea cliffs, he lived in a state of grace.

"I'll tell you a secret, Samuel. I too would be a lily if I could." Her fingers stroked the petals. "A bard came to my father's house when I was a child. He sang holy songs and also ballads of pagan times. He sang of lilies. Of the Virgin Mary's garden. Lilies that sprang from the tears of Eve as she left Eden. And of the pagan goddess nursing a baby godling—oh, how I listened!—her milk flowing heavenward to form the Milky Way and what trickled to Earth sprouted lilies. Innocence and fertility, purity and motherhood." She laughed softly. "Don't blush, Sammy. We are sisters." She clutched the lily to her heart. "Little Fool, little sister: I yearn to feel the milk."

Mara told him her soul.

§

Jeanette Wald was in her early fifties, trim and plain-faced. Red hair, fluffy but not extravagant. A narrow, assertive nose. She wore a baggy green pullover and jeans—not the best advertisement for her costuming acumen, but Albert was more comfortable with someone who looked like a gardener than with a purveyor of haute couture.

"Coffee? Tea? I make unforgettable chamomile."

"Glass of water's fine, thanks."

"Water. So be it." He filled a glass from the filter spout as she opened her portfolio on the dining room table.

"Lessee, okay." She leafed through it: both costumes and sets. "*Little Shop of Horrors*, Pinter's *Betrayal*, *Seussical*, *Twelfth Night*, *Noises Off*. Pretty conventional stuff."

True: conventional, quite professional, some clever touches. But as he surveyed the layouts, he watched her poker face flash glints of memory. He could almost see that the director of *Noises Off* was a total jerk, that the cast of *Little Shop* might better have hopped into the maw of the cannibal shrub, that in *Betrayal* there had been that sweet backstage moment. Her face was liquid. He heard Lainie's words at Salt Point as she watched the water swirling into the tide pools. "My God, the ripples are going seven different ways. They run right through each other and nothing stops." What brought that to mind?

Albert nodded in blank acknowledgement. "So I haven't—It's been a while since I've worked with another costumer. My wife Lainie always did the costumes. I don't really know a gusset from a gizzard, although one of 'em's a chicken, I guess."

"So your wife—"

"Lainie passed away a year ago. We always had a— Funny, we'd fight like fools, and sometimes the only thing we agreed on was that we disagreed completely. But, same time, we knew that we were both looking for—" He put on the brakes, took a breath. "We always knew we were in it together, whatever it was."

"No, I hear what you're saying, I think."

"Even scraping cow shit out of the treads of our hiking boots, we could keep the boots and lose the shit, I guess." He grappled for a thread. "No, but I think I'm pretty easy to work with, at least when I don't keep babbling."

He stared at the portfolio. He couldn't look in her face while she was looking at him. Her renderings for *Betrayal* were panels with huge shadows of intertwined hands.

"Frankly, the project is pretty vague at this point. Why I'm even talking to anyone right now— I oughta be out in the garden pulling weeds, or in a straitjacket, maybe. I'm not sure where it's going. It might be totally crazy." He fell silent. She closed her portfolio. He waited for her to run for the door.

"Well, it sounds different. I'd certainly be up for doing something different." Her expression—preoccupied, vaguely amused, and that assertive nose—suggested that she might indeed be up for something different but gave no hint of what *different* meant to her. "So I'm busy for the next five weeks, working on a show, but after that it's possible."

They went out to the studio to look at the puppets on display stands: characters from *Frankenstein, Orpheus, The Tempest*, and some of their children's shows. "We worked a lot in live theater," he told her, "but we kept coming back to puppets. They're non-union, scab labor. I love the little bastards."

She examined the faces and body structures. Albert wondered if he was telling the truth: did he truly love the little bastards? He looked over to the half-formed head on the work bench. "But this piece, it's— It'll happen. I once had a friend, Arturo, lost both legs in Vietnam. And he described the sensation of the unscratchable itch in a limb that wasn't there."

"I've heard of that, it's called—"

"Worse than pain. You scratch whatever you can reach, and I guess that's what I'm doing right now. And then I just say, 'Chrissake, Al, stop thinking and go to sleep, it's just a puppet show!'"

Jeanette Wald tilted her head, half smiling. "So are you sure you actually want to do this thing? Somehow you don't sound thrilled."

"No, that's just the way I—" He managed a faint chuckle. "So I'm thinking, how about fifteen hundred, would that work okay? Or say, two thousand? Plus materials?"

From her blank stare, it was clear she'd expected far less from a two-bit North Bay gig. She nodded. "That works. I guess that means you actually expect me to exercise some, like, creativity?"

"Sure, that's permissible. Why not?"

This time they both smiled.

"Okay," he said, "I'll give you a call when I've got my head a little more together." He realized after saying it that he'd forgotten to lie about interviewing someone else. She gave him a card. On the way out she stopped and gazed a long time at his lean-faced, unbearably innocent Creature from *Frankenstein.*

"Beautiful," she said.

Albert watched her walk out to her dented red Corvette and drive off. Funny to see a sports car way past its prime, like a wrinkled old movie star. Then he looked at her card and realized that he'd been calling her Joanne.

§

Sir Galahad and Lady Mara sat at their midday meal. For formal gatherings they sat at opposite ends of the heavy oak trestle table but at other times at one end directly across from each other, while the high-back lord's chair at the head of the table loomed with the weight of care. She waited for her husband to speak. All week he had said little, never came to her bed, sat late by the fire, sometimes in the company of the Fool, sometimes with the small child who had appeared on that terrible day and who said few words that anyone could comprehend. At these times it was best to wait for words to be spoken.

He fingered the crust of his trencher. *(No, let him have a wooden bowl. Who the hell knows what a trencher is?)* He raised his bowl to sip the savory stew of hare, leeks, and a grated peasants' cheese that he loved. Then he set it down and met her eyes.

"I have had dreams," he said. Nothing more. He tore a piece from the loaf, scooped in his bowl with the crust as if to feed some starving beast within him. *Let you go begging . . .*

Minutes passed, no sound except his swallowing. The bowl was empty. "More!" he shouted, and a servant came to fill it.

Finally, Mara ventured, "Do you wish to tell me?"

"Do you dream?"

She lowered her eyes. Was it proper for wives to dream? The subject had never been broached. Strange to speak freely to a simple fool and not to the man who enfolded her body and her heart. "I have had dreams of childhood," she said at last, "and of loved ones who are gone." The tremor began in her hands. "When my lord is— When you are absent, I dream of you." He made no response. "Should you speak to the Priest?" she asked. Galahad rose and left the table.

Lady Mara ran her finger along the rim of the bowl his lips had touched, as if touching his face. Not the dark steel visage in shadows thrown by the fire, not the heavy countenance abraded by his forty-seven years, but the face she loved: the visionary, the sacred warrior, the gentle lover who groped for words as he gazed at her in wonder. The man who might still seed her children. That was the face she held in her waking dreams.

§

The face was on its armature, late afternoon. The cheeks were fuller now, the lower jaw fleshier. Albert still worked at sculpting the mouth. The lips were narrow, teeth clenched. The soul had taken on a simian cast. Its blank eye globs stared into a sleepless world.

§

Later, past midnight, the somber Knight sat at the rough-hewn plank table in the kitchen where the servants ate. He dipped his bread in the leftover bowl and nibbled. A scullery maid snoozed by the fireplace, and the Fool stood leaning at the portal, doing a shuffle dance at intervals to keep himself awake. Galahad looked up and beckoned to him. The Fool smoothed his tunic and minced across the stones. He stood before his master, nodding his head.

"Why are you nodding?"

"Stirring my brains so they don't get a crust."

"I'm in no mood for jokes now, Sammy."

"That's good," he said in a singsong chirp, "cause they can get some sleep and feel jokier in the morning."

Then he saw Galahad's face. This was no time for sport.

"Sammy, we spoke of dreams. Do you have bad dreams?"

"Sometimes."

"What do you dream?"

"Maybe big ducks chasing me." That was no joke: it was true. "Or I poop my pants." That too had been true.

"If you had very bad dreams, would you tell the Priest?"

The Fool didn't know what to answer. Some of his very bad dreams involved the Priest squawking, "If thine eye offend thee" to the shabby felon. He risked a pinch of frivolity. "Maybe tell the Priest, and he tells the Pope, and the Pope tells God, and God gives me clean breeches."

The Knight didn't laugh, but he didn't frown. He sat a while longer, got up and left. The Fool went back to bed and tried not to think about ducks.

Next night, by the hearth in the dining hall, Sammy played softly on his lute. Galahad drowsed. The crone put a log on the fire. Her name was Skuld. The Fool saw her as one of the fabled Fates, feeding log after log to the pyre as if logs were human souls. It would be his turn some day, a little dry stick that would cost her no effort at all.

When the Priest appeared, the Fool pretended to fall asleep. Galahad seated himself in his chair of authority, gestured for Father Olyver to sit at his right, and told of his dreams. "The dreams arise from the death that I commanded," the Knight conceded. "The Peasant." (The dead peasant was now capitalized.) "Yet how can this be punishment? How can God punish us for a righteous act?"

The Priest chose his words with care. "Your dreams may not stem from that act." He slicked back his slicked-back hair. "Years ago, there was dispute within priestly circles regarding your vow."

"My vow?"

"Your vow to seek the Grail."

"I confessed my sin in forsaking the pursuit. I received absolution."

"But perhaps a sacred vow—" The Priest trembled. "I might query the Bishop, if you please?"

Galahad sat rigid. "Father, I must ask if what I feel in my heart at the present moment is a sin. Whether I might be at risk of my soul if I am not shriven at once."

"What is in your heart, my son?"

"I feel the overwhelming urge to rise up and bludgeon you."

The Fool stifled a laugh. He knew a good punch line when he heard it.

The Priest gave urgent thought to controlling his bowels but made no outward sign. He appeared to consider the matter. "I will confess you if you wish, but I find it understandable. I think we may wait until our regular time."

There were times the little man hated his God.

§

Albert pressed the glass orbs deeper into their sockets and sat back in his chair. Could he feel the man's dreams in the clay? Their knobby horn buds, their dribbling jowls? He had imagined the Knight was simply haunted by guilt, but he was Albert's creation, shaped from his own mind's scraps and sausage-ends, and in Albert guilt was no big deal. He was a pretty forgiving soul, even of himself.

Not guilt: fear. Galahad's deepest fear was . . . what? Being baked alive in his suit of armor? His own reflection in beggars' eyes? Finding himself in the gut of an endless puppet show? Or a death in pain. A death alone. A death on the toilet. A death in the midst of a sneeze. A death that made a mess. *What do I fear?* Albert asked himself.

§

"My lord, what is it you fear?" The little Priest was a noisome thing, but at times there was a soul astir behind his dull pig eyes.

"What do I fear?"

"Forgive me, but I see fear."

For an instant, the hapless Priest saw the visor lock down over the warrior's face, the sword spring into his hand, the fire-light flash red. But then the Knight's eyes softened to an infinite weariness. "Father Olyver, if the Church tells me I must seek the Grail, and you are the voice of the Church, then I ask you, what is the Grail?"

The drowsing Fool peeked through slitted eyes. He loathed the Priest, but he was curious to know the answer. He saw the little sphincter mouth squeeze tight. "The Grail is the sacred cup that the blessed Joseph of Arimathea brought to this land."

"But what is the Grail? *What is it?*"

The Priest rose. Questions outside the Catechism were snares, yet he could not fail in his duty as steward of answers. "My lord, I believe it to be the vessel of God's grace."

"Grace? What is grace? We are told that grace is freely given of God, not earned. Yet from infancy I was told that to obtain the Grail one must be pure, sinless, unstained. Now I have feasted, I have lain with woman, I have killed—"

The Priest ventured again. "Grace is the gratuitous gift that—"

The Knight exploded. "Babbling the same babble in different words, Priest, is no answer!" His eyes were spikes.

"I will inquire of the Bishop," the little Priest mumbled in terror, envisioning himself hung naked as a ham in the larder. Galahad made a vague gesture of dismissal. The Priest whisked himself into the night.

Sammy pretended to stir awake. He moved to sit on a joint stool by Galahad. At times, he felt like a humble wife, open to her lord. The crone stirred the smoldering coals and set another log on the fire.

Galahad spoke to the rising flames. "In my youth, I had a mad passion for the Grail. It could only be achieved, they said, by the man whose purity was a flood bearing him on its surge. The nuns raised me fatherless, motherless, no sin at my charge except being born of woman. In prayer I would turn my shuttered eyes upward and feel the same spasm of joy as when, in battle, I killed my first man. I began a quest, knowing the promise of the Grail, lust for the Grail, but nothing of its heart." His breath was short and deep, as if climbing a mountain. "Do you know the tale of the Beast of the Quest?"

Sammy scowled. "A big funny monster that's all different parts. It's got dogs in its belly barking."

"And am I, too, questing the Beast? Not the Grail? What if the quest is for the Beast?" He stared into Sammy's eyes, and the Fool began to shiver.

§

Scribbling in his notepad, Albert hit a dead end. He had an ear for the Fool, but he couldn't get Galahad right. Maybe it was his own voice he was straining to hear. What stood in his way? *What two-bit Grail do you seek?* Albert asked himself. Was he asking directions that nobody knew or waiting till the fares went lower? Did he believe that the Grail was a myth, a failed hope and that no amount of striving could deter his ultimate critics, the worms?

He sprayed the clay to keep it wet, covered the befuddled Knight with plastic wrap, picked up his notepad, and shut off the light in the studio. He went into the office, checked email. A note from Mara: *Thinking about U!* In her own terse manner, she was sending a note of comfort on the anniversary. May 10th. Only twice today had he even thought about it.

Time to get supper on. Maybe a pork chop tonight. He started toward the kitchen, then stopped and sat on a low stool by the fireplace. He hadn't made a fire there for months. The vase of ashes stood at the near side of the empty hearth. Mara had selected it at a local crafts fair during the two weeks she was there, insisting that it not be a standard cremation urn. A lidless round vessel with a dark purple crackle glaze, its rim drawn inward to a hand's width, it held nearly all four pounds of the remains.

"Do what you want with the ashes," Lainie had said in the final week. "The worm bin could use 'em. But give some of me back to Mama." She meant the ocean. The last two handfuls they scattered at Salt Point.

He fingered the grainy gray substance. The Grail couldn't

have been a cremation urn, since Jews didn't practice cremation. There was a logic to its being the Last Supper's goblet, but then what about the bread? Why wasn't there a quest for the Holy Platter? And what would you do with the Grail if you found it? Kneel before it, swig booze, or just set it by the fireplace? What would it bring you? Eternal bliss or digestive relief? These days, he could think only in question marks.

He went on skimming his fingers through the gray flakes and bits of bone. Something more was needed. "Lainie," he said. Then a moment later, "Hon." Then, "Love." The only things, as far as he knew, that he'd ever called her. His voice sounded odd to his ears. For a breath, he saw her face looking up as if to say *Is there a problem?* Then she melted into the slurry of fog that filled his eyes. He went to the kitchen and started a potato baking.

VII

Of two Maras and how One became a Fool

Mara—the daughter Mara—was up early. Her dad had sounded strange on the phone. She didn't need to be at work till noon, so she brewed an espresso, sat at the keyboard, started with *Dear Papa*. And stopped.

It occurred to her to check for news of the show her father was working on. She opened a tab to The Fisher Folk website, but everything was at least two years out of date: two shows for K through 6, study guides, testimonials, awards—a dead site now, frozen in time. And then she clicked a nearly hidden icon labeled *Album* and fell into the labyrinth of memory.

Papa, Mama, and baby Mara; the van; stages and back-stages by the score; herself as a little girl, helping to pack up props; the goose puppet staring up at the Eiffel Tower; on and on. And the tormented Caliban, the one-eyed Odin, the nearly-featureless Eurydice, the spectral Lady Macbeth, the biker dude Gilgamesh—strange encounters after *The Ugly Duckling*.

Her earliest memories were from a nest on the floor of the van, her parents driving at night to another city, another show. She loved listening to their talk, their anxieties, all the secrets they shared. She put up with their whispered quarrels because tomorrow they'd laugh and hug and buy a pizza.

Papa had started out doing kids' shows. After college in San Jose, he'd landed an accidental job with a puppet troupe. A few years later, he went solo. Mama had majored in theatre but was mostly playing the role of waitress in Oakland. When they joined forces, he began to reach beyond the birthday party circuit. By the time baby Mara came along, her dad was starting to grow sick of the kids' puppet shows. She remembered he'd railed about a sponsor complaining that the fox called the pig *dummy*, which might wound the pig's self-esteem. "It's a fucking pig," he muttered. In the back of the van, three-year-old Mara stifled her giggles.

She lingered over a photo of Mama in her forties. Touching the screen, she wished that photos were still things you could hold—crinkly paper you could splotch with tears. All she could hold was the memory of her mother's fierceness in cutting to the core of the issue, whether it was teenage Mara dithering on a term paper or Papa grousing about being unable to risk serious puppetry for adults when kids' stuff was paying the bills. "Do it or stop talking about it," she said in that low back-in-the-throat voice that cut through all objections. "Shit or get off the pot!" Nothing delicate about Elaine Scott Fisher.

It was a seismic shift. The kids' shows continued, but the duo began to work on *Orpheus*, which put them on the map and paid for Mara's braces. Their *Macbeth* had lasted a couple of years on tour. *Frankenstein* was an almost wordless text with haunting faces. But the touring market for off-beat theater was dying, and Mara recalled those audiences: passionate, deeply moved, and small. Her dad was writing a new script called *Search for the Lost City* when the diagnosis came. Five months later, Mama was dead. The lost city stayed lost.

A year ago, she flew to California, led Papa like a zombie through his days, directing him to sign papers and file forms, despite her own red eyes and bottomless ache. If she hadn't chosen the urn, the ashes would still be in a cardboard box.

Having lived so long in the shadow of Papa's churning obsessions and Mama's iron will, Mara had always considered herself lightweight. No matter that she read serious literature in great gobs and carried on passionate debates with friends over politics, cinema, and sex. Yes, she spoke three languages better than most people spoke one, had a Bryn Mawr education, and once she'd stood gazing so long at a Rembrandt self-portrait that she felt she'd married the dude. But she wanted more. She wanted to embrace a wild freedom—earning her bread by waitressing, teaching English, stage-managing for exotic dancers, and now writing low-brow culture news—but also to fulfill that pit bull sense of purpose that she knew was bred in her bones. She felt like two people on a one-seat moped. And it didn't help that the gifted female of thirty-one years that she knew herself to be was always scrambling to pay the rent.

She should have told Papa about the house. They were buying a house, or trying to. Alejandro had a small inheritance from his grandmother, and a friend had told her about this place in a town twenty kilometers from Madrid: an old squat stone bodega, with two huge rooms that could be partitioned, an attached stable and tack room, an incredible view, and enough work to drive them nuts for the rest of their lives. In America, they'd call it a fixer-upper. Here, it was a hovel.

"Vamos a comprarla!" Alejandro had shouted.

She was grateful to Alejandro for being such a fount of messy emotion, so unlike the father she loved. But save the news for next time. Time for work, and she still hadn't written more than *Dear Papa*. She would try calling later.

§

Albert skimmed his notes: *G. tells dream to priest, priest to bishop, bishop to cardinal—word comes back down the line.* He might stage this with hats, all the way up to the Pope. Maybe the lost kid's dad could be a hat salesman who saw the world as a flurry of hats. Or not.

But this was Arthurian Britain. A priest didn't email the bishop: there would be a formal letter drafted at each stage, and the transit would take weeks. Filtering through the primeval bureaucracy might take months. Galahad would rise every morning with nightmares seared in his head, shuffle through the day, stare into the fireplace to burn his eyes clean, then face the dog teeth of another night. Albert remembered the thirty-two hours of Mara's birth: leaving the hospital, rushing home to check the answering machine and feed the dog, moving through tasks dumbly, helplessly, as if on a single breath. And so Father Olyver sent word to the bishop, the bishop to the cardinal, and Galahad awaited the diagnosis.

For the Lady Mara, the days moved with a limp. She sought modes of killing time, even as time killed by slow degrees. During these weeks, her husband barely touched her. At mealtime, he told her news from afar, gossip from the village, prospects for the harvest, or some wry comment about the Priest. She tried to listen, to insert a word of cheer, but could only hear the beats of her heart. As the evening deepened, he clouded over, stared at the fire, bade her goodnight as if they were figures in the tapestry on the wall. A few times he came to her in the dark, buried his needfulness in her, sobbed and departed. She held back her tears until he was gone.

*Hear me, Lady of Sorrows. Once we needed no words,
I and my shining Knight. We spoke eye to eye, touch
to touch, and that sufficed. I knew my station, my
duties, my destiny hand in hand with my lord. I loved
him for his youth, his promise, his vision.
Now he fades. I must make peace with my barrenness.
Help me, Holy Mother.*

Now, in the waning afternoon, she sat in her room by
the window. In the whole castle, hers were the only three
small panes of precious glass, fashioned by distant artisans—
Galahad's anniversary gift. It gave the same view of the forested
hills that she saw through open shutters, but seen through crystal
those hills were a magical world. When it rained, the rivulets ran
down the panes like tiny erotic tickles, or else the drops would
surf ferociously like soldiers against the battlements. But the
magic was gone. The rain beat at the glass, an impenetrable
membrane, taunting her with an untouchable landscape beyond
her prison. *Prison?* She rose to the window with fists raised to
shatter the panes, to let herself bleed, cry out, pour free. But she
could not shatter a gift of beauty.

She often called Sammy to her. He would sit there for
minutes or hours, gazing into the void. She might work at her
embroidery, then speak, ask him to stir the charcoal brazier or
pull the curtains shut, but she never bared her thoughts as she
had on that day in the garden. *Sister?* Her sister was dead. All
sisters. "That was the way of it," her father had once been fond
of saying.

One day the Fool, sitting in silent attendance, took out his
juggling balls and began to practice a new trick. It would be
folly to do unbidden tasks in the presence of nobility, but folly
was permitted to a fool. And Mara was mesmerized. She had
never seen a juggler rehearsing, honing his craft. When the Fool
hesitated, feeling her gaze, she motioned him to continue. He
dropped the balls, tried and failed, tried and failed, until at last
his hands began to master the stunt's hocus-pocus.

"Teach me how," she said.

The Fool stopped. The balls dropped, bouncing three ways.
He stared like a squirrel frozen before a wolf, no whisk of move-
ment. She repeated her request.

At last, he whispered one word: "Springtime."

Then he began the teaching. Starting with a single ball, he
showed her how to toss it from hand to hand without moving

the hands out of place, trying each time for the same arc. The first day, she never caught it once. That night she prayed to the Holy Virgin to help her catch the ball. Next day she caught it three times.

"Father, Son, and Holy Ghost!" she cried joyfully.

That was the start of it. A trifling feat, yet within her a portal inched open, a vague pathway outside her peripheral vision. The sun set the crystal panes aglitter, and the hills brightened—a magic set free by impulsive frivolity. At times the strange little boy wandered in to watch them. She didn't mind. Strangeness was welcome.

At first, as they practiced, she spoke only as needed, but soon she began to chatter away, though her heart was all in the juggling. She scolded the balls as unruly servants, and when that didn't work, she soothed them as birds she was trying to tame. The Fool rarely spoke, but at times he paused, stared at the floor and murmured, "Springtime." He never looked at her as he said it, yet she always heard. She came to think of her name, her true secret name, as *Springtime*.

One day, on the verge of winter breaking its grip, she directed Sammy to sit in her chair, draped her own shawl about him, snatched up his droopy fool's cap, and put it on her head. Circling around the chair, she mimicked his mincing gait, announced in a squeaking tremolo, "Springtime!" and performed her simple three-ball juggle as if it were the most astonishing miracle ever pulled off by the saints. As the newly minted lady of the castle, Sammy applauded madly, and they lost themselves in laughter—cascades and ripples and peals—late into the afternoon.

"Now teach me to dance the way you dance, Sammy, and teach me the songs. Teach me to be a fool."

§

During those weeks, Galahad prepared for the day he would receive the dreaded verdict. In their tales of quests, minstrels would sing of lone knights wandering in the wilderness, but a canonical Quest required much more: logistical support, lines of communication, scouts, and an armed force sufficient to settle disagreements. It required that the Priest prepare villagers and peasants for heavy taxes to finance the enterprise, to see it not as their master's whim but as the implacable Will of Heaven. To tempt them to the venial sin of discontent, even to the mortal sin of revolt, would be sin chargeable to Galahad himself.

They must see the Quest as theirs and Galahad as merely the instrument. The stewards began to lay up stores, commission the forging of arms, and recruit the vassal knights and twelve-score shabby grunts wielding quarterstaffs, scythes, or teeth. The Priest began the sermons.

On a cool spring morning the week after Easter, word came down from the cardinal, via the bishop, into the trembling hands of Father Olyver. Yes, Galahad's nightmares were punishment for breaking faith. He had sinned in consecrating his life to the Grail, swearing to find the Grail, and then forsaking the Grail. To fulfill his vow, he must renew the Quest.

The official document came with an extended codicil laying out the ontological, teleological, and theological justifications of the Quest. Father Olyver translated it from the Latin with some difficulty: he was educated but not very bright. As the little man stuttered his way through the tortuous prose, Galahad paid scant attention. He simply wanted the nightmares to end.

And so did Albert. He was sick of dreaming Galahad's nightmares for him, and he was sick of Sir Galahad. How could he sustain interest in this has-been or never-was? A smug, self-satisfied dolt blaming God for the onerous burden of being rich. Better a show where he beats his wife, whereupon the Fool brains him with a poker and runs off with the Lady to become an itinerant duo playing the first Punch and Judy show. Why invent a hero who's the quintessence of everything you despise in yourself? Self-centeredness, self-righteousness, self-pity, self-hate. *I know in my deepest heart how pathetic I am, but somebody love me, please!*

"Stop that right now!" He spoke it out loud: the words Lainie would say. He knew her lines by heart. Get on with it. Send the poor skunk on his errand. Let him find a souvenir beer mug, at least. Give us some hope.

Hope. Always the challenge. They both saw too much despair in the world to want to add to the heap, and they agreed in wanting to offer glimpses of light, even if only the dimmest candle flame. But they loathed easy answers, fatuous optimism, cheap hope. They wanted whatever hope they raised to sprout from reality, to run the gauntlet, to be earned by blood and sweat. "Hope should be steel," Lainie said once, "not smelly cheese." She was no writer, but she had a way with words.

Galahad seemed to hear those words. He sat in a sequestered alcove at a small writing desk, with a quill pen and a scrap of vellum trimmed from the codicil, struggling with penmanship.

Though the nuns had taught him to write, important documents were always drafted by the Priest or an apprentice scribe, with the Knight simply adding a flourish at the end. But the theses that the clerics had sent to justify the Quest were convoluted nonsense: nothing he could proclaim to his vassal knights, much less to the commoners. Men needed something that would inspire them, send them forth with dignity. He strained to hear the faint echo of a long-forgotten hymn. Clumsily he inscribed the words *Every man,* then scraped out the ink with his knife.

He sat there all afternoon, compelled by the voice in his head that sang *Give us some hope.* It was dusk when he finished his call to arms. He read it over, astonished.

This we seek of the Grail:
All men live free.
None suffer want.
None taste fear.
All wounds heal.
All know peace.
Love is the law.
Young, old, women, men, the humble, the strong:
We are kin.

Those were not his words. They were some exotic fruit he'd never tasted. They were an old madman's words: a hermit, a babbler. Words he'd heard as a child, the words of Jesus spoken by an itinerant priest who'd visited the nunnery and was never invited back. *Unless ye become as little children . . .* The nuns told their young crusader that those words were the Devil's words, that children were befouled with Original Sin, that Jesus would never utter such nonsense. Yet the words had bred in a cavity of his heart, the distant, ringing canticle of the Sangreal. He expected utter bafflement when the herald read them out to the summoned throng, but they were the meaning of the Quest. Either they or the peasant's curse: *Drink your own tears.*

One morning—midsummer by then—Knight and Lady sat across the heavy oak table from one another. Neither knew what they might speak. In an earlier time, without words, their hands would have reached across that narrow board, but now even their touch was mute. He had told her his startling litany, and she heard mad words of her own that she longed to speak aloud: *Let me show you my magic. Let me juggle, strike laughter out of the stones. Let me conjure a joyous Grail.* But she could not force her lips.

"I have made the vow. I must fulfill it."

She heard a distant cackle. It was only a branch breaking in the orchard, but she heard it as demons mocking her bewilderment. He had no belief in the Grail: he believed only in the nightmare that had gouged all love from his eyes. She had held to her fantasies of the future, to her ache for a child, to a promise whose murmurs grew fainter and fainter, to a faith that from her secret juggling and songs and foolery might spring a simple grace.

"I fear you must," she said.

A servant had placed a vase of bright pink and azure blossoms at the center of the table. Why could not the two of them reach out, finger the petals, pronounce the Quest fruitful and done: a journey to simple oneness. The portal stood open. Then it closed. She knew he would never return, not as the man she had loved.

§

All was prepared. Galahad donned his full armor, his squires adjusting the straps and buckling the burnished steel. A few miles down the road, he would change into practical traveling gear, but a lord's departure called for spectacle. The force of three hundred men was slow to get itself arranged. The vassal knights were to ride at the head of the column, followed by Galahad himself. Archers and pikemen would trot behind, and the conscripts and mule-drawn supply train would follow up at the rear. The whores' wagons would meet them outside the village. Galahad saw the peasants standing by the roadway, muttering to one another. He knew they would be grousing about the new taxes. But what was he to do? He had made a vow.

The Priest blessed the long procession. Then a dispute. The Priest waved his arms, protesting, while Galahad sat rigid. It was clear: he had ordered the Priest along on the journey. The little man whined, but the Knight stood firm. A groom brought a saddled ass and heaved the speechless Priest into the saddle. A herald read out Galahad's proclamation. No one understood it, but it sounded fine. The muttering ceased, but the Knight felt eyes staring down: some old god or demon. He heard the thunderous voice of the Puppetmaster:

"Get your tin-can ass off that horse and go back to hug your wife! Don't inflict your nightmares on the whole damned world! No more hero stories! What the world needs is a break from heroes and a few short minutes of peace!"

Galahad was filled with awe at the uncanny roar but grasped not a word. The old god Albert turned his eyes to the Lady.

Lady Mara sat at her window glass to view the departure. She stared at her husband's distant face, into the shadowed hollows where his eyes might be. They had made a formal farewell, but a tearful public display would be improper. That was the way of it, her father would have said. The Fool stood passively behind her, having been left with her as a consolation. He held his silence.

"All gone! Sammy, all gone! The deepest sin, they say, is despair, and it strangles me. I would suffer his quest—I have loved him for it—but not a quest born of nightmare."

She saw her young knight, eyes of amber, luminous in the sun. And she saw a heavy-cheeked man who bulged out the sides of his breastplate, rattling at the joints as he waddled out the door. She felt a blunt stab in her gut, dreading an alchemy reversed: that her golden lover was transmuting into lead. He had not yet lost all luster—she had read the strange words of his proclamation—but what would remain?

"I believe, I want to believe I love him. Still."

She had seen the Knight's soul flicker alive only when, rarely now, he opened his eyes to hers. Its luster still shone, and she nurtured it as best she could. Without her, she saw it shriveling in the sun. The Priest perpetually proclaimed the worth of the human soul, besmirched but immutable as gold, though she could barely hear the Priest—that porcine, pock-marked little man who greased his hair with what smelled like chicken fat and stared at her bosom as if ready to take a nibble. And yet she clung to a faith in immutability, as do those who believe in love.

"I lost myself in frivolity. I juggled, secretly played the fool as my husband languished in Limbo and plunged into Hell. I might have—"

She might have juggled for him, done a funny dance. She might have posed conundrums, sung ditties, pulled silly faces, plunked the lute. She might have risked baring her naked soul. She might have done what she longed to do: she might have risked laughter.

"I am helpless now. No salvation. None."

§

Albert knew he was in trouble. He loathed his hero, and the wife would surely lose our respect, taking the blame on herself.

She should be more independent, more self-actualized, more 21ˢᵗ century. But the Lady Mara wasn't aware of those failings.

Sammy edged forward timidly, leaned close to her ear, and told her what to do.

VIII

Of the Host setting forth and the Fool's Plea

Galahad's horse raised its hoof for the first step on the Quest, then froze. The army strained forward like a tractor-trailer parked on a steep decline. Albert heard the cell phone beep from the office. He fumbled to finish his business, pull up his pants, and stumble out of the bathroom to quell its insistent cackle. The horse was poised, hoof aloft. It would have to wait.

"Hello?"

"Hi. Jeanette here. How's it going?"

For a moment he thought of offering a detailed report on his bowels but checked the impulse. "Oh. Hi. What's up?" Standing at the phone table, he finished zipping his pants. Just as he'd expected: she must be calling to say she couldn't do it. Blessed relief.

"So when can we talk?" she asked.

It had been three days since their meeting. He did not like to be rushed. He did not like people with an itch. He did not like people as pushy as himself. It was the perfect reason to tell her he'd made other plans.

"I thought you said you were busy the next five weeks."

"I multitask." That same flat voice, like a piece of plywood.

At least let the poor bastard get his parade out of town, he wanted to say. Secure his supply route, get rid of the little kid and the clueless tourists and the scummy Priest. Get rid of old Albert looking down from the sky like a senile God the Father.

"Weren't you working on a show?"

"*Sound of Music*. It's boring."

He could hear in her voice how much she loathed boredom. They had that in common, at least. "Boring? You get bored with projects?"

"Didn't you get bored playing *Donald Duck* a thousand times?"

"*The Ugly Duckling*."

"Oh. Sorry."

"But you have a point," he conceded.

"So I'm doing a bunch of cute Austrians and cute nuns and cute Nazis that will, how do you say it, manifest the director's vision? If I can discern one. But frankly I have to admit that I hate that fucking show."

Albert too hated it passionately. They had too much in common. He'd be way more comfortable with some faceless lady who could sew a straight seam and loved *The Sound of Music*. He checked his calendar. "Well, say next Thursday? Hard Core Espresso, down on Bloomfield Road? Noonish?"

"That works. I have to be somewhere at two. I'll bring some sketches."

Sketches? Sketches of what? "Sketches?"

"Just ideas."

"But I don't even have a script yet."

"No, just images from stuff you said. See if I'm heading the right direction."

He couldn't recall saying more than five words about the show. *Galahad. Grail. Fool. Weird. Puppets.* Not much else. "Okay, see you then. Thanks, Jo— Jeanette."

He wrote the appointment on the phone pad, then stood a long time at the table, aimlessly clicking the cell phone, trying to tell it that next time it should come along with him to the can. He knew damn well what he'd done. He'd sent himself an injunction—cardinal to bishop, bishop to priest—to force himself to the Quest. He'd stepped into the bear trap of responsibility so that he could spend the next five months chewing off his foot. The army was poised to depart, awaiting the fall of a hoof.

What hath God wrought?

§

The parents had been two days in their bed & breakfast. The dad kept flipping on the TV, channel-surfing a minute, flipping it off. The mother had brought along a paperback *Jane Eyre* for something appropriate to pass the time in England, but a third of the way she'd forgotten all she'd read. Their wheels were spinning in sand with no one behind the wheel.

They went down for breakfast at the posted time, returned to their room to wait for the police, and ventured to a nearby pub for other meals. There was safety in the fog, the half-life, the dead zone. They hugged but couldn't feel each other near. They waited for the Puppetmaster to tell them what to do, but they seemed to be forgotten. Even if Bobby came back, they might not know it.

§

Albert sat in his chilly studio, space heater puffing. He had just written the boy's parents into the same gelid state in which he found himself. He closed his notepad on their vacant faces. The phone jangle with Jeanette had spurred a brief surge of panic, deflected into scribbles that led him straight back to staring at the studio's rubble. He wondered how Galahad had coped not merely with failing to find the Grail but with sitting on his ass during all the years that followed. Failure: that was to make the long perilous journey up the mountain and slay the dragon, only to find that the Grail had been pawned by St. Peter to pay the gambling debts of St. Paul. Stasis: that was to rot at the foot of the mountain with rampant diarrhea. A whole army was set to march, waiting on one raised hoof.

His work table held the half-finished Galahad and several rod puppet mock-ups, good enough for temporary use. In the middle of the floor stood a green card table with a pad of newsprint, charcoal pencils, two pages of the scenario, and several hand puppets from shows long past. He had pinned some red-and-yellow-striped linen to the one representing the Fool and a blue silk scarf on another as the Lady. What could he use as stand-ins for the tourists? He dug out an old Hansel and Gretel. From across the studio, the Knight stared with empty eyes.

When Albert was young, he could daydream shows. Images came to him unbidden while walking or eating breakfast. Now it worked differently. He might scribble on his drawing pad at breakfast, but his brain was a cement wall, windowless, until he stepped to the center of the studio, picked up a puppet, and began to play. As he floundered, ideas popped forth. A door would open the moment after he stumbled through it.

He took the rod puppet mock-ups from their stands. Rickety PVC supported the waist-high playboard, six feet from left to right—the surface of the puppets' Planet Earth. As Bobby, he set a stuffed monkey on the end of the playboard. The Lost

Boy might remain a doll in the final staging. Keep to a primitive style.

The army's departure. To the left he placed Lady and Fool, and the monkey shouted, *"It's a parade!"* Maybe he'd improv with the audience as crusaders: *"Sit up straight! Atten-hut! Wipe that grin off, soldier!"* He didn't mind sounding absurd.

Cheap joke. Instead, he fixed an aluminum frame to a tabletop and pinned bleached muslin to it as a shadow screen. He set the Lost Boy facing it, watching the soldiers march.

"Okay, so I'm back of the screen, pulling silhouettes through the groove. *Warm spring day, ladies and gentlemen, perfect weather for this historic occasion.* Or a motorized loop across an overhead, and then I could be out front interviewing. *Hi there, what's your name, big guy?"*

He grabbed the monkey, wiggled its head.

"Bobby. Well, Bobby, you must be on vacation. Where do you live? Home? That's great. And how do you like Sir Galahad?" He stopped, plopped the monkey face down. "Jury's out on that."

Better idea: the army as cut-outs on a felt board. Add them in clusters while reciting draft notices. *"Greetings. You are hereby ordered to report . . ."* Then roll it up like an olio drop to show Galahad on his steed. Hobby-horse head attached to the front of the puppet, or maybe a full-scale rocking horse, gun barrels out the nostrils, steel-trap teeth, and for Galahad a gleaming tin halo, batteries for brains. Or the army: ten finger puppets, head on each finger, prancing around the parents, popping like popcorn. Or a castle of Legos with Lego soldiers, and the puppeteer looming overhead, bearded like God—

Neat ideas, dead on arrival. The Knight's hypothetical horse had lifted its hoof to start the journey, but it stuck in midair as Albert ran through his inventory of cast-off gimmicks. Why build an army of finger puppets or shadows or celery sticks to illustrate that the army was ready to march, when he could just say it? "The army's ready to march." Was he trying to tell the damn story or to prove how clever he was?

One thing stuck. The aesthetic of the show might be a kind of throw-away, very loose, no concern for the fine points of manipulation, just an obsessive, relentless telling—a dramaturgical peristalsis—with the Puppetmaster under no illusion that he even had an audience out there to witness this solitary mad rite. That might do it. At least it was honest.

Back at his work table, Albert stared at his terracotta bugbear. Galahad had evolved like a shapeshifter who couldn't make up his mind. The firm-set jaw had become grotesquely prognathous. His center of gravity bulged upward, spawning beetle brows worthy of King Kong. Then it all smoothed into a clear-visaged, cherubic Humpty Dumpty. More work, and it became a small bony rat-face with jowls. It took Albert a moment for the memory to snag him, and then he saw it: Galahad's half-formed face was the spitting image of his father. He hadn't thought of Al Senior for years, but the poor dead louse must have been lurking in his brain, aching for attention. If that's how he conceived Galahad, he had a serious problem with his hero. Carefully plucking out the eyes, he mashed down the nose and kneaded the rat-face into a featureless lump. Start over. Try to get into the heart of this guy or find out if he has one.

§

The world held its breath, awaiting the fall of the hoof. So many centuries, so many hooves coming down—the column of horses, the fluttering banners, the soldiers' dead eyes. And just before the moment of release, when that hoof would slam the earth and the horde start its clatter forward, a shrill cry rang from beneath the castle's portcullis: "Me too!"

It was Sammy the Fool. He hobbled forth in his mincing half-trot, waving his arms, his cap tassels bouncing. A knight called out, "Sammy! Sammy Shit-pants!" and it became a chant, three hundred raw voices in ritual invocation: "SAMMY SHIT-PANTS! SAMMY SHIT-PANTS! SAMMY SHIT-PANTS!"

Then the army hushed, except for the clank and rustle of horses held in check. The Fool trotted breathlessly up to the Knight in Shining Armor.

"What is it, Sammy?"

"I come too."

"Sammy, no."

"I can help."

Galahad smiled in spite of himself. "No, Sammy, go back and stay with the Lady. She will be lonely. You keep her company and make her laugh."

"She says go with you. Or you'll get sadder and madder and not empty your bladder."

Galahad looked unamused. "The battlefield is no place for juggling, boy."

"She says Father Olyver isn't a big enough fool. You need

another." The Knight glanced at the sour Priest, perched on his donkey. The Priest squeezed out a titter.

The chant began again, more insistently: "SAMMY SHIT-PANTS! SAMMY SHIT-PANTS! SAMMY SHIT-PANTS!"

Abruptly Galahad gestured, and a squire lifted the Fool into the saddle behind the Priest. The trumpets sounded, and in an instant the surly peasants forgot their grievances, their woes, and their scarecrow children. Like their fathers and grandfathers before them, they waved their hats and cheered their noble master setting forth on his sacred Quest.

In a distant window high in the castle keep, Galahad discerned a figure that must surely be his Lady, raising a frail hand in farewell. He waved in acknowledgment. The white steed's hoof came down.

IX

Of Daughters, Demons and Dreams

"So how's the house business? Is that coming along?"

"Don't get me started, Papa."

"Well, either I get you started or you get me started or else we squat like stumps on opposite sides of the planet."

Albert was sitting in his usual coffee shop with his usual sixteen-ounce Americano. He hated people who nattered on their cell phones in public, but right now he was the sole natterer. Mara had emailed him news of the house, but he hadn't spoken with her in over a week. When he was working on a script, he had a repertoire of avoidance mechanisms that usually involved the Web or the fridge but minimized direct connection with other human beings. He resorted to humans only when the loneliness became so unbearable that it inspired him to be flippant.

"So you've found your dream hacienda," he said.

"Well, the bank says that the mortgage is coming through but they don't know when, and then the signing will be sometime, maybe, possibly, we hope. I have to be out of my room by the end of the month, so in the meantime we're looking for someplace cheap to live. Then the renovations, which are gonna last the rest of our lives, although for a start just being able to turn on the lights and find a place to pee. Or we could leave the lights off and pee anywhere, I guess."

"What's weird to me these days," Albert said with mock incredulity, "is people buying a house before they're actually married."

"I know," Mara said, "I'm shocked."

"But I guess it's the ultimate test of a relationship. If you can survive a renovation, you can survive anything." He'd have to remember to use that line.

They continued small talk about the house, Alejandro, and the evils of the banking world.

"What baffles me," she said at last, "is you'd think an utterly corrupt criminal industry like banking would be more efficient. I mean, isn't it to their advantage to rip you off faster?"

Albert saw that they were veering into politics. He'd long ago resolved never to project his own sociopolitical despair onto his only child. "But on the bright side . . ."

"On the bright side, what?" She nailed him. Dead silence, but she granted mercy. "So you didn't say how the show is coming."

He knew that she knew: if he didn't talk nonstop about a project, he was in trouble with it. He made a few hemming-hawing sounds, said something about its getting bigger than he'd planned, some kind of deep-angst thing, as if anyone needed more of that. He described the kid's parents dithering in their B&B while the Knight rode off on his two-bit crusade.

"I just had an email from a friend, Joe Cook, remember, from Baltimore? He's doing a show about lizards. That's a much better idea. He's already claimed lizards, so I might consider bonobos."

"Papa, when you start getting facetious, it usually means you're hanging on by a thread. Is that fair to say?"

"Well, that's what spiders do. Call me Daddy Long-legs." He waited for a laugh but got a brief snort. "Okay, when I launched into it, this thing was going to be funny and simple. Then I start getting ideas, and there's nobody to tell me how dumb they are, so they sink roots. My whole head is crabgrass."

She suppressed a laugh. "Interesting."

A slim young woman came into the coffee shop with a baby in her arms and went to the counter. The baby twisted around to see the old goat sitting alone with cell phone and coffee mug, a vision of what might transpire in its scary future. Albert waggled a finger at it. The baby hugged tighter to Mommy.

"Look, I'm aware that this is a nutty project and that I'm bitching and moaning, not entirely unlike you did whenever you had a term paper due, if I remember correctly?"

"So you inherited my genes?"

Excellent riposte. He knew that she knew him. She had seen her parents in their worst lights and their best. From the time she was a toddler she'd traveled the worlds they created. She could probably still recite the lines of every show better than he could. Once, their tour host had recruited a babysitter for the four-year-old, but the babysitter wanted to see the show and sneaked into the back of the auditorium with little Mara. As Lainie's Red Riding Hood stared at Granny and took a dramatic pause, a tiny voice from the back of the house piped, "What big teeth you have!" You still couldn't take a pause with Mara: she'd tell you what you were going to say before you said it.

He glanced around the coffee shop. A few young people were caught up in the Web. An elderly couple—a matching set—stared at each other's coffee cups. By the window, two women discussed divorces, enlightenment, and constipation.

"Sweetheart, actually, let's talk about lighter stuff, like war in the Middle East." What he couldn't say was that he felt a loneliness like acid reflux searing his gullet. And that launching solo into this project felt like Lainie's second death. And that his night-time palavers with Sir Galahad had brought him no closer to finding that man's soul. The Knight rode forth in obedience to the Church: whose edict was Albert obeying?

"Are you, like, finding any companionship, Papa?"

"Well, I don't really think—"

"Maybe you should."

His reply was abrupt. "I get your point." He didn't mean it to sound so sharp. "Okay, I admit I'm a little lost doing this on my own, but I'll figure it out." With heavy-handed lightness: "In any case, I'm pleased to report that I haven't had any alcohol for a considerable period of time."

"Yes?"

"At least since yesterday midnight. But I think Galahad drinks more than he should, so it's tax-deductible as professional research."

There was a pause. "Papa—"

"Yes, I know. Thanks for your concern." He took a sip from his empty coffee mug to indicate his temperance.

Enough said for now. The conversation had hit a speed bump, the vehicle registering EMPTY though the tank was full to the brim. They accepted each other's love on trust till a better day, hung up, and tried to blink away the grit in their eyes.

§

After lunch, Albert refilled the cat bowl and sent Mara a quick note. He hadn't quite been able to brush out the grit.

*Good talking, sweetheart. Sorry I got testy. Right now
    I'm off to the graveyard, but don't worry, I'm coming
    back.*

A quarter mile down the road, he sat on a stone bench in
the cemetery, his notepad on his knee. The marble vault that held
rack upon rack of ashes—what did they call it? a *cinerarium*?—
stood thirty feet off, shading the sun. There was still a chill in the
air, and the stone bench was cold. He rummaged in his shoulder
bag, took out a friend's manuscript he had promised to read,
and tucked it under his butt. His page was blank. In his younger
days, Albert imagined that writers decided what they wanted to
say, then said it. For himself, though, he could only spew out
words and then decide if he wanted to say it or if he even knew
what it meant. He scribbled some random phrases.

*What about Merlin? Hero ensorcelled in the wizard's
    steel gaze.*

First atrocity heard by Lost Boy.

Get rid of Mommy & Daddy.

Across the grounds, an elderly woman hobbled after her
dog, a reddish-brown corgi. As she approached, he recognized
the purple hair: Edna, Ellie, something like that. One of a small
group of women—sometimes five or six, sometimes two or
three—who stood Friday noons with peace signs on the corner of Main and Bodega. She had come to see one of his local
shows, and he had talked with her several times but never knew
quite what to say. An eighty-year-old with bright purple hair
outdid his sense of daring.

She greeted him. "Is this your writing place?"

"Don't I wish." He waggled his notebook to indicate its
blankness. "No, but I like to walk through, sit here, stuff."

"I too. And Rosie enjoys it." She bent down to scratch the
dog's head. "She loves to defecate among the dead." Sudden
alarm: "Oh, but I wasn't thinking— Is your wife— Is she—"

"No, she's not buried here. She's in a local potter's pot."

Edna, Ellie, whoever, smiled. "That's wise. My husband
was buried in Vancouver, and he never comes to visit. It's too
far even at senior fare."

Albert didn't really want a conversation, but he'd have to
swipe those lines. *Defecate among the dead.*

"Well, don't let me interrupt. I can see you're working.
That last play you did, I really— Well, a lot of people love what
you do. I hope you keep going."

"You too." He mimed holding up a protest sign.

"I pretty much have to. It's a helluva job to stop all the wars when they keep starting new ones. And then, betweentimes, I have to feed Rosie."

He laughed, this time for real. She hobbled on, the corgi straining forward on its stubby legs. War: now she had him thinking. An old lady peacenik with a silly dog was inciting tumult in Camelot. He started to write.

> *You judge my Quest? Look in the mirror. Judge what your taxes buy: death from the skies, bombs seeding the Earth like Easter eggs.*

> *Simple for you who never commanded men, never ordered an attack or a flogging. You call our world the Dark Ages, yet you who live in the most murderous days, who wield titanic fists and babble homilies, who view all the flickering madness at dinnertime— You judge me?*

Okay, Albert, get it out of your system. War is bad, knights are cruel, life is tough. He scratched it out. Lainie would say it was the playwright preaching. His ass was going to sleep on his friend's manuscript. The cemetery's quiet was too distracting.

One trick when he hit a brick wall: pretend to give up. Grant that your brain is dead in the water, that you've signed the surrender and pulled down your pants, then just write a few more words, whatever spits out of your brain, just a doodle to test your pen.

> *I was the child of Launcelot, chosen by God—a deceiving God?—to redeem. I came to Camelot. I drew the fateful sword. I traversed the Waste Forest and glimpsed the Grail.*

> *Was humankind redeemed? Did mercy flow like warm honey, or armies, naked as children, cavort in the autumn leaves? The poets sang lies. No rapture, no choir, no light. I stood in an empty chapel, cold as death. Look in the mirror. See my face.*

Again, he scratched out the words. He was still unsettled by the phone call. Mara had nailed it as mercilessly as Lainie ever had. She had asked about companionship. That was the grit in his eye.

He couldn't imagine living the rest of his days alone, but neither could he imagine another woman. Not that he didn't notice them or want them, or that he felt beholden to a dead one. In her last weeks Lainie had said, "For Godsake, stay alive. You've had a mate all your life, so you better find another." Her actual words. He knew what she meant. Keep running on all cylinders. Work, play, carry the torch. So he wasn't blind to women, but they seemed as far removed as Galahad's sorry goblet.

Before marriage they had both had a respectable number of affairs, but after, while declaring themselves tolerant of other liaisons, it never happened—except for two brief encounters he'd had at festivals. And she'd had a fling, during the year he toured a solo show, with a younger guy named Dan. Nice guy, and if he'd been a performer, Albert imagined being madly jealous. But Dan was a technical writer, so he didn't count as rivalry. She never told him about it, but she must have known that he knew. It was rocky when her affair broke up and she needed comfort: hard to offer condolence for what he wasn't supposed to know about. In fact, sex with Lainie was juicy, but their true marriage bed was the work. They had met in the work, they lived in the work, and that's where they opened to each other fully.

So the concept of female companionship—its swell, its fiber, its nap—was beyond sex or the prospect of better cuisine. It was woven into a life that was now grainy gray ash in a dark red ceramic vase that sat to the right of the fireplace.

§

For supper he fried a hunk of fish, baked a potato, shredded some greens, and listened to the news, which made his food taste good by comparison. Early to bed.

Something in him was cracking open: the locked, barred door that shielded the hearts of white middle-class males, including himself and his godforsaken Knight. Was he the little Lost Boy? All the heroes, maybe, were little lost boys, and Eliot's hollow men were just Peter Pan's lost boys grown up. All history might be one endless chronicle of little lost boys.

Forget it. Early to bed.

In her last weeks, Lainie had told him of a dream. Nightmares were her lifelong bedmates, and once she'd said she had dreamed every horror movie before it was ever made. But this dream was very simple. She was driving at night, and suddenly she had no idea where she was or where she was going. No road signs, no lights ahead, not even a bardo demon snarling an uppity snarl. Only the car's rumble, the moan of the tires, and the endless dark.

"Is that death?" she'd asked.

"Check the gas gauge," he replied. She laughed, but the nightmare lurked in her eyes.

Now, facing the night, he felt himself looking through those eyes. He was safe enough driving straight ahead, but would he see a bend in the road? He felt sleep enclosing him, and then a lightness as if gravity had lifted. And then, with no headlights, wrong lane, the dream came hurtling at him.

He was in Spain. Night. A field lit by fireflies, then searchlights and a screech of feedback. He was facing a stage. From the left wing, a band of prisoners entered, with soldiers in matador hats. *Matador* meant killer. He saw Mara.

Mara, his daughter. Mara, the child of Lainie. She was with the prisoners, and after a moment he understood that she was one of the prisoners. He was a hundred yards away, watching the dream at arm's length, an old movie projected on a basement wall. She had volunteered to teach Spanish to African immigrants, and that must be illegal now that Franco had returned. She raised her hand to her father in apology and smiled. *Well, Papa,* she was saying, *shit happens*. He shouted out her name, but he couldn't hear his own voice.

It was only a film. Grainy black and white. They were lined at the edge of a quarry. The men in hats faced the prisoners and raised their machine guns. A prisoner reached out dramatically as in Goya's *Third of May*. Others posed the way tourists pose for snapshots in Pisa, pretending to prop the Leaning Tower. The soldiers laughed in spite of themselves. It was only a film. They fired. The film showed scratches. Mara's face exploded.

§

Albert woke in a sweat. He took a deep breath of blackness and after a while another. He was shaken, yes, but more astonished than horrified. He rarely had nightmares beyond being late to a gig or lost in endless hallways. Somehow his subconscious was ringed with razor wire to foil jailbreaks. Not even Lainie's death had opened those gates, yet now he was being pried open by rabid monkeys and the horrors were swarming like roaches. He felt his bond with Galahad.

The adrenaline should have kept him stark awake till dawn, but he drifted back to a dreamless sleep that held till the rays of sunrise. He woke feeling oddly spirited, maybe just from the sight of blue sky above the front yard's palm tree. It crossed his mind that Mara was buying a house. That was reassuring. The bank would have a financial incentive to keep her alive.

X

Child and Knight prepare for Show-and-Tell

Early afternoon of another plotless day. That morning, at the coffee shop, the barista had glanced at him and said, "Sixteen-ounce Americano?" He was becoming utterly predict- able: the walk downtown, the coffee, the walk home, the left- overs for lunch, the stumbles and mumbles around the studio, the extra glass of wine at dinnertime. Routine.

He'd once asked an ex-priest friend who'd spent a couple of weeks at a Catholic hermitage, "What do the hermits actually do at a hermitage?"

"Nothing!" his friend exclaimed gleefully. "That's the whole point!"

Now, Albert thought ruefully, he was achieving that col- orless existence. Then he remembered he had a four o'clock appointment with the costumer, Jeanette Wald, she of the frizzy red hair. The appointment had been changed twice and was now back at the studio instead of the coffee shop, which robbed him of the excuse for a blended mocha. She must have a busy life, or the need to create the impression of a busy life—something didn't quite ring true. But at least he now had the first half of the script, though he'd probably strike out most of it by four o'clock.

Albert was at a dead end with the parents, who lay at the end of the playboard, Hansel entangled with Gretel in quiescent communion. What in fact do parents do if their child disappears in a restive third-world country like England? They were stuck in perpetual stasis at their B&B, frozen, numb to the touch, barely able to see out their clouded window. They counted the hours of a dim eternity, suspended like bugs in amber. Of course, he might comfort them by changing the story. "With every bright idea, a weed is planted," he'd once joked to Lainie. Countless options, all goofy. Scads of notions, all lethal.

The parents had never dreamed they were vulnerable. He should reassure them that there was little danger to their son. The crusade was a low-budget show with no big special effects. The puppets might get scuffed a bit, but he packed them carefully between shows and never allowed the audience to molest them. He couldn't answer for emotional trauma: Bobby could depend on getting lots of that at home. But, as educated people do, the parents just sat there accepting inevitabilities. Albert had brought these creatures into being, as thoughtless of what he might engender as adolescents in the back seat of a Buick.

But it was only a story, for chrissake. Let the parents go hang. They'd done their job, had their headline moment, and they didn't require further notice. They could bump their way to the back pages and out of our knowing. Focus on the kid. We left the kid at the castle gate. Pick it up with the kid.

§

I'm by the castle gate. They're going off to war. The Lady is up at the window with the funny guy Sammy the Fool. I like when he juggles the balls but he sounds like a girl. The Knight in Shining Armor looks sad. So does the Lady. Father Olyver is kind of mean. A dog in the yard growled and I was scared.

Now the Lady isn't at the window. Sammy the Fool runs out the door. He runs to the Knight in Shining Armor and everyone yells *Sammy!* They put him behind Father Olyver on a horse with big ears. They start riding off and soldiers marching. It's like watching TV. Once I had a monkey doll and I set it where it could watch TV but the monkey doll got lost and I was scared.

I want to go home.

Then Old Cookie comes. They call her Old Cookie because she's old and she cooks. There are lots of cooks at the castle but she's Old Cookie. She doesn't know I'm Bobby. I'm wearing funny clothes. The castle people thought my real clothes were funny so they gave me clothes like they wore. Old Cookie grabs my arm and pulls me onto the back of a wagon. I say Mommy and Daddy will miss me. She says a bad word for Mommy and Daddy to do.

We ride a long way. It's fun to ride in the wagon. There are little houses like in fairy tales. They don't have cars in England or Burger Kings. I don't like England much.

I ride in the wagon except when we stop and give the soldiers food. I run around with bread and cheese. Old Cookie says go fast and I do. Later I help stir a big pot of soup on a fire. The soldiers come and eat the soup. They don't wash their hands before they eat. I have to scrub the big pot. I never did that before. Old Cookie gets mad and hits me. Nobody ever hit me before. I cry but then I stop. I sleep in the wagon. There's a bunch of tents close by with ladies inside. They make funny sounds at night.

Next day we cook more stuff to eat. I ask what it is and Old Cookie says, What does it look like, stupid? In school you can't call people stupid even if they are. Then I get in the wagon and ride. I don't see the Knight in Shining Armor or Sammy the Fool. They're way up ahead.

Old Cookie gives me a little cart. She puts in some bottles and a big bag she says is wine. I take it where soldiers are. They're happy for the wine so they let me watch.

They catch a man that was a farmer. They say, Tell us. He says, Tell what? They say, We'll hang you by your thumbs. He says, I don't know nothing. They take him to a tree and tie knots on his thumbs and then they pull him up. He looks like he didn't know it would hurt. He makes a shout like Hah! then a sound like a snore. He twists around in the air. They let him down and then they jerk him up and he's yelling loud. I guess he doesn't know what the answer is.

He acts like it hurts. It looks real. It's like TV. I hate England.

I start to cry and the soldiers laugh. But then Sammy the Fool comes there. The soldiers yell, Hey Sammy! but he takes my hand. He says I don't have to clean the pots. So we go up front. He takes me to the Knight in Shining Armor and says to call him Sir Galahad so I do. Sir Galahad looks sad but he says hello. Then Sammy the Fool juggles some balls and says he'll teach me to juggle. He says I can sleep in his tent so I do and he holds me like Mommy does. I feel better now. It looks like his little beard is falling off his chin but he sticks it on.

Sammy the Fool says Sir Galahad is seeking the Holy Grail. It's a cup or something. It might be at some castle but the people want to keep it so he has to fight and get it. I hope we can get it and then go home.

So the way it goes is like this. We come to a castle and ask, Do you have the Holy Grail? They say no. So we say, Prove it, but they can't prove it. So then we have to fight. Father Olyver does blessings and curses. The curses work pretty good.

I get to watch it some. Sammy doesn't want me to but I tell him the stuff I saw on TV like robbers and killers so he says okay. They have a big log called Ram and they take it up to a castle gate and bang down the gate. It's like Scottie who had lots of toys but he broke my robot kit and then we got in a fight and Mommy said not to play with Scottie. Toys don't bleed but people do, she said. I didn't know what she meant but now I do.

I didn't know castles catch fire. The fire is big. The soldiers come back all dirty. They've got a big girl like my babysitter Allie. She looks scared. Sammy the Fool pulls me back behind a tree. The girl says, Please no please. A soldier says, Say please. She says it louder. A soldier says, She's saying please, she's asking for it. There's lots of scuffle and the big girl is crying. Sammy the Fool is crying too, it looks like to me.

When the soldiers are gone we come out from behind the tree. The big girl lays there with her eyes wide open. I wonder if I ought to tell this for show-and-tell.

Sammy doesn't say if they found the Holy Grail.

§

At precisely four p.m., the grungy red Corvette pulled into the driveway and coughed to a stop. Jeanette came up the path, wearing the same green pullover with cargo pants—no fashion plate, she. Odd that he noticed: he never noticed clothes. Their first meeting, her red hair had been frizzed out, not to fright-wig status but definitely assertive. This time it was in tight pigtails pinned into a cluster, with a green silk scarf melting off the top.

They came into the studio, and she went immediately to the mangled wad of clay that had sprouted only lips and a chin. "I kinda like it this way," she said. He thought she was smiling as she said it, but he wasn't sure.

"State of the art," he replied.

"Well, I don't know what you're visualizing, but here's some ideas." She placed a file folder on his writing desk and brought out a sheaf of pencil sketches. A fusion of knights-in-armor and steampunk—top hats of steel, Victorian morning coats with epaulets, a ruffled shirt front over chain mail, a medieval damsel in a gown imprinted with corporate logos, a fabric swatch that glimmered like an oil spill—images that sent tentacles out in a dozen directions, but with a sense of gravitas in their lines, and at their heart a sense of worlds in collision.

He was stunned. He stood silently, then rummaged for word as he shuffled through the sheets as if to break the spell of her blackjack dealer's rhythm in laying them out. "How'd you know I was thinking, I mean, I guess, in these terms?"

"Well, I didn't, really."

"Neither did I."

This woman posed a major problem. She was good. She was too good. He could say, "Fine, let me think about it." He could say that he'd have a script in a couple of weeks. He could admit he was a total fraud and scared to death of working with someone who pushed him past his limits. He could say that actually he was going back to rework *The Little Mermaid.* He couldn't hear what he actually said, but it seemed to offer encouragement while buying him some time.

He shuffled back through the sketches, chuckling, taking it in.

"It was something you mentioned, I guess," she said. "Big Lake? Just some way that you said it, I was seeing that weird French cartoonist, what's his name? Kind of sci-fi, kind of mythic."

"Big Lake," Albert said with a flustered chuckle. What the hell did ruffled shirt fronts and chain mail have to do with Big Lake? "No— Well, it doesn't really have anything to do with—"

"Big Lake?"

"Yeah, I guess I was eleven, must have been . . ."

"So?"

The point being? No reason to tell it, except to keep talking. He stared at the sketches so he wouldn't look at her.

"Yeah, well, if you're asking, okay. So I was in Boy Scouts, very first week. Troop Nine met in this church basement. Three patrols, and they put me in the Panther Patrol, which was the best patrol, according to them, very gung-ho, like *We'll tie knots in anything!* But that night I came home with a serious problem. Serious for an eleven-year-old, anyway."

"Did you." Silence. "What?"

"Well. The patrol was going to go on a bicycle hike to Big Lake, outside town, and I knew my mom would say no. I knew it. She wasn't overprotective, but a hike out in the woods with older kids— And so we went at it: *You don't know those kids, what if you got lost, what if it rains, what if you run into hoboes?* We fought on Wednesday, we fought on Thursday, Friday, but anything I could say was just water off a duck."

"But you went."

"I had to. Some compulsion? Some kind of— You're hungry, but you don't know what it is you want? Yep, she let me. I just became the saddest little guy on the face of the planet, and she couldn't stand it. *Well, if it's not going to rain, we'll see. Six in the morning? We'll see.* So I got my tires pumped up, pack ready, and rain was predicted, but it couldn't rain, I mean at that point I still believed in God. And, of course, on Saturday morning, it rained."

"Of course."

This woman was listening to him, but Albert didn't want an audience. He wanted to bury himself deep in the story and finish the telling unheard. He gazed into the mist of six a.m.

"Just a little mist. Of course Mom would spend the day worrying herself to death, but that was her problem. Like any little selfish bastard, I had a life to live. It wasn't just a bike ride. It was a rite of passage, pilgrimage, quest? This kid, Vernon, said that once at the lake they snuck up and saw a guy and a girl doing it. He didn't say what was the *it* they were doing, but I got the general idea. So I rode off, and we all met at the church and started the five-mile ride. Whole new world." He could see it, even as he was fixated on Jeanette's sketch of a hollow-eyed Merlin and feeling her gaze on his hollow-eyed self.

"We got to the asphalt parking lot, and there was just a sprinkle, so we started along a trail by the edge of the lake. Lifted our bikes over big roots, under limbs or up a cliff, I guess heading around to where the guy and the girl had been doing it. Galahad's sacred quest: to see'em doing it."

"And then it rained?"

"You were there?"

"Similar journeys."

He had never told this story before, not even to Lainie. Especially not to Lainie. It was too dumb and too naked to tell, except to a stranger. Hard to believe how deeply it had sunk into his bones.

"Yeah. It rained. Definite rain. Gentle, then harder, like the schoolyard bully, Buddy his name was, who'd push his thumb in your bicep: *You feel that?* Harder: *Feel that?!* We were wet, then drenched, then drowned. And all of a sudden, like a flight of geese, with one mighty honk, the bunch of us turned around to scramble home to our mommies. Clearly no one would be doing it in the rain."

The bluffs were clay, the mud was superglue, clinging to the tires, jamming under the fenders. He would scrape it out so the wheels would turn as he pushed a few yards forward until they jammed again. Then he was lugging the bike, skidding down the banks and scuttling up. He no longer had shoes, just great gobs of mud at the ends of legs that lurched onward through seventh grade, eighth grade, ninth. It was years until he saw the roadway's broad expanse of asphalt, scraped out his tires one last time, and rode home. His mother said nothing, just tossed his clothes in the wash and made supper.

"Course, now I know what the guy and the gal had been doing. But I wonder what they were saying, you know? Their dreams, what happened the rest of their lives? How that came to mind I have no idea. Maybe Galahad rides a bike?"

How much difference was there between a farcical anecdote and a sacred quest? They stood a while in silence. There's one kind of silence, he thought, where there's nothing to say, and another where you don't know how to begin. He gathered her sketches, straightened the sheaf, handed them to her. "Nice. Very nice. Beautiful."

"So this is kind of a general direction, yes?"

"Yes. Yes," he murmured. Nothing more to say, but he needed more words. "So, listen, I can't really ask—"

"Ask what?"

"Well, I can't really ask."

"Oh, okay. Well, something like, why am I scrounging for penny-ante jobs in the North Bay?"

"Something like that."

She grinned, shrugged. "Well, so you asked me, so—" She held the silence and her eyes glazed, staring into the past. "My own hike around Big Lake."

They sat at opposite ends of the decrepit sofa, and she began to narrate the intertwined history of her career, her crises, and her hairdos. In college, she'd bounced between theater, commercial art, and getting drunk. In her twenties, she had been a prodigy, assisting a movie designer and moonlighting as a rare female artist on superhero comics. With a relationship crash, she plunged into depression, bounced back designing upscale party garb, which led to her first affair with a woman, which led to another crash-and-burn. Deciding that her problem wasn't gender but human beings in general, she got a cat. The cat died.

"Sounds sad, but I wasn't crazy about the cat."

Moving to San Francisco for an ad agency job that dematerialized, she ricocheted through illustrating children's books, costuming for theater, and bookkeeping for a dentist because she needed dental work.

"And one day I realized I was fifty-two years old. So I got another cat. This one's a keeper, I think."

Picking a loose thread on her knee, she seemed to be at the end of the chronicle. It would make a great puppet show, thought Albert, but how to capture that mercurial face?

"But the whole movie thing, and the comics, ad agencies, commercials, why wasn't that on your resume?"

"That was a different person."

"So who are you now?"

"Jeanette Wald."

So there it stood. She was fine with having no fixed performance date and no rush. Albert promised to have a full outline as well as a contract in a couple of weeks, with a first payment. He half expected that he'd call her to cancel the project, and he half expected her to call reporting that her cat was depressed and in no condition to pursue the Holy Grail. And he half expected the utterly unexpected.

§

Sammy the Fool tucks me warm in a blanket. He says goose down. I say down where? He laughs. I sleep good. He's like a mommy.

Next day we stay at the camp. The soldiers have to bury dead men and look for the Holy Grail. I don't understand the Holy Grail. What are we going to do with it is what I wonder.

Sammy the Fool shows me how to juggle. He juggles pretty good. You start with one ball and then you do two. At the castle he juggled better than now. Maybe it's hard to juggle if you're sad. Once he gets up and does a dance but Sir Galahad says no. Then he tells funny jokes but Sir Galahad says no. He tries to make Sir Galahad happy but Sir Galahad stays sad. Sammy the Fool cries behind a tree.

I ask, Are you my babysitter now? Only if you're a baby, he says. I'm not a baby, I tell him. Then I'll be your little-boy-sitter, he says, and I'll sit right down on you. I laugh. Sammy the Fool is my new friend. He's funny.

We go to another castle. I hope it won't catch fire.

XI

The Fool's Deceit

Now I am Sammy, fool to my very soul. Holy Virgin, hear my squeak of a voice, for in this harsh new world I must speak by no other. When I was the Lady Mara, my world was cold stone, yes, but each morning, as I rose shivering, my servant enrobed me. I smelled the close-stool's odor through the civet, but I had never inhaled the third day of death on the killing fields. I loved my husband as a god.

I love my husband still, but not as a god. I love him as I love my hand, my breast, the flesh essential to my being. The fool's skill is not in his jokes or juggles, but in an instinct to become visible or to recede. I studied this as a wife. Now I am closer even than a wife, because a wife, however compliant, still asks that her husband see her. As a fool, I am expendable except as needed. I fill the empty hours when demons might enter his eyes. We touch rarely: at times he pats my coxcomb.

"You be me," Sammy murmured to me in his reedy trill. His chirp was a divine command. I made no reply. I did it without thought, as if we were already become one another. We changed our garments without averting our eyes. Each other's nakedness was our own. Seeing his unclothed, foolish body, a plucked chicken with a tiny dangling worm, I saw myself. He was Mara now, the beauteous Lady Mara, and I was Sammy Shit-pants.

The change commenced long before that hour. I had learned to juggle, to dance, to deal out the jokes, the tales, the melodies. We conversed long hours in his crystalline gibberish. I think I desired even then to be the fool, to lose myself in virginal lunacy, to juggle the world like an eggshell floating on air. Even now, far distant, I can jabber along with Sammy, plucking words like silvery moths from the darkness, twisting my fingers into snuffling animal snouts, whispering, "Springtime."

What impelled my folly? My devotion to my lord, my fear for his soul? My panic to flee my prison? My belief in a sacred crusade? A surrender to love? An evasion? A whim? Do I seek applause for my newfound jugglery? I am blind to what moves me. My soul is chaos: vagrant chimeras, a morass of meanders, a labyrinth. Bards sing of maze caves so deep that one wanders for days in the dayless night. Since the start of the Quest, I have seen no mirror. Nor shall I.

When the moment came, emerging from the archway in my coxcomb, wispy chin beard, motley tunic, and yellow breeches, I was Sammy the Fool. A remote, unsexed Lady Mara was framed in the glaring window, blinded by sunlight, as I cavorted before my lord astride his steed, pleading, cajoling for all my worth. And then I was lifted up, soaring away from my womanhood to consort with the bristling horde, clattering toward the dawn. I heard the mighty shout of brass.

Before you, Holy Mother, I strive to speak with what faint echo remains of the Lady Mara. I miss her now. I have exchanged clothing, rank, sex, my very mind, but one cannot exchange souls. Thus far I have made a skillful masquerade, but when will I answer for it? Will the paste of my chin beard hold before God?

I protect the Lost Boy. He was in Sammy's care at the castle, and he passes into mine, like an angel's whisper moving from heart to heart. He is a gift to this childless freak. I shield him from crimes that shame the sun. I tell him the cries are only a game of pretend. I nurse him with lies because truth is a poisoned sap.

And then I must tend Galahad. We move from village to village, town to town, keep to keep. He gives orders, then stares at the rising fire. Next day he wakes, gives orders, stares into fire, and I juggle to divert his eyes from the blaze. I speak when he speaks to me, as befits my role. He never asks me to sing, and no song comes. Holy Virgin, sustain me.

I feel my voice coming from other lips. The Father of Lies? How else to explain the slaughter, the spoiling of women, the dead reeking up their souls? Perhaps the Father of Lies dangles his dolls on strings to play out his hideous jests. Holy Mary, in your name they call them marionettes, but the strings are tangled, the dolls flail about, and the Father of Lies, like a small child breaking its playthings, bawls out whatever torments his mind. And we perform his mad squawk. We are his toys.

Or not the Father of Lies. It may be only some poor old floundering bard, caught in his own muddled tale and thrusting it on us. You know my heart, Holy Mother. Shrive him, make him see. Kindle in him a glimmer of dawn.

§

June 11th. The costumer—Jenny the Red, he privately called her—was phoning daily, wanting more script. Some progress on the sculpting, but last night he'd left Galahad posed on the armature with a chin and little else. He would have to take care that his defunct father's face didn't come peeking through again. Early morning, he popped out of bed, poured a large glass of grapefruit juice, and outlined a scenario for *Rumpelstiltskin.*

A much better idea, he told himself. Before the magical dwarf met the poor miller's daughter, he was a misshapen runt of a puppeteer, whose wife would sprinkle his dolls with tears of joy or sorrow and bring them to life. At night, in each other's arms, she whispered his silly name with a love that made it music. But then one day, blinded by sun on the seashore, she was swept away.

His puppets all went dead and wouldn't dance. So he took the first job he was offered, the first distressed maiden who wept. He spun the straw, took her necklace and piggy bank. Then, faced with the prospect of losing her to the king, he asked for her firstborn child. *A living creature is dearer to me than all riches.* A serious overreach: he should have offered to babysit and do puppet shows for the little prince, but he had to be grabby. And after he set her the riddle, he grew frantic for recognition, howling his name for all the world to hear, and wound up ripping himself in two. A professional hazard for dwarf puppeteers.

A new show in fewer gulps than a glass of grapefruit juice. What a relief to escape his bastard twin, to let Galahad swirl down the toilet bowl of history. *Rumpelstiltskin* had pathos, comedy, character, and a lesson that made it marketable. He could even cast it with old puppets from the bins. Mister Punch could play the hapless dwarf, and he would have no need for the talents of Jenny the Red.

Albert sat breathing deep relief, watching the mottled sunlight play across the window shades. Then, to his surprise, he rose, went into the study, tore the four new pages from his notepad, stuffed them into a file marked IDEAS, and shuffled out to the studio to get an early start on rehearsal. The hapless dwarf would have to wait his turn.

After an hour of rehearsal, he laid down the puppet that was standing in for the Knight and picked up the Fool's understudy—an old puppet named Wiley. Then with the Fool's hand—Albert's own naked hand—he picked up the monkey playing Bobby. Child faced Fool.

"I had a bad dream." The Lost Boy shivered out a whisper.

"Or the bad dream had you."

"I dunno."

"Your nightmare had a nightmare. It scared itself and turned into a duck."

Bobby whined, angry at being cajoled.

"And the duck laid an egg, and what do you think was in the egg?"

"No!" more angrily.

"Me!" Sammy waggled his head and Bobby laughed.

That scene might work. Maybe the duck was too cutesy, but there had to be some warmth amid the desolation. He hated the old saw about puppets appealing to the child in each of us, even though he'd used that phrase endlessly in publicity blurbs. But they did allow more extremities of love and rage and pain and joy than he saw in regular theater, where camp irony or identity crises prevailed these days. He'd need to reconsider the duck.

Enough rehearsal. He turned off the fluorescents and walked across to the house. The feral cats were poised outside the glass door, alert for their food. They could wait. On the voice mail, another call from Jeanette. She could wait. He had an early afternoon appointment to take the car in for an oil change and to have a rattle checked. (Lainie would have known what it was.) He needed to pick up cat food, then take back two library books that were overdue and mail a playscript. He shambled out to the car, checked his list, went back to fetch the car keys. At last, he pulled out of the driveway.

In the waiting room at the dealership, he sipped courtesy coffee, nibbled a chemical cookie, and scribbled a scene between the Priest and Galahad. The Knight would naturally reach the point they'd reached in Vietnam, Iraq, and Afghanistan, where your transmission whines, your carburetor floods, your muffler roars, and your tail pipe falls off, but you still can't junk your junker. How to admit being wrong, wrong, wrong?

It has to end, he tells the Priest: the torture, the killing, the rape. The cardinal had misunderstood God's will, perhaps: God was preoccupied and the cardinal hard of hearing. Or the phone connection was bad, so the cardinal couldn't tell whether God said "Go!" or "No!" Or the cardinal offered his message as a suggestion, which the bishop took as an opinion, and Father Olyver heard as a command.

"Whatever the cause," Galahad cried, "I am doing evil!"

What would the Priest reply? Albert finished his coffee and glanced up at the TV screen, which offered nonstop news whose rhythms, jumpy edits, and juvenile inflections seemed drawn from Saturday morning cartoons. But what could Father Olyver say that wasn't drivel from a flaccid asshole? Obtuse homilies about "God's will" would be true to life—never underestimate the human genius for cop-outs—but totally predictable. If Albert were to be stuck with the little Priest for the next four months, he didn't want him to smell that bad.

As the news droned in the waiting room, the Priest stayed mum. The Knight endured the silence. At last he prompted, "What have you to say?"

Father Olyver lowered his eyes.

"Speak!"

"What first inspired my lord to inquire about God's will?"

"Nightmares."

"Do you now have these dreams?"

"I dream nothing."

"Shall I then pray for your dreams' return?"

Galahad was silent. His revolt was at an end.

A woman in a powder-blue suit picked up *People* from the table beside him and lumbered away to sit under the TV. Albert watched the commentators in bilious diatribe flaunting their haircuts. One seemed to project a low-calorie greasiness, another the bitter aftertaste of artificial sweetener. Might the Priest be interviewed on cable news? TV spoofs were outworn but still got laughs. The little man would lean into the camera, grateful to set the record straight:

> *I believed myself a servant of the Divine. At night I lay*
> *in my cell smothered in God. As I took communion,*
> *I was one with the bread and the wine. I would lead*
> *all humankind to shout Yes! to the stars.*

That might work, Albert thought as he scribbled. The Knight's a cold fish, the Priest a pathetic slob, but they're both true believers. They still believe in this murderous puppet show.

Years passed, and my life became negation. I blessed, confessed, chanted words that no one comprehended.

My vow of obedience? Cowardice. Poverty? The food I eat would feed the shackful of peasants who grew the food. Chastity? Why does a loving God compel us to a test we must fail? I clamp my despair in my fist.

My love for the downtrodden poor is so profound I must insure that they stay that way.

Is religion only a scatter of whims, swarming like ants on a dead man's face?

Another monologue. Everyone spoke in monologues nowadays—the soul stewing in its juice, drinking its bath water, passing the hat for pity. In Shakespeare, it was the the plotters and ditherers who spoke their souls to appall us, but these days it was anyone with a gripe. They had to do monologues: no one had patience to listen. But it might work if pared to the bone. Albert heard his name called at the service desk, closed his notebook, pulled out his credit card, and checked his list of errands.

§

"Tell me a story."

The Lost Boy is crying as I crawl into the tent. I make a funny face, and he hugs me.

A slattern from the wagons had been ordered to care for him, so he stayed with her all day, hearing the sounds. Soldiers had brought a prisoner to a clearing across the gully. From the camp the boy could hear the snap of bones. "They're gathering firewood," the nanny said. By dusk she had wandered off drunk.

I lay my hand on his forehead. "Tell me a story," he whimpers and grasps my hand.

"You bet!" say I in my silly moronic voice. "The story of Sir Galahad?" The child turns away.

"Tell me about the battle."

"Battle?"

"The big one. Today."

"We won."

The boy begins to sniffle, then suddenly a flood of tears: grief for a lost mother and father, lost macaroni and cheese, lost Alex and Dylan, lost puppy, lost words from another world. With a sob I embrace him, my never-born son.

"Tell you what I saw," I say in a whisper thin as soap-bubble skin, "cause that's all I know." He goes silent. I speak in the simplest words. The surprise attack from the castle at dawn. The lion grace of Galahad, suddenly titanic, leaping to horse and blunting the surge. The grim struggle back to the walls, the assault on the gates, the victory.

"But what I did," I tell him, "was hide behind a tree. A big tree. Then I heard a noise." Should he be told this? Should he be no longer a child? But was not the goal of childhood to become no longer a child? "Somebody crying. I looked. A big boy. Big boys cry too. I sneaked out from the tree, and the big boy was lying there flat, all yucky. And I wondered, was he one of us or one of them? Cause all blood's red."

My Lost Boy is very quiet.

"But I wipe him off, and he says what sounds like *Gih wah*. I dunno what he means, but then he says *Gih wah* again and cries and cries."

"What did he mean?"

"Maybe that's what he meant. He meant *Gih wah*."

"No."

"But he goes to sleep, and he looks so happy to be asleep that I bet he never wakes up."

I press a hand to my Lost Boy's forehead. Might the true Fool have told it better? The framing of truth into story is an art it takes long to master.

A shout from a squire summons me to the fire. A gesture directs me to sit on a log at my once-husband's side. His breast-plate has been removed, but he still wears his scarred greaves and the grimy quilted padding that protects him from his armor. The bonfire seems invested with kingship: its subjects gaze in dumb attendance upon it.

"I have a letter from my wife." He speaks into the night.

"My gracious lady, devoted to her lord."

"She reports that all is well. Discontent with taxes, nothing new. She was obliged to send two men to the stocks for drunkenness and flog one for false weights. She accepts her duty, though I grieve her distress."

"God is so big that maybe He can't see his toes."

He pays my nonsense no notice. He runs his finger across the parchment. "This is not her writing. She is educated. Why does she make use of the scrivener?"

"Sore finger?" I venture.

He stares at the letter. Two knights approach, and he beckons them to sit. The squire appears with two stools. I make a deep, sweeping bow. Sir Bluffot reaches over and squeezes my head like a melon. "Good day fighting, Sammy? Kill anybody?"

Sir Firts guffaws.

"Sure did!" I cry. An audience at last, base though it be. "Ten flies, three mosquitoes, and a dead man."

"How can you kill a man if he's already dead?"

"Easy. He won't fight back."

"So you'd sooner kill dead people, huh?"

"Sure. They don't mind so much."

Firts and Bluffot are not verbose, except with coarse names for the parts of women. They take long swigs from the goblets the squire brings them, then Sir Firts hands me a wad of fabric. I hold it up: a woman's tunic. Deep blue linen, edged with embroidered vines. Elegant, except for a dark stain across it.

"No idea," Firts hastens to respond to Galahad's stare. "Found it."

"Dance in it, Sammy. Be a girl," Bluffot commands.

I look to my liege. He stares at the fire. I struggle into the strange woman's garment as the knights make amorous moans. The tunic is too long, but even over my motley it forms a feminine shape. I stand before the knights as a delicate female in blue, with coxcomb hat and a wisp of a beard.

"Dance!" they bellow.

I dance. I try to mimic Sammy's jiggly cavorts, but I feel the nameless lady's dress itself is dancing the dance, a dance of deep blue, a spirit swaying, yearning upward, lost in time. My Galahad raises his eyes to the moving figure and sees me.

For an instant. Then he springs to his feet, kicks his stool, barks, "Enough!" and I freeze. I stand in a bloody rag: Sammy Shit-pants, all elbows, no grace. Sir Firts and Sir Bluffot rise, excuse themselves, and depart into stinking blackness. The Knight stares at Sammy the Fool wriggling out of the tunic, then stumbles into his tent. The dancer wipes her tears.

§

Albert sat in front of the sculpture, trying to stare it into shape. He knew he was very drunk. He had hoped he might flush open the gates of inspiration with one great slosh of booze, but he knew damned well that tactic almost never worked. Better to stumble off to his tent.

He went into the house, opened the fridge for one last vodka. One thing he'd found he had in common with long-gone Albert Senior, though he hoped he had a bit more control: they both liked vodka. He poured a shot and set it on the counter. Better if it drank itself. He drank it, poured another.

Back pocket, wallet, photo of Lainie—wanting to ask her something but not knowing what. He dropped it on the floor. Down onto hands and knees, down to the crate supporting the microwave, down to the depths, fishing in cobwebs.

And then, with one deep breath and a flash of awareness that he was shamefully passing out on the kitchen floor, he did.

An hour or so later, an arthritic crayfish raw in the joints, he woke. In his hand was the photo of Lainie. "What are you doing under the microwave?" he heard himself mutter. Tried to laugh but went into a coughing fit. There's always tomorrow, he told what was left of himself, and tomorrow he'd hold off on the vodka.

He caught a glimpse of Rumpelstiltskin stomping in rage, ripping himself in two. All the same story. All stories were the same, so you might as well stick with the one you started. He paged through the script in his head to find that speech—*All men free*—but saw that he couldn't read it because he was asleep. He shook himself awake long enough to haul himself to his feet, hit the bathroom, then plunge from the great clay bluff above Big Lake to land crosswise in bed.

XII

Of a Wound in the Eyes

The morning after his descent to the kitchen floor, Albert woke on top of the covers, fully clothed except for a bare left foot. He sat on the edge of the bed and began to massage his throbbing forehead. Soon he was exploring the flesh, bone, musculature, his fingers in discovery mode. An hour later, he was in the studio, and the Sacred Knight emerged at one sitting. Now the noble creep sat eyeless but resolute, prepared for eight layers of papier mache.

But Albert needed more than a puppet skull. He required a black-and-white commitment to move the Quest forward and discourage himself from passing out on the linoleum. He had emailed three Bay Area theaters where he'd performed before, suggesting they might host *Galahad's Fool*. He would create the show and they'd do promo, with a split of the gate. Replies trickled in. One theater had folded. One was under new management. The third wrote, *Sounds fantastic, but Twin Peaks Rep is reviving Camelot.* So he would have to rent some dark little shoebox, do his own promo, and hope for the best. Whatever the initial motivation, all he truly wanted now was to get this monkey off his back. He'd just have to chart a better strategy to stay off the kitchen floor. It badly needed mopping.

One potential funder had invited a full grant application— it would help at least to pay for the promo. Back in the office, he tried to craft it, but every phrase rang false and he gave it up. He had no performative strategy to subvert the dominant paradigm, adduce nonlinear perception, interrogate conventional structures of post-Hegelian thought, or bring peace to the Middle

East. Unless he could make headlines by committing a major felony, it was just going to be one more calendar listing. *Some kinda puppet show at the Garage? Naw, let's stream Netflix.* To his daughter he wrote:

> *As you well know, sweetie, I dramatize myself. I get a charge from seeing myself as the stalwart opt-out guy. I take comfort in knowing how richly I deserved the grant that I declined to seek, thus sparing myself the pain of rejection or the terror of assent.*

He meant it as a joke, but he heard its echo: the pain of rejection or the terror of assent.

§

"So why does the Lady disguise herself and go along with him?" Jeanette had asked last Saturday when she stopped by to pick up another sliver of the script. "How are we supposed to believe that? What's really her motivation?"

Because it's in the script, he wanted to say. If we say it they'll believe it. That's why they vote for gangsters. That's why they gobble carcinogens. That's why Jenny the Red had convinced herself that this show was worth the effort. Instead, he replied, "Well, who ever knows why we do stuff? Why am I doing this? I have no idea."

"That's not enough. She's giving up her life."

"What, her embroidery? She doesn't know who she is. That's what she's discovering."

"By serving this guy's obsession?"

She had hit a sore spot. He took a breath before finding his words and then trying to suppress them. "Don't you think that women ever behave like idiots?"

"You think women need a man to tell them that?"

She was one of those ladies who never punched straight ahead but had a mean left hook. He shrugged. "Well, you tell me. She has to do it, since that's the story, so— Would you do it?"

Her eyes grew distant, focusing on something he couldn't see. She seemed to have experience with inexplicables.

"I guess I might do it if the guy was headed to Maui or Bermuda." She smiled. The first time he'd seen her smile—she was a frugal smiler. "No, seriously, I don't know. I've gone on some of those trips and wound up asking why. She wants to escape? She wants something to believe in? She wants to hold onto the memory? Maybe she thinks you can keep a memory on life support."

"Well, I guess we try."

"Maybe she just wants to be a clown. I did once."

They were sitting on stools in the kitchen. Albert had cleared the old yellow table to hold new clutter and brought in the clay head and his tools. The sculpture was finished. He had tinkered some with the ears and the lobes of the nose, but the jaw spoke resolve while the cheeks sagged with despair. Jeanette stared at the bloated hero. Today her hair was entirely covered by a tight, furry white cap. She kept fiddling with its edges, as if worried it would pop, and tucked in a few strands that had gone astray.

Albert offered to make coffee. She asked for tea. He set the water to heat, rustled in the cabinet for the tray of assorted teas, and held it out as she made her selection.

"My wife and I, before we had space for a garden, we'd try to raise house plants and always killed'em. But somebody gave us this leafy thing with little white flowers, just before we went off on tour. Came back ten days later, it was stone dead. Brown leaves curled up like fingers praying for rain. I don't know what possessed her, but Lainie watered it anyway. Like watering burnt bacon. Two days later, new shoots were coming up. We called it the Lazarus plant. Twice more, same thing."

"You still have it?"

He shook his head. "Even Lazarus finally croaked."

They were silent as the water came to a boil. He poured water for her tea.

"But it's a question people will ask." Jeanette wouldn't let it go. "Her doing that, following along. The why of it."

Lainie would be the one to answer that, he thought, since she had done it herself. Her friend Nancy—not his—had always berated her about how she ought to be working on her own. *You're your own person*, was the mantra. "Well, I said I appreciate what you're saying, Nancy," Lainie told him, laughing, "but I have no intention of going off and having a baby on my own, just to prove I can do it." The memory brought back her laughter to his ears. "Sorry, Al, babe," she said, "you're stuck with me."

"Seems like right now I've got more questions than answers," he said. "I could have a yard sale on questions." Jeanette looked at the eyeless Galahad. "You like it?" he asked.

"It works, but there's more to him than that," she said. "It has to be in the eyes."

"I know that."

She ignored his abruptness. "And do you have any idea about the tourists? The mom and dad?"

"Very unformed faces, I think. We see'em, we forget'em. They just sit there. I'll do'em this week."

"And what about the Lady? The Lady Fool? I mean she's your main character. Nobody gives two shits about Galahad."

This was not the conversation he needed right now. We have to connect with Galahad, she'd said, and now we didn't give two shits. But she was dead right: it was the Lady Fool who might stir empathy. Galahad was invited to this party only as Albert's stand-in.

"I'll take it under advisement," he said, suppressing a hiccup of annoyance. "Other thoughts?"

Her eyes grabbed his and held. "The Fool adopting Bobby. She doesn't have children. That means something."

"So?"

"It's important to her. It needs to be stronger."

"You have kids?"

"Hardly." Her face went blank.

They talked a while longer: costume questions, puppet hair, the weather. They scheduled their next meeting, and he set a deadline to finish the script. He sensed an odd formality in their speech, like genteel Edwardians sitting naked in each other's presence, pretending not to notice. Was there an erotic spark between them? The crazy hair, the direct eyes, the intelligence— all that attracted him. But sex? He wasn't sure he remembered how to spell it. And her edging herself into collaboration? No. No, absolutely. Then, predictably, he heard himself welcome her along for the ride.

"So here's the deal. The way I work— I'm always confused. I'm always rushing to meet the schedule. I hate making decisions because I can instantly marshal a case against anything I decide. I'll surely finish the project, though I have no earthly notion why I should. And— Listen, I want to say, I appreciate your input, feedback, all that, or at least I think I do. No, I really do."

One more contradiction to pile on the heap. She smiled a second time and walked out to her car.

§

He wanted to call his daughter, but this week they were probably closing on the house and he was hesitant to intrude on her labor pains. Better to focus on his own. And in fact it was a productive week. His crackpot staging ideas were starting to make sense. He was finding a crude, almost amateurish style that matched his grizzled state of mind. Sometimes the puppets would have precise, fully animate gestures; other times they jiggled like dolls. He could flop one creature down on the play-board and start speaking the next scene's lines while slipping his hands into another. Two puppets could play realistically and then, with a shimmy and wobble and wag, he'd be a little kid making his soap dish talk to his rubber duck.

He would always be visible behind his puppets, he decided, back and forth between narrative and dialogue. Some scenes that had seemed overripe with sentiment began to work, his instinct told him, with the presence of the haggard old Puppetmaster adding garlic to the stew. He decided to run his own light cues from an on-stage laptop: Wagnerian opera from a one-man band.

The style was rooted in an audacious premise: here was an old guy with an obsessive compulsion to tell a story, no idea how or why to tell it, but unable to shut up. He was on his own, ignorant of the future, fumbling for a thread. That would work. It was the naked truth.

He still struggled with Galahad's eyes. All week he worked on the little glass globs, carefully painting the pupils, letting them dry; then the irises, letting them dry; then the whites. Time after time, he positioned them in the sockets, turned the head on the stand, checked from all angles, then plucked them out and scraped off the paint. Yes, he agreed with Jeanette, who had no goddamned right to say it: it had to be in the eyes. He was doing fine at capturing the heroic obsession, the will to penetrate fog, the valor to vanquish demons—but where was the wound?

Lainie had been into the mythic stuff. All the great myths were of wounds, she said: old archetypes dying, new forms in flower. And there was no lack of wounds. We make endless war, torment the planet, elect our own hangmen: a world awash with wounds. And here he was sending finger puppets against the Death Star. The odds were thin, so he'd better get back to work.

Yet another try at eyesight: the pupils higher, larger, slightly wall-eyed. They were dry enough and looked promising as he held them up to the sockets in the clay. He began to paint the irises. Larger, a darker amber with flakes of green oxide, a floatingness to it. But how to paint a wound that couldn't be seen, the wound as a shadowed fountain? What would Rembrandt do? Somewhere he had a book of Rembrandt self-portraits—eyes full of personal grief or simply gone dark from seeing the blacks and browns and yellows of life. He should look it up and copy. Then he thought better of it. One glance into that savvy Dutchman's soul and he'd never get out alive.

Waiting for the irises to dry, he fumbled under a paint rag for his sketch pad and the box of coffee filters he used for papier mache—tiny strips, strong, absorbent—and flipped his pad to the scrawls that stood for the parents. Cartoon faces, soulless, dumb with ache. He had seen a movie about a recluse who fell in love with a sex doll, basking in her light as she sat beside him inert and brainless. Maybe the parents could be full-size dummies, watching his puppet show as if watching TV. He could offer them news of Bobby, sheltered by a fool who was not a fool, a woman who was man, a frail, divided thing. Then Bobby would go back to school and report on his summer vacation.

§

Night. The cries of carrion birds dreaming the next dawn's feast. A numb lackey at riverside by torchlight, scrubbing stains from his master's day of killing. The soldiers in line at the whore wagons, next by next, seeding a diseased brotherhood. The air was chill and crisp.

Albert watched Galahad by the fire as best he could, though at times the wind changed and blew smoke in his eyes. Lost Boy and Fool approached. There was a distant, gravelly shriek. The Knight looked up.

"Vulture had a nightmare," said the Fool, flapping arms and peeping like a tiny chick. The child laughed. Their voices carried over the rustle of the encampment.

Galahad ignored the jest. He spoke in a low voice, barely hearing himself. "My falconer knows them. Bald heads, so their feathers never clog as they gorge. They eat putrid flesh that would kill other beasts. They piss down their legs to clean themselves. Servants provided by God to clear our leavings."

Another shriek sounded overhead.

The Knight was unshaven. A squire had removed his chain mail, but he still wore the sweaty padding. He drank from a pewter mug, but the wine seemed to have no effect. "Like them, I've gained weight on this Quest." He clapped his stomach and snorted out a laugh.

"Me too!" cried the Fool, commencing a pantomime of blowing up like a balloon, plodding like an elephant, then exploding into fragments floating down, twinkling in the night. Bobby laughed. Galahad smiled a bleak smile.

"You make a try, Sammy Shit-pants. You deserve a better audience than myself." He threw something into the fire. It flared, then vanished. "Another messenger from home. My wife writes of the weather, the crops, new babies, a Viking raid on the seacoast. Predictable reports. Dutiful." He cleared his throat, gathered sputum, spat. "Yet again, not in her hand. The pen of the vicar, perhaps, or a mendicant monk. And endearments, of course, copied from some book of amorous martyrs. Words without heart. Words that your parrot might cackle. Have I lost her? Tell me. She spoke often to you by the fire, in the garden, at the window glass."

The Fool shrugged. In sudden rage, Galahad rose, grabbed the small freak by the collar, shook him—then abruptly let go, waved an apology, sat heavily on the log with his back to the fire. The wind died, the trees went silent. Without looking up, he extended his arm, calling Sammy to him. Sammy sat at his side, and Galahad embraced the frail creature.

The Fool shivered. For a long time they sat together, Galahad's arm over fragile shoulders. The Lost Boy sat at the end of the log.

"Maybe she can't think what to say," ventured the Fool, "cause words are like cats, they don't come when you call." No response. The Fool huddled closer. "My lady was sad when you had to go. She told me go with you, cause she wanted to go but she thought I could juggle better. She said tell him I look through the window glass and I see him all the time. She said tell him I'm with him right now."

Something flickered in Galahad. He turned and saw love in Sammy's eyes, something like love: his own wife's face in this ludicrous freak of nature. He looked away. The Fool crouched lower, pressing the wispy beard to the chin. Galahad wept.

Albert for once did not begrudge him the tears.

They sat in silence. Bobby waited. He was sleepy but hoped for a bedtime story, and he needed to pee. He'd asked where the bathroom was and they'd said, "Wherever!" He went behind a large oak and relieved himself, nearly dousing a tiny tree frog before it hopped out of range. When he came back to the fire, the two figures were still huddled. Sometimes he'd seen his parents huddled like that. Maybe that's what you did to have a baby.

Bobby had heard the soldiers talking about Sir Galahad. They joked that he looked at the Fool like the little freak was a woman he wanted to screw. Bobby didn't know what it meant to screw, but he could look it up for show-and-tell. He worried how much school he was missing, if they might flunk him even though now he knew history really well.

The Knight looked toward Bobby. "I have no child," he said. "My wife desires children, but God has not willed it so. She visits each new mother, whether lady or peasant, to stroke the brow of the newborn, though most of them die, of course. She allows not even a litter of cats to be drowned. Some of my serfs have a dozen spawn, and I have none."

"Maybe God's run outta parts," said the Fool, pretending to rock a baby. "Maybe you gotta say please."

"We kneel together and pray for a child. But I know that God looks into my heart and sees that my prayer is a lie. How may I seed the future," he cried, "when I myself am soulless?"

The Lady Fool twisted out a daffy grimace and forced a cackle. "Everybody's got a soul, like everybody's got a butt. One each. Even me." The Fool did a finger dance, then the hands formed into the wings of a bird, fluttering upward. No response from the Knight, so the Fool grabbed her fingers, scolded them for bad behavior, and looked up to meet Galahad's naked eyes.

He stared at the Fool. "I desire no child. I loathe the thought of it." He looked away.

If Galahad had held his gaze on the eyes of the Fool, he would have seen a soul struck by lightning, dying, but he stared back into the blackness of the fire.

"When I took my seat at Arthur's table, the Siege Perilous reserved for purity, I was pure. No soul, no heart, no inner being, an unstained channel of power. I drew the sword from the stone and swore to claim the Grail. But how would I know it? By a halo, an emblem, heraldry? Was it of silver, gold, or wormy cedar? I rode into the labyrinth of my emptiness.

"And my emptiness issued the call. This Quest is absurd. A soul grows from seed, from stains, from excrement even. From the fervent, relentless pulse of the heart, not out of a blackened goblet. I should order them to torture me: under the searing iron I might divulge what I long to know.

"I have only contempt for peasants who bring brats into the world by the dozen, to be withered by thirst, to starve, to gouge their scalps for lice, to spit out their teeth. I too am tormented by need, by this vile obsession that ravages all I touch. I will sire no child in my image."

Galahad turned to the shivering Lost Boy. "Take him, Sammy! Journey home! Return him to his parents and bring me news of the Lady Mara. Carry her this kiss and bring her kiss to me." He grasped the Fool's trembling hands and in each palm bestowed a kiss that burned like Greek fire, endless and unendurable. Then he turned away.

The Fool drew in a breath to plead, but the woman who looked through Sammy's eyes knew that words were useless. The Lost Boy must go, and the Fool would return to the madness of the Quest to nurse a sterile husband. The fragile creature rose, took Bobby to the tent, said that in the morning they would journey to Warwick Castle and find his parents.

"They'll be mad at me," said Bobby.

"They'll be glad to be mad," said the Fool.

§

Albert touched the whites to see if the eyes were dry. They were. Gently he placed them in the sockets, adjusting the angles, careful not to scrape the paint. And at last he saw what he had intended: eyes slightly out of focus, bent to the side as if avoiding what lay directly in front. The subtle asymmetry of the cheekbones and brows and jaw defined a mighty face straining against itself, frozen in the instant before it yawned open its mouth to cry for its mother.

Deep in the eyes, he could see the wound.

XIII

Of a Journey to Nowhere

Fool and Lost Boy wended homeward through the land of Anachronica. It was hard going. Time zones were shuffled like playing cards, millennia ran amok, eras frisked with epochs, and aeons curled into the primal womb to be born again. No reason to be surprised, then, at eighteen-wheelers barreling over the broken, weed-infested Roman roads. They might have tried hitchhiking, but in the Dark Ages that was ill-advised. Risky to bum a ride from an anachronism.

Albert had always disliked shows that muddled chronologies, though puppeteers seemed to love that stuff: Prince Charming with an iPhone, the Three Little Pigs as Three Little Stooges. But now he couldn't stop chasing every incongruity that streaked naked across the road. Ferocity, depravity, absurdity—those he could only depict in images from the floodlit Dark Age he lived in. His hikers trekked under a gathering smog.

Their journey, he knew, was a theatrical blunder, leaving his hero slouched on a log, mired in a tar pit of gloom, as the playwright danced an allegorical hokey-pokey. At this point, if the audience weren't on the edge of their seats, they'd want to go out for a beer. But this was a journey the Knight commanded—a quest within the Quest—and the Fool complied.

Bobby remembered the teacher reading a King Arthur story. "Why can't Merlin fly us home?" he asked. The Fool said nothing, fearing to deny the existence of that compulsive shapeshifter—now an old hermit, now a mossy cairn, now the lissome Lady of the Lake—always a presence, always a menace. Yet while magicians could fly, they couldn't ease the landing. They could open doors but couldn't tame the demons lurking behind. Like puppeteers, they could summon godlike power, but that god might smear you under its thumb. "Couldn't he?" the Lost Boy repeated. The Fool was silent. She held the child close to quiet him. It began to feel strange to think of herself as *she*.

They trudged on, their foodstuffs dwindled, and the bleak landscape offered them no sustenance. From time to time, they came upon a deserted Quik-Stop but couldn't assemble a meal from the ravished aisles. Fried candy bars? Boiled potato chips? A soup of peanuts and Pepsi? They passed through vacant housing developments: acres of mud and concrete slabs with placards dubbing them Ravenswood or Edensgrove.

They came to an arroyo under an outcrop of rock that resembled a massive hand. The Fool recalled that the army had once camped nearby. Troops from the castle had swarmed to attack, led by a dozen heavily packaged knights, but they were no match for Galahad's archers. There were still patches of scorched earth here and there, but brambles grew rampant over the battlefield, gorging themselves on the gore.

The corpses had been stripped, the bones picked clean by wild pigs and bleached by the sun. It should have taken years for the skeletons to dry, whiten, and sunder, but Time flayed its victims swiftly in Anachronica. Someone had sorted the bones, heaping fingers, thighbones, and pelvises into piles. The spines had been cleanly detached and placed end to end to form a labyrinthine spiral around a center pyramid of skulls: a labor of love or madness. The Lost Boy asked if he could take a toe bone home for a souvenir, but the Fool said no.

With a tunic bought from a miller's child, who ran home naked clutching a dollar bill, the Fool fashioned a comic garb for Bobby. They worked out a dance between Fool and Baby Fool. If danger loomed, they might save themselves by foolishness, though Sammy doubted a comic dance would charm a pack of wild dogs.

They met no wild dogs. Highway signs alerted motorists to the presence of deer or wandering cattle, but no such creatures appeared. Except for that miller's child, the populace stayed hidden. No insect chorus even: apart from the brambles, the land was devoid of life. Had the Quest rendered it thus, or had they made a wrong turn and arrived in a lifeless future? They passed a farm with a huge faded banner between two trees. CHOOSE YOUR OWN PUMPKIN, it said.

Now there were billboards. Food in colossal florid sizzle. One gaping maw with a cheeseburger poised on the flapping tongue: BURGER ME UP! A whooping cowboy riding a wild crustacean: LOBSTER RODEO, BUCKAROOS! Two intertwined lasses on syrupy pancakes: HOTTIES FOR YOU AT IHOP. They proclaimed a world rife with food, teeming with food, bleeding food out of every pore—a magical kingdom where hunger's rat face was unknown.

The Fool had once partaken of feasting, of abundance every day. While she had known there were people starving, she saw them only through her crystalline window glass against the glaring sun. Now, at the base of the towering billboards, something stirred: shadowy creatures, colorless, clustered, refugees scraping amid the rubble of derelict cars and barrels leaking a shimmering waste. One raised a hand toward the burger, the lobster, the succulent girls.

The travelers stood at a fork in the road marked by a megalith. The Fool smelled peril. Fairy tales were rife with forks and crossroads. A hooded beggar sat leaning against the rock. Raising great hollow eyes set in a bony face, the creature extended a hand, huge and spidery, splayed out from a skeletal arm: a perfect beggar's hand.

"Food!" croaked the beggar.

The Fool emptied a bag on the ground, a few crusts and rinds, and the supplicant ate.

"More!"

The Fool shook the bag again and out fell an apple core, a wizened potato, a chicken bone. Bobby's eyes glazed over as the beggar wolfed the offal. The Fool was bent with hunger cramps.

"I'm hungry," the Lost Boy whimpered. The Fool hugged him close and told of kingdoms with mountains of candy, gullies of custard, blizzards of chocolate ice. The Lost Boy dreamed his belly full.

As if in recompense, the beggar pointed toward the right-hand fork. The travelers continued their journey.

§

Food. The fridge could always lure Albert away from work into munchy procrastination, but he had no appetite now. He had written these souls into a hunger too deep to be fed. He was seated at Lainie's desk again. He had been sleeping on her side of the bed. He riffled absently through a stack of receipts and sent his duo onward.

§

Each day they felt deeper thirst. From the road they saw a shimmering stream, but the banks were too steep to descend. They came to a stagnant ditch, filled a bottle, and drank. By day they licked their own sweat, by night the dew from the grass. They dreamt of mountain waterfalls, awoke with cracked lips.

Billboards again: beer, wine, colas, organic smoothies. Dark figures beneath, like shadows shed by their wearers. A second megalith, taller than the first, marked another fork. A second beggar: a woman, bald, with pale blotches on her face as if dribbles of bleach had branded her, and the same hollow eyes. Must be, thought the Fool, that all mendicants by turns shared one pair of eyes.

The hag reached out a dry hand with sharp knuckles and wrinkled skin. "Drink!" she cried.

The Fool drew out the bottle filled from the roadside slough. Bobby remembered the baby bottle he hadn't seen for years—*your titty-bottle*, Mommy called it. The derelict sucked the last trickle.

"More!" she squawked.

The Fool produced a can of Pepsi they had found in the rubble and pulled the tab. The liquid, condensed to a syrup, flowed into the harpy's maw. The Fool's lips cracked deeper as the last drop vanished.

"I'm thirsty," said the Lost Boy.

The Fool wiggled her fingers like water. The beggar, thin lips grinning, pointed the way. The travelers took the right-hand fork, continuing homeward.

§

Albert saw where this was going. Nowhere, fast. Why the passive acquiescence? To prove that all journeys are circular? Was that a bit of wisdom his audience really needed or just the whine of his own futility?

§

Sunrises, sunsets: the fireball rose and set in every direction. They could place no trust in their senses. If they took even a shallow breath, the craving was roused, the cramps and desiccation. Pain was aswirl in the air, a poisonous mist. Like pilgrims across the millennia, their feet went numb. They deepened the road's ancient groove.

Again, the billboards loomed. Myriads now, markers for the dead. They covered hillside, meadow, and sky. No, the Fool told herself: she had covered her eyes when the killing began, but there could never have been so many. The Quest was the work of a small battalion, not the onslaught of Huns. The billboards pitched messiahs, presidents, electronic gadgets—a landscape of buoyant dreams. Each bore a single word: HOPE.

Predictably, a fork in the road and a third beggar crouched beneath a rough-hewn stone. The travelers were caught in the implacable trigonometry of the fairy tale: three bears, three billy goats gruff, three little pigs. The beggar's head was hooded, its caustic voice sexless. From the sleeves stretched no hands. "I despair!" croaked the supplicant.

The Fool's words formed on her lips, though her lips were mute. *I leave here my hope. My laughter, my dancing, my joy. My sense of the rightness of things. The certainty of sunrise. My desire for a child. Embroidery, truffles, songs. Hope for this Lost Boy, for all lost children ever. I leave it.*

Me too, the Lost Boy nodded. *My bike, my dog, my mommy and daddy and story books. My birthday coming up, and when we visit Grandma she makes a chocolate cake. And going to Heaven some day, where Kathy is.*

In other tales, such encounters brought gain: a ring, a wand, a feather that might save the hero's neck. In this tale, only a finger pointing to another deep-rutted road.

"I'm cold," the Lost Boy said. The Fool wrapped his tiny shoulders with the empty sack.

The travelers took the right-hand fork and resumed their trek, having shed all hope of reaching home. A slant of sunlight let pour a tide of shadow, and the greenery blossomed cankers. Old memories arose—an embrace, an odor, a smile—and they could only pray to blur them out, mutely shouting *No!* A fork to the right, another fork to the right, another. The old god Albert Fisher watched his characters plod on. At sunset they saw, silhouetted against a bonfire, one hunched figure on a log.

§

How do you give up hope? Albert was on the back porch filling the water bowl for the feral cats. These beasts would never do that. If he failed to feed them, they'd trot off and raid a neighbor's garbage can or try to snag a mole, but they'd be back at the trough for vespers. With the threat of hawks and raccoons, the winter rains, the scourge of fleas and hookworms, the great metal hunks roaring over concrete, how did they retain their idiot faith in Providence?

Well, Providence provided them cat food for one more day, but he couldn't promise forever. Lainie loved to sit and purr with her brood. None except the black furball would come to be petted, and then only when she offered him a bite of tuna. Albert felt no responsibility to these freeloaders. Grantmakers rarely offered support for multiple years, and that should apply to cats. Yet they nourished their hopes.

But his own faith was at an end. He was writing theatrical roadkill, scenes he could never stage. Right turn, right turn, right turn, and the Fool's journey had brought them back full circle to a rust-bound dolt on a log. He had trapped his characters in a Dark Age so bleak that none could escape. They were dragging suitcases filled with concrete through seasons that washed backwards, winter to fall, fall to summer, summer to spring to winter, for no reason except to reflect the confusion in their creator's head.

No more Galahad. The show was dead in the water. Leave the poor stiff staring into his bonfire. The burning desire, the loneliness, the lies—it was like that duo show they'd done years ago, *Scar Tissue*, which a dear friend had told them was beautifully written but impossible to watch: too full of bitter self-mockery.

Who would notice if he quietly put the project out of its misery? His daughter, yes. Mara knew that her father lived for his work, that it kept his fire alive. He would have to endure her pain, or he would have to lie. He'd probably lie.

And Jeanette. He knew she was on a roll with the designs, but it wouldn't be the first time she'd been dumped. Their contract had an exit clause, and it would be generous to offer her half the fee, more than generous. If she insisted, he'd give her the whole damn thing as a ransom for his freedom. He'd kidnapped himself, so it was only right that he'd have to pay the ransom. Just before sitting down to supper, he picked up the phone and told her what he'd decided.

A long silence, and then she said, "Let's talk."

XIV

Of the Puppetmaster's Astoundment

They met the following afternoon at the coffee shop. He had rehearsed his apologies and his rationale with an absolute determination to end it then and there. The flat inflection of *Let's talk* promised unpleasantness, but it had to be faced. If he could survive Lainie's pitbull tenacity in their artistic skirmishes on problematic inspirations (Eurydice's resistance to returning from Hades) and half-baked baloney (Hades as a shopping mall), he could survive anything.

Jeanette arrived five minutes late, in a loose black work shirt over jeans, her hair drawn back in a ponytail or as near a ponytail as frizzy red hair would agree to. It was the first time he had seen her raw, without makeup. She came directly to his table. As he started into his prepared remarks, she snapped, "That's bullshit."

She spat out the words: *self-pity, despondency, crying the blues, head in your armpit.* As eyes rose from scattered laptops around Friendly Joe's, she cut off her salvo, lowered her voice to a sibilant whisper. "One of my so-called relationships, a very nice psychopath named Gerald—dear Gerald—we broke up. I missed two deadlines. I sat hugging my pillow, crying nonstop. I didn't take the garbage out for three weeks, and then you know what I did?"

Albert kept his eyes fixed on hers. He let it come. He owed her that. "Yes? What?"

"I took out the fucking garbage and I did my work."

There was a gnarly silence. She was still standing at the table. He made a vague gesture toward a chair, and after a pause she sat, staring at a painting on the wall behind him. He couldn't recall what it looked like. Almost from the start, he knew that, okay, yes, of course, he would do the show. In fact he barely heard her words, only felt the passionate surge. There was no appeal.

"You're right," he murmured. "Yes. Okay. The show must stagger on, as they say." He heard the whine in his voice. "I mean let's go ahead with it. I mean if you're willing."

She spoke under her breath. "This is important work, goddammit, whether you think so or not. It's not about you, it's about the story that's being told. I shouldn't have to tell you that."

"Right. True. Okay."

"I mean it!"

"I agree. I just said I agree. Let's do it if you're willing."

"Oh, just like that?"

This had too many echoes. It had taken him years to understand that a quarrel had its own music, that a crescendo couldn't be chopped short by a preemptive, *Right, okay*. He had cut her to the bone and it had to play out.

"Jeanette?"

"Yes?"

"As you were well aware, I loathed this guy, my so-called hero. And now I'm identifying with him too strongly. Right, it's not about me. But on the other hand it is about me, and I wish it weren't." With an effort, she shifted her gaze to him. He continued. "I don't do introspection very well. I guess my neuroses are in my characters. All I can say . . . ." A pause. "Not sure what it is that's all I can say."

"You can say let's do it and stop with the crap."

"Let's do it."

The wrong thing to say. Or right thing, wrong rhythm. He asked if she'd like some tea. She nodded yes. He went to the counter. When he returned with the cup, she was sitting with both hands folded symmetrically.

"I'm okay now," she said. "Possibly."

At some point, he suggested that they move back to the studio out of mercy to the coffee shop, but they arrived in his living room instead. As he opened a bottle of sauvignon blanc—in celebration or in compensation?—he confessed his brief affair with *Rumpelstiltskin*, and she said, "Interesting." From the first glass of wine to the opening of the second bottle, they both knew they'd regret it. Albert never drank before dinnertime, and Jeanette started to wobble after half a glass.

They spoke of Albert's choice of the Galahad tale, that it wasn't accidental. And why the Lost Boy had popped into his head like a casual drive-by bullet. And why he'd named the Lady after his daughter when there wasn't the slightest resemblance. He started to talk about Big Lake but realized he'd already told the whole story.

And she began the tale of her stint in the comics industry as an inker of musclebound superheroes, then tried to remember the relevance of that subject to the matters at hand. That sent them into a fit of giggles as they realized they were getting very loopy. Long before they ever touched, they were making love.

"So you said, what was it, a week or so ago, maybe . . ." Albert tried to focus as she poured herself another glass. "No, I was gonna say . . . Okay: you said how the Lady wanted a child, how that was important to . . ."

Her voice was a low murmur. "I was . . . I guess I was just projecting my . . ." She stared at her wine glass, took a sip. "So after a split-up, hey, turned out I was pregnant, *Oh God, what now?* Then a miscarriage. Second trimester. What good fortune, I thought. But it hit like a ten-ton truck." She sat a moment with the remembrance. "No, I don't know if that's relevant to the Lady, but there are so many layers to a person, try to get it clear, try to—"

A sharp sob from Jeanette. Automatically, Albert touched her shoulder. She put her hand on his, and somehow they came together.

Sex had been no part of their dialogue, but it was there in the rhythm of their speech: a music, an intercourse, the spree of a milkweed pod. It started with hair. He felt her hair, the red of it, and she fingered his long, tangled gray. At the start, the lust was only to hold closer, to burrow in, to find shelter from swarming memories. They kissed a tentative siblings' kiss, and he heard his own pointless mumble, some buzz in his head, "You think how attraction, it's the strangest thing, how it happens . . ." She kissed him again, deeply, as if to shut him up.

Somehow they landed in bed. Albert wasn't sure how they got there or what to do about it. They were kayaking on a boozy river, seeing the rapids ahead, thinking, *Well, what the hell!* Getting naked, the sleeves and pant legs seemed to multiply, invert, and tie themselves into the clove hitches, bowlines, and sheepshanks that Albert could never master in Scouts. Some things once learned are never forgotten, like riding a bike or making love. But Albert had never biked while shedding his clothes, and Jeanette seemed equally clueless despite her years and her lovers. A zipper snagged, an elastic clung to a wrist, and they became all elbows and extra limbs. They rolled over snaps and hooks and a Gordian knot of cotton, polyester, and one stray tangle of silk. Both sensed that the scene involved two people in amorous grapple without knowing why or how. It was a flat-out fumbling, with all the grace of a squid making out with an armadillo. A few epileptic spasms, something approximating intercourse, and the wine god claimed victory.

They lay flattened against the rumple, empty, exhausted, awaiting a sob or a wail. Instead, there came a moment when both took a breath, held it forever, then gave it all up. One of them laughed, then both, and the laughter wove its own mad tangle of jazz, in duets and silence and solos, gentling to spurts and trickles, and at last a quiet breathing. Albert pulled a sheet over their twilit nakedness.

In the course of time, Jeanette spoke. "This wasn't my intention, I don't think."

"Nor mine," said Albert. "Are you okay?"

"Unless I stop laughing." And she laughed.

Their mutual gaze explored the irregularities of the shadowed off-white ceiling.

"I'm just curious," she said, "what you're thinking right now. I know that's kind of an unfair question, but I guess we're—"

"We're both old enough to answer unfair questions."

"Yeah. Though for me, it's been a while."

"And for me. You want to know what I'm thinking?" He smiled. "Well, to be perfectly honest—"

"Something about the show?"

She was right. Truth could be embarrassing, usually was. His brain had been weighing the merits of first sculpting the Lady and using that model for the Fool, or vice versa, and how many separate heads, given the challenges of change, would be needed for Fool and Lady Fool.

"You busted me," he said. Propped up on his pillow, he outlined his thoughts on the matter.

"Whatever," she said when he finished, in a flat noncommittal voice.

"Whatever," he said.

She spoke in a perkier tone. "So are we going to talk about puppet heads, or about . . . this?" She placed her hand lightly on his chest. "Or maybe we're not in a condition to do either. I haven't quite landed yet."

"Me neither." Something in her tone suggested that he had survived the honesty. "The only thing you can expect is the totally unexpected," he said, then wondered if he'd said it before, or written it, or thought it. "It's a wild ride, whatever."

"Wild ride," she pondered. "I knew a woman who wrote a song called *Wild Ride*. She was one of my own wild rides, in fact. Beautiful song. Never got out there, of course."

And he was remembering high school, walking home from the first date with the girl of his dreams. Tree branches were etched across the moon, and he was thinking how life was just about to happen, if he could only—

Jeanette rose to make her way to the bathroom. Albert caught a passing glimpse of the dark aureoles of her small, pert breasts, and filed the memory among other places he would like to travel again. When she returned, they untangled their clothes and shuffled back into the fabrics and fastenings. They found their way to the kitchen. The wine was still hanging in there but trailing off. He suggested tea. They made small talk about tea and coffee and yerba mate, then sat steeped in silence. She sipped her tea attentively, as if testing it for accuracy.

"You want to stay for supper?" he asked. "I can make either spaghetti or spaghetti."

"No, I need to get back."

They had come to a fork in the road without a beggar to point the way. It might be that the only thing lasting from their erotic collision was the laughter. Much later, they would talk about the impulse, the leap, the tangle, as if describing scenes they had read in books or seen in films, startled to find that those characters seemed to resemble themselves. The obvious question—what further intimacy was implied—didn't arise. They had work to do.

"So I'll have the rest of the script, I guess, in some shape or other, what, next week? Friday? 1:22 p.m. Pacific Time?"

"I'll work on the sketches."

They gave each other a friendly hug. Jeanette walked out to her car, turning to wave. They were bonded somehow, but neither seemed to know what lurked beneath the *somehow*. Later, as

Albert straightened the covers, he was struck by a tide of emotion—not joy, not pain, just a purely undifferentiated tide—that flattened him face down on the bed. With Lainie, he had made one child and thirty-odd plays, each born of their coupling, labor, and strife—the strife of a chordal dissonance that somehow moved through a cadence to its resolution. Now suddenly, a farcical roll in the hay, the briefest coitus, and a new genesis: a presence, a risk, a woman he barely knew, a pushy understudy replacing his lifemate, a tangle of redheaded contradictions. He lay a long time with his cheek to the coverlet, fearful of turning upward to face the ceiling or the sky.

Worlds away, the Fool and Lost Boy came within sight of the camp, the solitary silhouette against the fire, and the boundless silence.

XV

Of the Plague

At the first turn, the Fool had known they were going in a circle. Stories were like that: they formed patterns, and you found yourself woven into the tapestry before you knew it. From her earliest memories of lessons with tutors or bells calling the family to prayer, she had felt the entrapment of pattern and the drainage of time.

Wherever soldiers had touched the rolling hills, they left dark blotches, gluts of rubbish, staleness. Approaching the encampment, the Fool expected to see a sprawl of bonfires and tents, but the twilight squalor they entered was silent, save for the hum of blowflies. Vacant tents were pitched helter-skelter, and a stench arose as from the vast, rotting corpse of a god.

They came to the smoldering campfire. Shirtless and sweaty, Galahad mutely acknowledged their presence. The Fool led Bobby to a water keg, and they drank. She found a piece of jerky and cut strips to chew. The Lost Boy curled on a stray blanket and slept. Sammy sat at Galahad's feet.

"We went back, but Mommy and Daddy weren't there, so he was scared."

Galahad stretched to poke the sputtering coals.

The Fool told him the news. Lady Mara was happy but sad. Crops were cropping and babies were being babied. No one was stealing the chapel bell. Everybody was living happily ever after. She made no mention of the beggars or the forks in the road. The Knight accepted the lies without a word. At last he spoke, in the listless voice of a bard telling a tale that his hearers already knew.

One night, a young sentry had screamed and roused the camp. They lit the torches, grabbed their weapons, prepared for surprise attack. The sentry stood shivering amidst the tumult.

"What did you see?"

"The Angel of Death."

The prankster got ten lashes for being drunk.

But next day they began to die. Some never rose from sleep. Some felt faint, feverish, then tiny buboes flowered in their armpits like poppies in spring. Others hopped about in the gawky dance of the Plague, the staggering hiccups of drunken fleas. Enraged, their comrades fell on the villagers, hacked dead every creature that moved, and at night by the fires they drank themselves senseless and vomited out their bile. Galahad shook off his torpor. He moved from tent to tent nursing his men, captaining the burials. *Am I blest, being immune to the Plague? Or curst, being the source of it?* In three days, there were scores of dead.

He called on Father Olyver to say mass. Knights, pikemen, archers, common soldiers, muleteers, whores (a growth industry now, filling five wagons), assorted pages, scullery boys, cooks, and two lunatics they had taken along for sport—all gathered on a rocky hillside to plead to a merciless God. The Priest rattled out the ritual, his thin voice cutting the chill. Few understood the Latin, but they knew the words were holy, and a flux of hope rippled through the throng. Their crucifix was only sticks bound together by cord—a deserter had swiped the original—but for those few knights who had seen the great cathedral's altarpiece, the Priest's hollow eyes stood in for those of the suffering Jesus. In this hour of dread, the scurvy little Priest seemed transfigured into a man of God.

He came to the homily. Keep it short, Galahad had told him: preachments were pointless. But the words came uninvited to Father Olyver's lips. They spoke themselves. He was astonished to hear himself speak the truth and to feel its unstoppable flow.

"My children, children of God: a loving Father does not kill. It is we who flay ourselves. If I cast myself to the rocks, I am killed by the force that takes me. God has only created the rocks and the force; He does not cast me down. He gives us a world, and we make it a killing field."

The wind shifted. The smoke from the fires drifted over the assemblage. A murmur, then silence as he spoke.

"God assigns us our station. To some He gives command, to others obedience. To some great estates, to others stony fields. Some dine on venison, others on roots. Unequal measure, yet all receive His abundance."

As the smoke rose, they saw dark clouds gathering in its wake. The flogged sentry, crouching at the edge of the throng, dug at his eyes to expunge the hideous angel's beak.

"Yet His children are discontent. The rich swell with rage at the greed of the poor who scrape the dregs of their gruel. The Grail might bless us like the sun, free to all, but no, it must be seized. It brims not with the blood of Christ but of those slain for the prize. *If others hunger, I may glut. If others die, I live.* The logic of lunatics. We press our brothers into the raptor's maw."

Murmurs, low chuckles, curses, the shuffling of feet. The Priest knew he should stop, but the words kept flowing like pus from an unbound wound. The sun went black.

"Once a Prophet entered our night. He cried, *I see it! It's there! Follow me!* And we caught Him, fell upon Him, nailed Him right up where we wanted Him to hang. We worshipped His death, not His life. And I am one who has babbled the lies, fueled the fires, praised the wars. I am priest to the buboes."

Muffled grunts. Scattered hisses. Distant thunder. The soldiers didn't understand his words, but they caught the gist of it. They began to drift away. The Priest raved on.

"So I ask not God's mercy upon us, but our mercy upon ourselves. We it is who spawn our own sores. Look in your heart. See what you see. You know the worms in your bowels, but there are more. There are worms in the heart, in the lungs, and there are found among children the eggs of worms in the eyes. What is the face of a mother seen by those eyes? Will you not understand?"

Father Olyver stood pale, sweating, drained, his voice a hollow croak. His congregation had filtered down to three soldiers—call them Larry, Moe, and Curly. They weren't the historic Three Stooges, of course, and they never indulged in violence just for laughs. This Larry, Moe, and Curly were simple souls. They couldn't follow Father Olyver's logic, but it seemed to make sense. They knew what they'd done. In the early days, the killing was good honest work, and afterwards you partied. But they were sick of the torture, the screams, the women's eyes glazing over. Now their buddies were dead or drifting off to die, and the Priest was telling them to cleanse the world. They knew what would come of that: peel the onion down to the core, there's nothing left but peel. They stared at the little ranting cherub. Maybe time had come to purge the world of ranting cherubs. *Silence over the Earth for a day and the passing of days.*

"Let's bonk him," said Moe.

They took him down a forest path, deep into the tangled woods. From time to time he asked where they were going, but they made no reply. They came to a rock outcropping with an undercut that formed a cave, partly obscured by a huge fallen trunk. A fierce cicada rhythm set in, like a brewing storm, a dense fog of noise to blot the scene from the ears of humankind.

The trio encircled the little Priest. Moe slapped him. Larry pulled his ear. Curly poked him in the nose. Then they stepped back. Larry swung his quarterstaff.

§

No, Albert: concentrate. He scratched out three pages of notebook scrawl. The last thing anyone needed was another atrocity. Better if Larry swung his staff, missed the Priest and whacked Moe in the rump, launching a donnybrook as Father Olyver wandered into the wilderness preaching to the trees. Suffice it to say that the next day Larry was dead of the plague, Curly was hanged, and Moe deserted to seed future generations.

It had been a hot spell, even for mid-July, and the studio was stuffy. He turned on the fan to get the air moving and wished he could do the same for his head. Not that he lacked bright ideas: they bred like the feral cats, litter upon litter, chasing their tails into the night. His mind kept chewing old dead bubble gum. Was any of this necessary? Violence and nudity in the movies—strictly necessary? A guy stops the show and intones, "To be or not to be"—quotable, but necessary? Why must we visit our parents on Sunday, care for the elderly, the disabled, the unemployed? Do they serve a purpose? Don't we already have plenty of humans? Seen one, you've seen 'em all. A horrible thing to say, but it's said on a daily basis.

In a burst of inspiration, he rose and threw his notepad twenty feet across the studio. A wild bird-flutter, a satisfying touch of melodrama that might be useful in the show. He fetched the tattered notepad and made a note in it. He had been seeking some potent moment of horror that nailed it, but would that stop the world's butchery or merely raise our threshold for nausea? Maybe see the Lost Boy watching it from a distance:

the Puppetmaster narrates, the puppet reacts with no more than a tremor, and we read the horror in the blankness of his face. It's the seeing that makes it horrid. If children see it, they might have nightmares. They might grow up to be us.

Tomorrow was his Friday deadline, and while he'd been writing words, words, words, he was no nearer the end. The stuff was all detours and cloverleafs, unusable, never a straight shot to the finish. He had always started with a scenario, expanded the outline, then brought in the dialogue, honing it to the bone. Now the words swarmed like army ants, and the show would be ten hours long.

He sat back in his squeaky chair—that squeak had to go— and it came to him why he was grinding his gears. It was three days since Jeanette. As they parted, he'd actually had a moment when his faith—faith in the show, in storytelling, in life—felt as if it were on the mend. Once he had thought of his work as revolutionary action, changing the world one puppet at a time. At a certain age he saw that the world wasn't about to change and that the powers of evil were outspending him by billions. So he simply went on making stories because they were asking to be made. "We can entertain ourselves debating the purpose of life," Lainie had said, "but we don't stop living just because we can't decide." Now, for a few moments, all it seemed to take for renewal was one wacky romp in the hay. Yet that brought its own uncertainties.

He hadn't called her. He didn't want to seem pushy. Scattered through these three days had been moments when he'd sit back and think, *Well, that was a memorable episode, no big deal.* And then he'd be hit by a longing deeper than time. It had something to do with sex, but more with what sex had something to do with: the risk of closeness, of nakedness, of being seen. Their tipsy ride on the bumper cars was mostly comic relief, but it was a wild ride, and he didn't want it to end.

But what did he offer to any prospective bonding? A curriculum vitae six miles to nowhere? An obsessive hobbling on wobbly knees? A firm Germanic jaw too full of words? A thin skiff of humor over a chasm of pain? Clearly not a whole lot of positive self-image right now, though he might order some online.

Or he might just stop whining about what he had to offer and go ahead and offer it.

§

The Lady Fool returned from her journey bereft of Hope. She was with her husband now, no more army to distract the Sacred Knight, so why prolong the masquerade? If the Knight learned the truth, he would not beat her or cast her off. They might return together. In the darkness, under the festering drone of the flies, he had spoken the words she longed to hear: the Quest must end. The horses were dead, the men, the comfort women. Old Cookie was dead, who had bounced the toddler Galahad on her knee and received from him the nickname *Old Cookie* when she wasn't yet past thirty. What earthly reason had the Fool to urge him on?

She was barren now: no hope. Her spirit was chill wind through withered leaves. She had changed faces long ago, and now she was Fool to her very soul. Beside him on the log, staring into the fire, she watched the faint smoke wisps of the lost Lady Mara's girlhood.

As a girl she had heard of a warrior queen who fought a great conquering horde. She read of an ancient poetess and a nun whose hymns brought tears to the eyes of God. She was told of a duchess nursing victims of plague, female saints who worked miracles, and virgins who ruled vast lands. She wept for joy at the lowly woman who anointed the Savior's feet.

But in the glare of day, she had followed the well-trodden path: writing dutiful meditations, strumming the lute, finding a dash of skill in embroidery. She was praised for her fair complexion. If she bore a daughter, she vowed, she would discourage dreams: they led only to discontent.

In her Sacred Knight she had once found her soul: fierce vision, courage, ardor. True, she loved as a slave might love, but service to a master was the calling of all, from peasant to Pope— all bound to the service of God and His Holy Mother. She was blest with a consort whose flesh fulfilled hers, whose tenderness soothed, and whose obsessive passion gave meaning to her life.

As his amber eyes clouded, worn by mundane cares, she felt pangs, stabs, chokings of loss, relieved only by her impetuous gusts of foolery that whispered a promise. Then suddenly, the priestly decree. Her world collapsed, and she stumbled across the courtyard in her motley coat and coxcomb.

In the days, weeks, months of the Quest, she had one desire only: that her master laugh. Even as counterfeit fool, she wanted to spark laughter. She danced, she juggled, she spoke in silly tongues, she went all bug-eyed and stroked her wispy beard like Moses on the mountain. But there came no cough of mirth. In the bleak night hours he might hold her hand, though he knew her not. The deepest anguish: to offer a gift and no one to accept it.

With her lost Knight, she stared into the ashes at her feet. A scrap caught her eye: a charred strip of vellum. She picked it out of the ash. *This we seek of the Grail . . .* The words had survived the flame.

No hope, but something more vast. A resurrected vision. A miracle. The Fool thrust her fingers into the ash and touched her forehead. *Memento, homo, quia pulvis es . . . and to dust you shall return.* A mark of grief, but the words of the Knight were living still. They were blurred by the ash, but they spoke truth.

Now the Quest was hers. It needed no army, no battering ram. The Grail was the oneness of life, the love she still bore to the dumbstruck soul beside her, the future she had imagined in the child she had never borne. The Grail was promised to Galahad's hands, and she would bend his fingers to grasp it, for the sake of the young, the old, women, men, the humble, the strong—all kin.

After midnight, she dreamed of crossroads and megaliths and dark silhouettes. Then his words—strange even to himself— came to her again as glowing coals in the ash. *Heal, peace, no fear, free . . .* The Lost Boy slept dreamlessly beside her.

§

Nearly time to start dinner. Albert was tired of spaghetti, but he could stand it one more day. He left the props scattered, picked up his notepad, flicked off the lights. A frustrating day: too many ideas. He trudged into the house and started a pot of water heating.

Standing at the stove, he mulled the question of the Lost Boy. The tyke had served a purpose, but now he clogged the works. Fate's hand had a way of reaching in and plucking out characters. Some malignant storyteller had zipped Lainie from Albert's little tale without a second thought. No deeper meaning, no mercy, just Nature's whim that this woman who filled his life with joy and challenge and tasty dinners was not worth her time on stage. He might just as easily deep-six the kid.

Impulsively, as the water boiled, he called Jeanette.

"Hi?"

"Jeanette?"

"Well, yes, as far as I know."

Why was he calling? What was an acceptable reason? What was he interrupting in her life? "This is Albert."

"No doubt about it."

He had stepped straight into the swamp. "How's it going?"

Silence. How was what going, Albert? After a moment, her voice: "Well, I haven't done that much since we talked, but I'll be collecting some more swatches on Saturday."

"Well, actually I just meant . . . life."

"Life?" she asked. "I'm not sure. I'll Google it."

Albert tried to backpedal, said he was having a staging problem, would like some feedback, and asked if she might come over. Tonight? Tomorrow? Whenever?

"Let me check."

He endured dead silence. She must be bringing up a schedule on her screen, paging in her datebook or consulting the Mayan Calendar.

"Soonest would be Monday. Though you're dropping off the script this Friday, right?"

"Well, could you spare a little more time than that?"

"Well, Monday?"

Soonest would be Monday. "Monday, fine, good. Give me a call." He was shaken by a shock of raw desire, then an aftershock of emptiness. He clenched his teeth, cursing the wall of professionalism he'd erected between them, both before and after their fumbling transgression. He wanted to tell her what he felt, even if she didn't reciprocate, even if she made a joke. He wasn't even sure what it was that he felt, but if he could just blurt out some words, he might know.

"Hey, today I pretty much finished the Lady Mara's head, all in one go. I'll cast her and then do the Fool from that."

"Good."

"She looks a little bit like you. You at, say, thirty, maybe. Although a little more upturn to the nose, more touch of chipmunk."

"Gee, and I thought I did chipmunk pretty well."

"Or no, actually not that much resemblance." A lie: it was her and she would see it.

"Well, I've always aspired to be a puppet. It must be kinda restful."

He mumbled something, she mumbled a reply, he hung up and put the handful of spaghetti sticks into the bubbling water.

He saw the Lost Boy raising his hand to ask either for a life-or-death verdict or for a bedtime story, but Albert tucked him in to sleep. One more mouth to feed, but let him live. At least till next Monday, when the little brat could be arraigned before Jeanette and her capricious hair.

That night in bed, drifting to sleep, he saw her face again. Close up, vivid but deeply shaded, the slant of the brow in a single straight line down the nose, the hair frizzed out full. Her lips were moving slightly, as if murmuring some crazy language all her own. Her eyes were in shadow. He strained to see if they were looking at him, but the pupils were elusive, like some dark creature peering out of the brush at dusk. He'd spent months trying to capture the eyes of his hero, but it wasn't till now that he could see hers. He always felt she was staring at him straight on, but she never was. She was looking past him or more deeply into him or into herself. But the eyes were not her center. The soul was in the mouth: thin lips pinched forward, a tension at the corners, a noncommittal Mona Lisa tilt upward. That mouth could bite you with no ill intention but with relentless intensity.

This woman was the utterly unexpected that he'd half expected, one more plot twist to worry about. It should have been no surprise, given his loneliness, his confusion, and his running battle with his hero. Another roll in the hay was the last thing he needed right now, much less an emotional bond, and very much less the likelihood of being told no. He reached across the bed, drew one of Lainie's pillows to his jumbled pile, and pulled the covers up tight around him.

Yet somehow, stalled in perplexity at a fork in the road, as Jenny the Red's sharp-etched image faded and he breathed himself into the dark, he felt a sharp twinge of joy.

XVI

Of a broken Tooth and blind Sightedness

Me and Sammy tried to go home but went round in a circle.
I was hungry and thirsty. At night the stars were bright. God's
candles, said Sammy. We saw billboards and scary people. I
wanted Mommy and Daddy. Maybe they don't remember me.
I'm different now.

So we came back. Sir Galahad is here. The soldiers are
all dead. I heard him cry in the dark. Knights in Shining Armor
don't cry but his armor wasn't shiny now. I asked Sammy but
he was crying too. Why do grownups cry? It's not so noisy now.

We just sit here I guess. I try to juggle but I drop the balls.
Stuff stinks a lot. Sammy said it's the dead men that ought to get
buried but nobody's left to do it. The undertaker buried Grandpa
with lots of flowers and we prayed. I really want Mommy.

Last night Sir Galahad drank a lot. He yelled at Sammy,
Make me laugh! Sammy said funny stuff and did a dance and
I laughed but Sir Galahad didn't laugh. Sammy did the juggle
where he drops the balls but they bounce back up and he keeps
dropping balls till they disappear but Sir Galahad didn't laugh.
Sammy stood me on a rock and got behind. I hid my hands and
he put his hands under my arms so it looked like his hands were
mine. I just stood there and he made salutes and cutting off
people's heads and then his hands started pinching my nose and
bonking my head like they were mine, only he was just pretending. Then the hands were flapping like wings and I laughed and
then Sir Galahad laughed.

I never saw him laugh before. He laughed a long time like
he wouldn't stop, and then he said that's enough and he stopped.

Sammy told me to go to bed. I think they were up all night. I heard them saying stuff but I didn't hear the words. When you get to be a grownup then maybe you hear the words.

We're getting ready to go but I don't know where. Things don't stink so much now or maybe I don't smell it. Sir Galahad doesn't look at me. I wonder if I'm dead.

§

Galahad's papier mache head was cast from the clay with eight coats of paper shreds carefully laid down. The shell was dried, cut in half, pried free of the clay, and assembled. The sockets were drilled. The eyes had been painted, needing only to be glued, and then Galahad could see. Meantime, the Lady Mara was finished in one fell swoop, and her Fool self was well on the way.

Jeanette had picked up the script on Friday, except for the last four pages, and Monday she came as planned. He met her in the driveway, unsure whether to give her a friendly "Hi" or to offer an embrace. She saved him the decision, saying as she emerged from the battered Corvette, "I can't stay for rehearsal. I broke a piece off a molar. I've got to get it looked at. It's kinda tickly."

"Tickly?"

"Meaning it hurts like hell."

"Sorry. Bite something the wrong way?"

"I was eating a banana."

"That'll do it every time."

He followed her into the studio. The broken tooth side-tracked his weekend fantasies of fingers in russet hair. Despite the dental crisis, Jeanette had brought new costume sketches. She laid them out on the table, and they were all that Albert could wish. The Knight's first garments were pure fairy tale—a mix of High Middle Ages with ancient Britannia—both elegant and primitive, agleam with virtue. The second rendering was of the grim crusader: breastplate, chain mail, and heraldic surcoat with Napoleonic gauntlets, a World War I Sam Browne belt and holstered pistol, and a general's hat over a coif of quilted padding. The third costume contained remnants of the second, with the breastplate gone, the heraldry bloodstained, the chain mail blackish with mold, and a helmet the shape of a stovepipe. To make the changes, Albert would build three bodies. The first head was completed. From that clay model he would age the man progressively into a ravaged shell.

"Beautiful," Albert said as he scanned the drawings. "Perfect." Jeanette's lips curled into a one-sided grin, as if distancing themselves from the broken tooth. He turned to her. "How many ways do you do your hair?" Today she had pulled it flat at the top, with bushy ponytail festoons on both sides of her head. Strange, with her mechanic's gray coveralls.

"This is my little-girl look for the dentist," she said, "and the coveralls are for cleaning the basement." She seemed friendly but not in a mood to be bantered with.

He repeated his admiration for the sketches, trying to delay her departure. "This is better than he deserves." Something in that choice of words darkened her eyes. "I'm joking," he said.

"We have to care about him, Albert, his journey—"

"I agree, I agree, yes yes yes—"

"I mean it!"

They seemed to be caught in repeating cycles, like a long-married couple where each knew the other's lines verbatim. As the words flew back and forth, Albert fixated on her eyes: greenish flecked irises somehow forbidding entry. A peculiar slant to the lids, suggesting a shared conspiracy yet keeping a female's distance. Whatever he said, it seemed to calm the flurry, or maybe it was the tooth that did it.

"Okay, so I don't have my schedule book with me," she said at last. "I'll email to set the next meeting."

"Great."

"Glad you like the stuff. Sorry I can't stay." She gathered her sketches. "Maybe you'd better have an honest talk with your hero. You guys need to come to an understanding." She gave him a quick hug—he was grateful for that—and walked out to her car.

§

And so that evening Albert sat at the end of the dining table, with the shell of Galahad's head beside him, and booted up his laptop. Hold off on the wine until you've written at least a page, he told himself. Staring at the screen, he visualized the Knight hunkered down at the fire. Too easy: the guy hadn't done a thing for weeks except hunker down. Let him at least take off his boots and clean between his toes.

An honest talk with your hero. But a dialogue meant nothing out of context. His hero needed to be up, active, struggling against being swallowed. He might be seized by madness, charge around the camp, command the corpses to fall into ranks.

He might be doing the practice routine with a two-handed long-sword that he'd done daily since adolescence—thrust and feint, parry, riposte, bastard cross, pommel bash. He might—

He saw the Priest's carcass. The little man, left for dead, had crawled back toward the camp before going stiff. The Knight found him broken, bled out. He had no love for the greasy creature, but he couldn't leave the corpse for wild swine to gnaw, so he began to dig the grave, stripped to the waist, sweating in the glare of the fire. He spoke no words, yet they flowed into Albert's ears.

> *What do you ask of me? A key to my ragged heart? I have none, only raw compulsion. First a dirt nap for this carrion, then— All men free . . .*

Galahad went on digging. The Lost Boy in Albert remembered digging. Eight years old, just for fun, he was digging with a spade. He raised it, brought it down, and chopped a gash between two toes. He staggered bleeding to his mother. He still had the scar.

> *My quest enkindled minstrels to sing beautiful lies. Lies: the sinews of kingdoms, the mortar of great cathedrals. One day I rode to a valley deep in fog, drawn by a force as fierce as the suck of death. In my path stood a gaunt old man.*

Short of breath, Galahad stopped digging. He had thrown himself into the task as if into battle, but his lungs were no longer a warrior's. Albert listened, obliged to hear him out.

> *It was Merlin. Not the Merlin of Camelot, but the older Merlin, the haggard scarecrow of crossroads that formed before roads were laid. The Merlin deep in the bone. None taste fear . . .*

Albert imagined a Merlin robed in filthy black, white hair blown in a wind that blew nothing else. Galahad heard only his horse's breath and his heartbeat. He dismounted, followed the mage to a lean-to thatched with reeds and sealed in mud. The elven geezer crouched like a beast by a low peat fire. His eyes were thick with cataracts.

> *You are sterile, the Sorcerer told me. A housewife may scour the stove, make the bed, dust the altar, but the house is not sanctified by cleaning. The stove was made for cooking meals, the bed for love and sleep, the altar for prayer and praise. Those are the sacraments. All wounds heal . . .*

Galahad stopped digging. A ribbon of smoke from the fire wreathed the scene in a delicate veil. He pulled himself out of the pit and approached the patient corpse, took it by the arm, dragged it across the ground, and eased it down to its bedding. A sigh arose from its lungs. Galahad began to fill the excavation. Father Olyver disappeared, another of history's broken teeth.

§

"Have an honest talk with your hero," she'd said. Clearly she was telling him to challenge himself, and there was no love lost between Albert and Albert. Yes, he had spent a lifetime in pursuit of a vision, had enlisted Lainie in his obsession. Yes, he was trapped in a snarl of conundrums. Yes, he could recite the atrocities of his own sex and race and nation and species. Yet as Galahad would keep stoking his sooty fire, Albert would keep on building puppets. He gave up on further questioning.

He drifted out to the spacious deck behind the house. It was months since he'd stood in the back yard at night. The crisp air bit him; he welcomed its bite. A half dozen tall redwoods, several apple trees, a vast cottonwood, its branches rife with mistletoe. The unkempt vegetation had a scruffy charm, inspiring a friend to exclaim, tongue in cheek, "How very Pre-Raphaelite!" He and Lainie would sometimes come out and drink wine in the moonlight. He had thought of scattering her ashes beneath the apple trees but knew that some day he would have to move.

What if— His notions kept bending toward Dadaist perversity. What if the show ended by demolishing itself? Suddenly the puppeteer would tell Galahad that the Fool was Mara in disguise, denounce him, denounce the bovine stupidity of theater, denounce Death, and sit with a gallon jug of Chianti drinking until the befuddled audience left? Just lay it all out there. All the despair.

No. His daughter would fly across the Atlantic just to kick his ass, and Jeanette would be— No. He cursed himself for assigning this woman a role she could never fill. Unfair: she wasn't applying for the job of co-creator.

The Fisher Folk had shared bonds without number: the bed, the work, the travel, the meals, the luminous girl child, and the pain. Especially the pain. In Austin, Lainie broke her ankle, and they had to cancel the last four bookings of the tour. No big deal: a cast and crutches and three days' drive home. But the first time on crutches up a curb, she twisted a sinew in her thigh that made every crutch-hop utter hell. He had never, even in her arduous childbirth, felt so keenly both the impotence and the privilege of care. He would lift her into the tour van, help her as she inched to the motel room, fetch the carry-out food, support her on the toilet, massage the muscles that screamed at the slightest jiggle.

"This is humiliating!" she cried.

"You're mortal, hon," he whispered.

"Since when?"

And for years, so many years, she had been a crutch to his own mortality. That bond was gone. It would not repeat. He had no map for any new trip. Best to think twice before getting behind the wheel.

Lainie?

What?

Talk to me.

He looked up into the trees. Their webwork silhouettes were dark against the moon.

Lainie?

Older by the minute, Albert sat on a stump gazing into a bed of white calla lilies that caught moonlight on their lips. He saw himself stalled at the gate to his own underworld, bargaining with the gatekeeper for a brief tour, meals and tips included, but no extended stay. He hadn't yet written the end of the play. He knew the ending, but something in him resisted. The Knight would have to see it, and Albert still had to glue in his eyes.

The full moon was high in the sky, roaring down. Again he looked up and couldn't stand it. He rose from the stump, chilled to the bone. It was 9:40 p.m., still too early to call his daughter across the time zones. He went indoors, opened the freezer, took out a bottle of vodka, set it on the kitchen table, and then, instead of pouring, perched himself on the stool by the microwave and just stared, like his Knight in Creaky Armor. If you're too stupefied even to pour vodka, he thought, you're truly fucked up.

His father stared at the bottle.

When Albert was two years old, his dad deserted. The guy had worked construction jobs all over the West, with Mom and Baby Bertie following once he'd landed in Denver or Yakima or Wichita Falls and rented a trailer. One day, without a word, he disappeared.

Until little Bertie was twenty-nine, and his dad showed up on the doorstep. The man had boozed his way across four continents, working construction on pipelines, refineries, highways, and bridges. He had migrated from country to country, job to job, bar to bar. He remarried, deserted the second wife when she came down with cancer, and looked up his son.

The would-be Odysseus was guilt-ridden, might have felt better if his son had punched him in the face. But Albert's only feeling was curiosity, and Lainie's presence had smoothed it. The man wasn't an articulate soul. In the two nights of his visit, the son had written down what he felt the father was trying to say, so the words that Albert remembered were his own, though they came from his father's presence. The man's eyes spoke a wordless curse:

> *You can't help fucking your life. Scarring your women, twisting your kids. You search in the bars. You search on the streets of Tulsa at three a.m. You search in the beds of wives and girlfriends and whores, but when you have a woman, after the coming there's a vacancy sign. It's a going, not a coming.*

> *You hear a party's music from the street, but no door to enter. In a trailer in Ecuador you drink till the weeping stops and then empty your seed in the toilet bowl. Searching is no guarantee you'll ever know what you're looking for.*

Now he knew why the man's face had emerged from the clay. Hearing words that his father never spoke, he knew he had inherited that perpetual quest. It had sunk deep—too deep to touch—into his own musculature and into his cloistered heart. But the emptiness that had cursed the father had blessed the son. He had found a partner for his journey. He had walked the teeming streets within himself, interlaced with the myriad stories of Orpheus and Eurydice, gods and monsters, rabbits and ugly ducklings. He had forged a life from his father's twisted genes. He had banged at the steel portal of his dreams and yelled, "Lemme in!"

It may have been half an hour that he sat staring at the Polish vodka that served as his long-dead father's Grail. Then he stirred, picked up the bottle, and set it back in the freezer. He would need it tomorrow, no question, but not tonight. Tonight was the full moon, and for the first time in many moons he felt almost hopeful. Ready, as in the begetting of children, to accept the ordeal without knowing its future. To feel the joy of the rising sap, the bite in the pulp, the swallow. To enter the dance, to swim in the waters that pool in a lover's eyes, rapt in the overflow.

It was near midnight when he shuffled out to the studio, mixed epoxy from two sweaty tubes, and placed the hero's eyes in their sockets. The Lady Mara—with this woman Jeanette Wald's unfocused and penetrating gaze—watched from the end of the table. Galahad blinked awake. He gazed at Albert Fisher with merciless clarity.

XVII

Of a Hawthorn Bush

Next morning, there was an email from Mara. Albert brought it up on the screen, read a paragraph, then went to the kitchen, made himself coffee, spread two slices of toast with marmalade. He returned to the computer, skimmed the news, then clicked on her email and brought it back to the top.

Hi Papa,

Too hot here, couldn't sleep. Tried to envision drowning in warm chocolate, but it didn't work—guess the chocolate kept me awake. So thought I'd write, but remember, I'm never rational till ten a.m.

Thinking of your quest for the Holy Spittoon, whatever. You sounded a bit grim. Grim is fine, I'm a big fan of grim. But do I recall that you started with a comedy, then your puppets began rioting & now you're not sure whether to bring in the dancing elephants or a SWAT team? Something like that?

You know how much I love, honor & nitpick your work. I've seen you bashing your brains for a long long time, starting when I'd sneak out of the womb at night to peek in your notebook. But I'm feeling maternal toward my Pa. You seem a bit disgruntled beyond your usual disgruntlement. Should I send a glob of loving anxiety winging your way?

I did have some questions on the new stuff you sent.

You go back & forth with Galahad. He produces disaster, yet the Lady Fool forges on when they could just pack up & go home. I'm confused. Maybe she is too. I surely recall some of my own misadventures with impossible liaisons—remember Wesley? And Miss Minnehaha? yike! So in a funny way I maybe understand.

But this guy, it's fun to see the knight-in-shining-armor as knight-in-smelly-cheese-rind, given what hero worship has historically brought us. And I get that the Lady Fool sees something in him that's still alive. His litany—all men live free, that stuff—ought to inspire. But does it? Will it? Don't those beautiful words just go in one ear & out the other? Do we take it seriously? Do we have to be fools to believe it?

It's a play, so maybe your presence will give us the belief. I've seen you do that on stage. And you've talked & hugged me through hard stuff. And I you, yes? But you're going to have to believe it to the bone. I worry that Galahad is projecting your own self-image as a failed crusader. But sorry, Papa, self-pity is my hairy demon in a rancid undershirt, not yours. You don't have my permission to play with him.

One thought: I'm not big on battle scenes—I do too many of those, myself against myself, both foes heavily armed—but you might want fewer atrocities & more straight warfare-on-the-rocks. There are long boring passages in the Malory Arthur where one knight's horse is killed, next knight kills another knight to give him a horse, then knight after knight, horse after horse—kind of an implacable 4/4 Sousa rhythm. A lunatic banging his head on the wall is more terrifying than the rapes & tortures. Know what I mean?

Just out of curiosity & Alejandro asked too: why name the wife after me? I know how many times you've used the family's leftovers in your plays, so if it works for you that's fine. Maybe I should take up juggling, just in case.

By the way, Alejandro just got some welding work & I finally got paid for that article on squids, so we're rolling in small change. And the house, or the beloved hovel, looks like it might happen.

But know that I really love you for taking this crazy

*leap. These crack-brained quests are worth it. Lots
of people care. Do it.*
Love you,
Mara

Albert remembered the cats, went into the living room, slid
open the patio door to fill their bowl. "No, don't give me that
Where's-the-mackerel? look. Cats can't stand mackerel, didn't
I tell you?" He shut the door, returned to his computer, deleted
the spam, scanned the news, then hit REPLY.

Dear weird sweet loving child—

*Thanks for your note. I was going to answer it later,
give it the attention it deserves, but I'm clean out
of procrastinations. So let me give it a try without
thinking much, which is usually smarter.*

*Well, I really hate those questions because they're the
ones I'm trying to dodge. Answers are dribbling in,
but not at high tide. About Galahad: my costumer
Jeanette advised me to have a long talk with the guy,
and he tipped me off. Yes, he is me, or a caricature
of me. Is that just another form of self-pity? I guess.
But I'll get past it, or try to. Don't fear for my basic
sanity. Growing up in Iowa, we're equipped with a
gyroscope to keep us stable no matter how loopy the
carnival ride. You won't get any startling news.*

*I do like your battle idea, though I fear this show is
already about six hours long—cut down from ten.
My costumer Jeanette says make it ninety minutes
at most. Could I narrate a battle while the Marines'
Hymn plays and I juggle two knights and a horse?*

*So why does the Lady Fool forge on? Why did she start
in the first place? Not some fond memory of a hot
young stud, I don't think. Attraction would wear
thin as his armor grew potbellied. For that matter,
what induced your mama to hop aboard the leaky
boat with me, take up one of the oars, and urge us
on ferociously when I floundered? I doubt it was my
heroic jaw or my suave demeanor. "Impossibility is
no excuse." That was her line, not mine.*

*All I can think is that she dug the wild ride, some nutty
faith that playing a half-dozen Ugly Ducklings a
week—week in, week out—might be a life worth
living. But don't quote me on that. Probably we*

*glommed onto each other for all the wrong reasons.
Needy creatures, half-formed, we founded our private fan club, our two-bit Ponzi scheme, our mutual
deception. We made it work. And then she finked out
by dying.*

*Oh hell, sorry. That's a line that Lainie would say was
way over the top. I told you I'd write without thinking. But you're right: I have to bring a faith to it, a
belief. That's the hard part right now. Pick a Grail,
any Grail, and make it real.*

*Hey, remember Whit? I got an email. He and Katie had
twins.*

—Love from thy Papa

He hit SEND and wished he hadn't. The humor was forced, and the crack about Lainie's death was too raw. Reading back through the message, he cringed at every word. He and Mara tried to be honest with one another, but the family didn't walk around the house naked. Nevertheless, he'd sent it.

Twice he had mentioned Jeanette: *the costumer Jeanette.* Mara would sense his self-consciousness, a ploy to distance himself from this woman. Certainly his libido, which he thought had been pickled in brine, felt a stirring. He was frankly attracted to this acerbic, foxy screwball, but he found himself thinking about her dramaturgically, as if working on a play: what to do with the sexy costumer?

More email: a note from Jeanette with the subject line QUESTIONS. He opened it, hoping there might be something attuned to his train of thought: How are you feeling about our impulsive roll in the hay? Wondering what we're expecting of one another? Does Sir Galahad feel intimidated by redheads? When's your birthday?

But there wasn't. Just technical questions, which he answered rapidly:

*Yes, the Fool puppet uses both hands, but Galahad is
only right-handed.*

*No, we changed the Priest from a rod to a hand puppet,
but the perky little flounce on his cassock works fine.*

*No, we don't see the real Fool again, only the Lady in
disguise.*

The rest of the bodies will be ready on Thursday.

*Let's go with the red and yellow stripes for the Fool's
jerkin, but gray them down a bit.*

And at the end of his reply, after two or three false starts, he asked if they might find some time to talk, over a glass of wine. Just one glass this time.

§

Galahad finished burying the little Priest. A shallow grave, but by the time the beasts had devoured the unburied cadavers, they might be too sated to dig up one more. He sat by the nickering fire, soaked in wine to blur the keen edge of the moon. The hero had watched his crusaders—soldier and whore alike—die off, but he still mumbled his litany. *"Love is the law . . . All live in peace . . . No more want . . ."* He knew its naked absurdity.

But the Puppetmaster couldn't leave his hero flopped on a log, lumpish until the Apocalypse. He had to rise and slog on to the end of the show. The Knght's goblet was empty. He rose, swaying, to his feet. Tomorrow the drinking had to stop, so he needed to finish the flagon tonight.

He looked around to see the Fool hunched over, asleep at the end of the log. Distant, through the smoke, he saw the Lost Boy staring— a rootless, motherless child whose terrified, empty eyes, like a firestorm, sucked air from every hiding place. In that child's eyes Galahad saw the pitiful image of himself. Rage rose in his gorge like fiery bile. He gave out the howl of hounds at the flanks of the fleeing hart, raised his fists to launch an attack on the shadows: full slaughter, no mercy, all faces expunged.

His cry startled the Fool awake. Galahad staggered, flailing, away from the fire into the corpse-strewn night. The Fool scrambled after him, flung arms around him, and squeezed him to still his frenzy. The befuddled Knight threw off the puny arms, turned, struck the Fool full in the face. The Fool crumpled. Galahad reached up to mount a phantom steed, stumbled over a stump, and fell headlong into a hawthorn bush.

Fitting. It was hawthorn that sprang from the staff of Joseph of Arimathea, the bearer of the Grail to England, as he thrust the rod into the Glastonbury earth. It blossomed, brought forth a rivulet whose waters granted eternal youth. It was there that King Arthur was buried, below the tor at the gate to the Underworld. And there the drunken Galahad floundered, tangled in thorns, until the Fool, with a darkening bruise on the side of her face, lurched into the brambles and pulled him free.

The addled Knight lay on the frigid earth, sobbing, muttering orders, curses, a prayer. The Fool brought bedding, laid it out, and rolled him into it. He peered up into the marred face of the counterfeit jester. "Sorry, drunk . . ." Words the Puppetmaster's dad had said to the Puppetmaster's mom before waltzing into the dark.

The Lady Fool had seen the next moment many times. She would place her hand on his sweat-drenched brow, over the scar from a bygone joust, and press till a spark caught the tinder and memory flared. His eyes would widen in bafflement. She would pull away her wispy chin beard, and as his eyes cleared she would loosen her fool's cap, unbind her hair, let it fall.

My lord, my beloved.

What—

I am with you. I have been, always.

Mara!

He would know the depth of her love. His soul would awaken like a seed in spring. They both would know the Quest was done. As Christ endured three days in Hell, they had endured a Hell of countless days, let Hell sear their souls, created Hell. Now, the Resurrection. They would find one mule alive. They would harness it, load provisions, and start the journey home. Here, by the fabled hawthorn bush that would be blown away by war, then sprout again; be broken by vandals, then sprout; be paved over, yet still send up shoots from its ancient core. Here by the hawthorn, they would reach out and touch what the Father of Storm and the Mother of All had given them.

But it did not go as she imagined it.

§

I reach to touch his forehead. My red-and-yellow striped jerkin, gray with filth, cuts into my breast. I try to pull it looser. I cannot move my hand. My hands are not my own. We might return home, but the Questing Beast rumbles afar and I hear a baying, a bark, a spastic bleat. I shrink in a withering wind. My way is not homeward.

Once my Knight had the Grail in his grasp. Now his fingers are drained of will. His words are ashes, charred. Men, women, young, old—a song of promise. If I cannot grasp these words, embrace them, sing them, who will? To seek the Grail, I should be warrior, prophet, saint. I should be man, not woman; wizard, not fool. The words that lie in the ashes are his seed, now mine to nurture. But am I fit to nurse them? My breasts are dry. I am only jokes and juggles. I am Sammy Shit-pants.

And yet now the Quest is mine: a Grail not as a prize to be seized but the Grail of a woman's fruition.

§

"Get some sleep, guys," sounded the low voice of the Puppetmaster. "You've got a long trip tomorrow." Galahad rolled over on the blanket, then jerked up to dig his fingers under one of the greaves that he'd worn for weeks. The Fool loosened a clotted knot and flushed out a tiny brown spider that scuttled away in search of its hawthorn bush.

The chill of death hovered over the blackened camp, and the wind came up. The Fool pulled an edge of the blanket over her shoulder. *All live in peace.* She brought her fingers to her throbbing cheek, the pain partly dulled by the chill. *No more want.* Her mind considered what they should pack, what they should leave behind, what direction they might go, where she might see a new path to the Grail. *Men, women, rich, poor . . .* Pierced by the night, the bruised freak lay beside Galahad and pressed close to his body's hillocks for warmth, in the manner of spoons.

XVIII

Skirmishes on the Quest

Albert groped for a metaphor to start his characters onward. *Their land, a broken toy.* That worked, kinda. You tore off the Christmas wrapping and wham, you had this gaudy box with the fierce photo of the laser dazzle-blaster that you needed to achieve manhood and stand against the forces of Doom. And then you opened it: this plasticky gizmo whose ninja sniper-scope snapped off five minutes after you brandished it. Ditch the gizmo, keep the box.

§

Knight and Fool trudged down the road. Galahad had slept a few hours, risen abruptly. His eyes were glazed and his balance shaky, but he moved with the implacable resolution of the action hero he was born to be. As the sun rose, he kept a steady footfall. The Fool looked back to see the Lost Boy following.

Galahad's armor-plated torso clanked and chugged like a tank, but his will was numb. The Quest no longer had a goal, only an inertial force. It was the Fool—she of lost hope—who drove them on. Her eye was bloodshot and her cheek black and blue, but she was pregnant now with his clouded vision. *Holy Mary, let me see!*

"Where now?" murmured the Knight.

"Holy Grail, nuncle," said the Fool. "All men free, live in peace, that stuff."

"*All men free . . .*"

"Free like birds. Or butterflies, if the birds don't eat the butterflies."

"*None suffer want . . .*"

"Even howling kids that don't know what they want, but when they get it they do."

"*Peace . . .*"

"Peace, so you can't kill people even if they snore, but it's okay to pinch their noses."

"*Love is the law . . .*"

"Love is the cherry on top." The Fool began a sing-song chant, "Cherry on top, cherry on top," as they staggered on.

Not homeward: onward. Some time between dawn and the blaze of noon, the Questing Beast had shaken off its torpor and emitted its wild-goose honk over the baying of hounds in its belly, and the Fool led Galahad on the path that slanted toward it.

The sun beat down. They walked alongside a high stone wall that enclosed a great estate. At times Galahad stopped, put his fists to the stone, and shoved as if to topple it. It paid him no heed. Sammy, trying to stir a chuckle, scurried forward and pounded a tiny fist against the bulwark—"Bad wall! Bad wall!"—but Galahad never smiled. The Fool looked back to see if the Lost Boy still followed. The small figure dragged a stick in the dust and raised it to whack a weed.

It was mid-afternoon when they came to the gate: ornamental ironwork in foliage patterns laced through heavy bars, shut tight against the world. Through it they could see a tree-lined lane that led to a great columned manse from some grander millennium. The Fool rattled the gate, then called out a shrill "Halloo!" No answer. More calls, then her full repertoire of hoots, barks, a rooster's crow, a peacock's cry. At last, the Gatekeeper emerged from the kiosk. Brown uniform, bull neck, surly belly—a balding megalith. He stared at the tattered duo.

"I am Galahad," murmured the Knight.

"I'm Fred," said the Gatekeeper, and stood there.

The Fool came forward, bowing with a flourish, parroting the old lines. "Honored Sir Fred, my master seeks the Holy Grail—"

"*All men free*," mumbled the Knight.

"We have need of lodging, water to fill us, and a simple meal, if it please you."

The Gatekeeper stood expressionless. "We don't give to beggars."

"My master is no beggar."

"So why's he begging?"

"He pursues a sacred Quest."

"Who doesn't?" The Gatekeeper gave a mirthless chuckle. "My ass, my gut, my paycheck, sacred as hell, to me."

"Let us speak to your lord."

The Gatekeeper sighed. Talking was not his specialty. "Look here, Squeaky, the folks that go through that gate are the ones they want to talk to. You heard of the chosen people? So God chose His chosen people, and we choose ours."

"*Love is the law*," whispered Galahad through the narrow slit of his visor.

"Great. So I love you guys, you're sweethearts, just get the fuck outta here." The megalith was breathing in short, sharp snorts.

The Knight lowered his visor, raised his sword, and dealt the bars of the gate a mighty blow, as if to cleave a dragon skull. The blade shattered like chicken bone, and his momentum drove him to his knees, his stovepipe helmet wedged between the bars. The Gatekeeper took a small canister from his utility belt, raised the Knight's visor, filled the helmet with pepper spray, and slammed the visor shut. The Knight screamed. He wrenched off the helmet and writhed on the pavement, clawing his face. The Fool embraced him.

The Gatekeeper lumbered back toward his kiosk to watch the game. He didn't much like hockey, but it was better than the History Channel, which gave him nightmares. A distant Puppetmaster spoke, and Fred heard a voice in his head: *You're not a mindless lout, you're just doing your job.* "I'm just doing my job," he grumbled plaintively.

Heavy breath from the Knight, whimpering from the Fool.

Fred floundered, trying to form a plea, a cry, a malediction, anything to still the blaring hush. "Shut up!" he shouted. "You—" He had run out of his week's allotment of words. He knew he'd reduced himself to caricature. There are animals out there, he wanted to cry, and if I wasn't standing here they'd be swarming like flies on roadkill. There's too many people. People that have no call to exist except they want to. Cancers on the face of the planet. Blotches. Warts.

The Gatekeeper didn't think of himself as a violent man, but he struggled daily to resist drawing his 9mm and simplifying the world. He wouldn't just do it to Blacks: he knew that racism was wrong. He'd do it equal opportunity. He'd do it to these derelicts. He'd do it to his wife. He'd do it to himself. He'd make it so clean.

He lumbered into his kiosk, back to hating his hockey game, but kept watch on the smelly pair. After a while, the whiny little fag got up and helped the tin bum to a wobbly stance. They lifted their backpacks and started down the road.

"Hey! Good luck!" Fred shouted. He didn't know why he said that. He turned up the volume and leaned back in his chair for six years, watching hundreds of games, then died of stomach cancer. His granddaughter cried till all of her tears were gone.

The two crusaders hiked until at dusk the Knight began to stagger. The Fool helped him to a clearing among bushes and would have laid out bedding, but Galahad collapsed, immovable, so they curled up on bare earth. The Lost Boy was somewhere about. The Fool slept with open eyes. I've done that often, thought Albert.

Next day the journey continued. The Knight awoke, murmuring, "*All men . . .*" through cracked lips, but he blanked on the words.

"*Free*, nuncle."

The Fool helped him stand. He croaked, "*All wounds . . .*" and groped for the rest of it.

"*Heal.*"

They set out walking at the edge of the roadway: four lanes now, demonic behemoths hurtling past like meteors, whipping them with wind. The Fool longed to reveal herself, to embrace her Knight, to claim the Lost Boy plodding far back. She longed to feel her breasts free of the jerkin, yet she was locked into the mindless forward lurch. She knew only to follow the road.

Fog rose up, blending earth and sky, dissolving the hills. A great lake appeared, and the setting sun turned it to blood. Cries of water birds tore at a heart still female in its ventricles. Then a burnt landscape, yucca and sage, a plague of sand. Once a land of fairies, she thought, and we spread it with death. This vast ribbon of stone is the path of pestilence. We are contagion. But her Fool mind phrased it more simply: we made a big mess.

She bore the supplies and was crutch to the flagging Galahad. The Lost Boy was with them, she knew—she could feel his gaze—but nowhere to be seen. Perhaps he was watching through the magical window he had spoken of, worlds fitted into its frame, summoned and dismissed by the touch of a finger. In his land, they all had magical windows that showed whatever they yearned for but never could touch. He's watching our story, she imagined, and wondering if it's true.

At twilight, the roadway crested a hill, and they saw a vast plain of lights like frozen fireflies, stretching into the void. "Maybe the Grail is making all that light," whispered the Fool. Galahad mustered a burst of strength to break into a run, but the Fool held him back with soft words: they must rest here and come by day to the city, where cheering throngs would hail the Sacred Knight. They made their way down a narrow ravine to a grove of oak. The Fool laid out bedding, and Galahad fell upon it with the weight of a thousand days.

He paid no mind to the Fool curling up against his spine. For herself, she was beyond desire. It was animal warmth, the breath, the heartbeat, the way cats huddled against the winter's chill. As she drifted off she could hear him babbling under his breath. The words formed and dissolved, trickling out like urine down an old man's leg: "*All men free . . . none fear . . . young, old . . . shelter . . . peace . . . love.*" He still believed.

Next day, on the outskirts of the city, the odd pair trudged long blocks past drive-ins, dealerships, motor homes, and vacant shopping malls. At last they came into the city's bowels, dodging fierce traffic and clusters of people blindly walking past them, into them, through them as if they were dream stuff only. The Fool saw dark figures in doorways with blankets and bundles. This must be the pilgrims' lodging, she thought, and stopped to ask a grizzled old man, sprawled on a piece of cardboard, where might be the monk in charge.

"FUCK THE SHITFUCKING JESUS CHRIST IN THE FUCKING ASSHOLE!" he exploded. "WHO THE PRESIDENT IS, FUCK THE SHITSUCKING PRESIDENT AND HIS ASSHOLE FUCKING DOG!"

The derelict rose to his feet, spewing venomous spittle. He floundered into a lane of traffic, dodged an oncoming bus, then reeled back and slammed against a parking meter. The meter's red flag flipped up.

Fool led Knight through the multitude. She saw street entertainers—a silver-faced bird-creature, a girl singing in a pimply voice, an elderly man bowing a one-stringed instrument. Each had a hat or a dish into which passers-by threw coins. If she juggled they might get food.

She found a street corner bereft of entertainment. A wave of people would cross from one direction, then lights blinked red and green, and a wave would cross from the other. The Knight, still clutching the hilt of his broken sword, sat hunched on a fireplug, though he had no name for that knobby cylinder of iron that rose from the gray stone earth. The Fool set their single soup bowl in front of him. To his befogged memory came a blaze of sun and a peasant's curse—

Let you go begging on bended knee!

She who had been Lady Mara was now pure Sammy Shit-pants, no trace of herself remaining. She began to prance around the fireplug making shrill rooster sounds and flapping wings, announcing, "The Knight in Shining Armor!" A couple of brown kids paused, grinning at the craziness, and a teenager bonked his knuckles on the hero's helmet. Others lingered, uncertain whether the Knight was real or a dummy. "Make him be happy!" squealed the Fool, pulling out three balls and starting to juggle.

The sparse crowd began to disperse. The weird costumes had hooked them, but the juggling was not that special. The Fool juggled for an hour or so, accumulating a few coins in the bowl from passers-by who felt the beggars deserved some reward for pretending not to be beggars. She took the coins to a street vendor and returned with a can called Diet Coke and something on a bun that she guessed might be food. She opened the can, took a sip, and raised it to Galahad's lips.

That night, they slept in the doorway of a sporting-goods store and were undisturbed till morning, when a watchman rousted them. They returned to the corner, set out the bowl, and waited until the streets began to teem. One ball was missing. The Fool searched frantically in their bundle. Then, just as the lights blinked and a horde came surging toward them, Sammy squealed, "A juggle by Sammy Shit-pants for the Knight in Shining Armor!" and began to juggle two balls and the empty soda can.

A hit. Sammy's instincts jerked awake with the challenge of the unfamiliar—the weight, the grasp, the trajectory of tumble. Someone picked a tennis shoe out of a waste bin, and that took the place of a second ball. A shopper tossed in an organic grapefruit. A new game was born on the corner of Market and Stockton: *Stump Sammy Shit-pants.*

In the hours that followed, the Fool juggled a basketball, a hammer, and an iPod; a keychain, a porkpie hat, and a dummy hand grenade; a purse, a high-heeled shoe, and a bra; a hair brush, an Egg McMuffin, and a baggie of dogshit. Money poured into the bowl. By the end of the day, they could treat themselves to falafels, two cans labeled Pepsi, and a roach-ridden room in a transient hotel, where they filled their canteens from the rusty faucet.

Coming out of the bathroom, she saw Galahad sitting on the bed, still in his helmet and chain mail, staring into the sack of artifacts she had kept from the day of juggling. He reached into it, as if into a sacred place, and drew out a gold-plated trophy with a tiny bowler in the act of flinging his missile pinward.

"Is it . . . the Grail?"

He must have known it wasn't. He gazed at the water-stained walls, the window open to a black air shaft, a dresser with two drawers missing, the glaring bare ceiling bulb. No miracles. No music in the air, just the pounding crunch of bedsprings from the adjoining room. None were free of want or fear, no wounds were healed, honor was a joke, and love was only the relentless thump of meat on meat. But at least for a night there was shelter.

On the morrow, the Fool held hope for the show-biz success that promised survival. But at the corner they were confronted by a blue-clad man with a badge, who told them they needed a license. His voice was kind but firm as he pointed their way toward the midmorning sun. Sammy took up the pack again, and they turned eastward.

As they came to the city's outskirts, the Fool kept glancing back but saw no sign of the child. Had she only imagined one? If she had thought to look toward the right-hand side of the Fisher Folks studio, she might have seen the Lost Boy flopped at the end of the playboard watching TV, purged from the show by an elderly puppeteer, never to reappear. She was childless again.

§

Albert pared the scene to the bone. He liked the Fool juggling improbables and impossibles, tennis shoes and dogshit, and the Lost Boy going up in smoke, but most of the city thing was social comment, depressive comedy, muskrat rambling. It could only be redeemed by the Knight rising up, shouting "*All men free!*" and falling on his face: big laugh, end of show. But he knew he was padding out the play to delay its ending, avoid making it real, risking—what?

He picked up his notepad, his empty coffee cup, the scattered pages of script, and took his existential confusion into the house for more coffee. For the first time since the start of this journey he felt a measure of confidence: if he had just now managed to excise ten minutes of brilliant self-indulgence, he might turn up a winner. He put on the water to heat and checked his email. A note from his daughter:

> *Hurray, hurray, our offer on the house is accepted & the*
> *bank says it's a go. We sign away our lives a week*
> *from Friday! Am I a grown-up or what!*

He had mentioned to her a few days ago that there might
be a connection evolving with his costume designer, though he
wasn't sure he believed it himself. After he'd written the email
and brooded over having sent it, he realized that he was doing
the same thing he'd always done with production ideas: start
talking it up, tell people you're working on it, set that proverbial
bear trap so you can step right into it as you're about to shit in
the woods.

Mara encouraged him, depending, she said, on what he
was looking for. She agreed that his doubts were real, that he
was surely taking a risk, and that he'd never recover fully from
his deeper loss.

> *But for that matter, Papa, it wasn't just your loss: it was*
> *mine & it was Mama's. She probably has a ton of*
> *notes to give you about the show, but it's hard to get*
> *a good connection with Skype.*
>
> *Anyway, I don't know if you're asking permission to go*
> *out on a date, but if you can't drink from the Holy*
> *Grail, then maybe you should settle for the holy cof-*
> *fee mug. Depends entirely on the coffee.*

XIX

Conundrums

"So how's it going?"

Widowerhood evolved in your friends' vocabulary. The first month after the death, you would hear "Omigod, Albert, I'm so sorry! If you need anything, just call." A month later it was "How are you doing, man?" Now it had evolved to "So how's it going?" Which meant that after nearly fifteen months you still bore the stink of death, but it wasn't for friends to mention.

He had read those sardonic articles cataloguing the babbles endured by the bereaved, and now he could add his own. He stifled the impulse to respond, "I'm bloody awful, you asshole, I want to die!" or "Fine, except for the hassle of my wife being dead," or "Fantastic! I'm free!" He knew, though, that he'd be just as baffled in finding words. A simple response of "Pretty well" usually did the trick. Grief forced you to have great compassion for your comforters' dilemma.

In those months, Albert had gone out socially only a few times—gambits of the groundhog to emerge from its hole, blind to the shadows—though sometimes he'd driven to San Francisco to walk among strangers. But today he'd accepted an invitation. Old friends had made a special plea for him to come to their housewarming party, and with six weeks before the opening of *Galahad's Fool*—September 7th, if the Governor didn't commute his sentence—he would grab any excuse to procrastinate. So here he was, having dutifully admired the balcony and the patio, hovering near the food table. Someone had brought deviled eggs to the potluck. He loved deviled eggs. He took one, intending after a decent interval to take another.

"So how's it going?" Some guy he knew from somewhere, Albert recalled, who sold solar panels or owned a winery or something.

"Pretty well. Working on a show. Mostly focused on that."

"Great. Send me information."

"Will do." He always did, but the guy never came.

"You're looking good."

"Well, that's the advantage of puppets," Albert said. "This is not me. This is a puppet version of me. Still need to touch up the bags under the eyes."

The guy laughed, raised his glass, and wandered off. It never failed. Tomas and Kym always assembled a menagerie of fascinating people: open, intelligent, bright-eyed. Why, Albert puzzled, did he never have a satisfying conversation with any of them? Invariably he'd be asked if he were doing a new show, and he'd say yes, and they'd say, "Sorry I missed your last one." Then a bit more small talk, and they'd find an excuse to move on. It was too much like the collegial butt-sniffing at professional conferences. It served a purpose—something to do while drinking—but it didn't scratch the itch.

What itch? It was too embarrassing even to think it: he wanted a gateway. An invitation to bare souls, to love, to peel away each other's rhino hides. He knew what turbulent life lurked in the blandest human being, the way a surgeon knew of the Gordian tangle of guts in the trimmest tummy. But surgeons knew better than to palpate the abdomens of party guests, and Albert always hesitated to ask a question that might open the veins. He wanted to be as close to human beings as he was to his characters. He wanted allies against the fishhook of death. He wanted to hop aboard the rattletrap truck bouncing along the ruts of other hearts, but he could scarcely even manage the butt-sniff.

Kym approached. A tall, sturdy blonde, she'd been through an appalling divorce three years ago but seemed to be happy with her newfound guy. She was one of those crazies Albert was grateful to know, however much he avoided them.

"You look like shit, man."

The best thing he'd heard in a month: the simple truth. "Don't mince words," he replied.

She hugged him. "Hey, I don't mean physically. You look great physically, sorta like a really healthy zombie."

"Mind if I use that line?"

"Be my guest. Are you still really that slammed?"

"Naw, just pretending," he said. "I want to be well rehearsed for when I'm totally fucked up." They smiled, hugged again, and for the first time in a very long while Albert felt true affection. Yes, there were people around who cared. "These guys who invite zombies to their housewarming," he growled.

She laughed, went back to the kitchen, and he ate another deviled egg. After a while, he looked up Kym's guy Tomas, a gangly Ukrainian-Mexican, thanked him, said, "I hereby declare your house *warm*!" and left.

Coming into his studio, he felt the bitter backwash. He had snarfed a dinner's worth of food and drunk two or three glasses of wine, but he'd never felt so empty. Isolation was his own court fool, and that fool was an insult comic, a doleful jester who'd been with him since high school. His daughter knew that when he was at his funniest, it was a sure sign he was grasping like mad for a fingerhold on the human race. He had found one of his tribe, married her, made a life, but now she was footloose in the clouds and he was a loner again. Ironic that his work had brought him into the intimate presence of thousands, hundreds of thousands, but no one was with him tonight except a couple of puppets on their PVC stands, dumb as turnips.

Albert picked up the third of the Galahad heads, the Knight at the end of the Quest: sunken cheeks, hollow eyes, stringy blond hair with gray at the temples. He had spread glue over cheeks and chin, sprinkled coarse coffee grounds over that, and brushed lightly with black and gray, achieving a perfect stubble.

He had made a third head for the wife as well. The first was the face Lady Mara expected to keep all her life. The second was her Fool self, altered slightly from Sammy's head: less twisted, with deeper eyes, hair tucked firmly under the cap. Albert picked up the last. Lips open as if, on the journey's last stage, she needed to breathe through her mouth. Stark staring eyes that had caught a glimpse of her fate.

The two puppets in hand, he stepped into the rehearsal space under the fluorescent light. It was folly to try to rehearse when sodden with food and wine, but the evening stretched ahead of him like a thirty-year mortgage. Like the last half-hour before the school bell rang. Like the week you waited to get the diagnosis. He stood a moment, then sat on a stool, took a breath, and began mumbling in subvocal gibberish, moving the puppet heads as if coaxing them to life.

Each puppet normally required two-hand control—one hand into the head, the second through the costume emerging as the creature's live hand—which for a single puppeteer with two puppets meant a radical shortage of hands. And so for most of the play, except when he put one down and slipped both of his hands in the other for a solo harangue, he used them as dolls. Mutter and waggle, mutter and waggle. He bounced the Fool about as if loading a backpack with food and the day's swallow of water. Galahad seemed to fumble with his armor, fasten the gorget at his neck, call the Fool to help him with the breastplate, give it up, kick away the plate armor and slip on his chain-mail T-shirt, buckle his empty scabbard, sheathe the hilt of his broken sword, and lug his helmet into place—all handless, hopping about like a crazed popcorn kernel. It was a crude storytelling, and the audience wouldn't pick up on specifics, but with luck they'd find it amusing.

He felt like a fool, aimlessly waggling a couple of heads in the chill studio, a humiliation of which the subject was the sole observer. Since childhood he had felt a pressure—in his lips, between his eyes, somewhere indefinable—to say what was urgent to say, but he could never feel that the words quite made it. His writing was a stab at pinning the tail on the donkey, a game he'd never won though he kept on stabbing. And what was he longing to say? Six weeks till opening night, and then he'd have to say it.

Albert played out his improvisation—the duo leaving the city—restoring some lines that he'd cut. The phone rang in the studio. That's what the show needed: every once in a while the phone could ring. He'd interrupt the narrative to answer it and say no to the damn solicitor, then carry on the Quest.

He picked it up. "Thanks, we don't want any."

A pause. "Well, if you don't want any, you can't have it." Jeanette's voice. She hadn't called this late before.

"Oh. Hi there. I just finished rehearsal, or something resembling rehearsal, and I was still back in the Dark Ages. Before the advent of consumer confidence."

"Sorry to call so late," she said. "I finished all the hand puppet garb, I think, and just wanted to check in."

"No, that's fine. I was just about to go get drunk and talk myself to sleep."

"Albert, I wanted to say . . ." She paused. For once she sounded on shaky footing. Careful articulation: "I kind of blew off replying to your note. About getting together to talk? But you more or less just stuck it in there at the end of the email."

"You sound a bit strange right now."

"Do I? I guess I try to disguise the fact that that's the real me: strange." She was treading water. "No, but seriously, you asking to talk, I was really touched by that. Or no, I should say moved. Or actually, Albert, really kinda pissed off."

"Is this multiple choice?" He had never heard her at a loss for words. To fill the silence he said, "It might help if I knew what your hair looks like right now. I've come to depend on that for a clue." Better to keep things light.

"I just washed it. I think I'll dry it in the oven."

"Great line. Can I use it?"

"Let me reboot here, Albert. I'm trying to say—"

"My email, you were saying."

"Your email. Okay. What am I trying to say? Don't tell me, let me guess. You know, it's been about three years since I've been in any sort of card-carrying relationship. Not that having a drink and talking necessarily implies that, but I mean we're not kids. I mean, what's happening with us here? That's what you're really asking, isn't it? Let's be honest, okay?"

"Okay."

"Problem is, Albert, look, you're still married. You remember what you said the night we made fools of ourselves? Which was, yes, actually it was fun, it was, okay. You remember? But look, you said it yourself: you've still got her clothes, a whole closet full of her clothes. And I realized what I felt: I'm jealous of someone who doesn't exist."

"Jealous? Well, that's a start." Albert's eyes went up to the flutter of a moth barking itself against the fluorescent ceiling lamp. "I'm watching a moth right now," he said. "It's very confused."

They talked a while longer, a dialogue that reminded him of one of those plays with the characters spouting words that demonstrate the futility of words, never getting to the point. Finally, they came back to the swamp of silence.

"You need some rehearsal help this week? I've got some time, I guess."

He gave her his next week's work schedule, making it up on the spot while scribbling on his pad so he'd remember it.

"So, well, dry your hair, I guess, if we haven't already dried it."

"No, it's still drooling down my neck," she replied. Albert heard a timbre in her voice that sounded oddly like himself. Was she truly a kindred soul or only adept at echoing his mordant rhythms? Then she surprised him. "I can't believe I actually made this phone call." A sharp breath, and then she hung up.

§

Enough with the adolescent angst. Albert had gotten Galahad off his ass, to dubious effect but still in forward motion, and it was time to stop dithering with this woman who'd turned up in his life. He was taking it too seriously, he told himself, trying to justify the redeeming social importance of gerontological lust while clinging to his lifemate's ashes. Why could he not just ask, in a simple and friendly way, if she was up for some fun? He had learned, at about age twenty-three, that women liked it too.

They met in the neutral zone of the coffee shop. They began with the weather and wandered off into speculations on whether the Lady Fool should have any suggestion of breasts. The decision was negative, but it took a while to get there, with detours through Jeanette's anecdotes about the challenges posed to costumers by the female bosom. One director had wanted a topless Titania. The actress was reluctant, so Jeanette was charged with creating fake neoprene breasts for her to wear over the real ones. After several recastings—the actress wailing that they looked like grapefruits—Titania's pride bested her modesty, and she opted for baring her own. Theatrical war stories: the strategy of survival. Nothing was said about the making of love.

He called late the next morning. The impulse had come the night before, but nighttime proposals seemed too desperate somehow. Better to say it in bright sunlight, straight out, unconcerned with setting a mood. He'd never been a *How 'bout it, babe?* type of guy, but he might plead senility.

"Yes?"

"Jeanette, hi. Listen, do you have about ninety seconds to spare, or more if desired?"

"This isn't about the show?"

Of course she could hear it in his forced cuteness. "Okay, I'm guilty until proven innocent," he said. "I'm just thinking—"

"Well, okay, I'll admit that I've been evasive if you'll admit to pussy-footing. You'd like to get together. Sort of a fuck-buddy thing?"

It took him a moment to find his balance. "Well, that's putting it right out there. Thanks for the prompting, although I didn't call for lines."

"I didn't intend that as insulting."

"I didn't take it that way."

"Good." Who had the next line? "Well, I have more than ninety seconds, Albert, if so desired."

"So could we maybe get together? Tonight? Tomorrow night? Sometime?" Okay, he'd said it. No chance for rewrites. The stage direction now said *Long silence.* What a relief if the answer was no.

"That's fine. Your place? Eight o'clock tonight? Curtain time?"

Simple as that.

§

One glass of wine each. A stillness. Tonight Jeanette's hair was held back tight in a clasp. She wore a loose ochre pullover, velvety, and a long paisley peasant skirt. The effect was something between hippie chick and meter maid. He sat on the sofa, she in the armchair, both sipping with tentative precision. He cleared his throat.

"We're making it last."

She nodded.

"I'm glad you're here right now. Otherwise I'd be drinking both glasses." He made a slight whiff of a laugh.

"I do strange things," she said to her wine glass, as if to a sister. "Rarely any regrets, but lots of puzzlements." A sigh that ended in a quiet laugh. "I tend to get involved with other people's obsessions. People with obsessions. It's not always a wise idea."

He was about to say something funny, but refrained. The silence held. They looked across the distance between them, four or five short steps, and their eyes met. Albert knew the way Lainie would lock eyes with one of the cats, sharing a simple presence, doing it so easily. Jeanette sipped again, and his gaze went back to the rug.

"I was thinking the way two cats can just look at each other," he said, "without embarrassment."

"Who knows, though? Maybe they struggle with it."

"Well, so." He had no idea what to do from there. He sat like a puppet awaiting a hand to give it life. She smiled in reply to what he never said. "Nice skirt," he managed to mumble.

She set her wine glass on a side table. "Well, somebody better move." She rose and came to him, standing close as he leaned his head to her midriff.

"Thank you," he said.

"You're quite welcome."

He rose beside her, took her hand, pressed it to his chest. Neither risked looking at the other. One stutter of a laugh came from him, she echoed it, and then they were silent. They walked to the guest room hand in hand, as if afraid to awaken their parents. Before, they had frolicked in the master bedroom, but that seemed too fraught a journey now.

They stood at the bedside. "You know," he said, "I've still got a few years, I think, of prowess in me, whatever you call it, but I can't offer any guarantees, except just—"

"We're here for what happens, okay?"

"How like life."

They undressed separately, unbuttoning, unzipping carefully, as if each garment was precious armor, except when Albert stumbled as he took off a sock. For each, the gaze was solitary, unfocused, and they each sensed without looking as the other came to nakedness. At last she unclasped her hair and let it blossom out. They turned their bodies to one another, allowed flesh to touch, and after a breath that drew in the whole sky, he brought his hands up to her narrow hips. They floated their quiet embrace to the bed.

The first penetration, each to the other, was through the eyes.

§

They lay around one another in a quiet half-curl. From somewhere came a muffled scuffle and growl.

"Sounds like angry clowns out there," Jeanette murmured.

"Raccoons. I forgot to bring in the cat bowl." He rolled over to free his arm and ventured to touch her hair lightly. "Or it might be angry clowns." The growling died away. "I guess they resolved their issues."

Each shifted to face the other. Words were slow to bubble to the surface.

"I should probably take off," she said. "I have to get the car in early tomorrow for an oil change, new tire maybe."

He made no reply. They continued to gaze at one another, as if surprised to find themselves in bed with a stranger. She seemed to sense his need to hear her voice. "I like that you're not reluctant to make noise at critical moments. I guess neither am I."

"Could we talk a little? Would that count as noise at critical moments?"

Jeanette heard what he was asking: where did they go from here? She turned onto her back and stared at the ceiling, then spoke with a forced calmness. "Albert, listen, let's have that conversation after the show has opened. Okay? I'm feeling good right now, actually kind of gratified. But let's wait for serious talking till after we've found the Holy Grail."

They left it at that.

XX

Preparing the Endgame

Suddenly, three weeks till opening. September 7th loomed. Albert saw himself riding the current toward the open whirl of the drain. The months had scattered like the cats when the skunk showed up at the food bowl, and he was still tormenting the script in his head as he repainted the Priest, glued Velcro to the Lost Boy's backside, and reset the O-ring on the neck of a dragon who'd made a last-minute guest appearance.

Since the play's first glimmer, Albert had been snapping at its final scene with the frustration of a terrier trying to sink its teeth into a cornered rat. He had the image of a gesture, and it seemed at times that the whole motive for months of toil was to make that gesture. The gesture was Lainie's reaching out.

Late evening, three days before the end, he was in her hospice room. Her eyes had changed and she couldn't focus, so he was reading to her. They knew these were the final days, and she had asked that he read from old playscripts they'd staged over their thirty years. The comedies were the hardest to endure. It seemed that every laugh was followed by a pain too exquisite for the morphine to touch. "I need the damned drugs," she said, "but I don't want to lie here feeling nothing." For Albert, it was almost impossible to flatten the cry in his voice, but as they liked to say, impossibility was no excuse. He'd swiped that line for Sammy.

He was midway into *The Green Bird*, a commedia they'd adapted many years ago, full of enchantment and love. It swept him into a memory of rehearsing the comic bits—the clown eating flies, trying to kill himself without farting, hiding his monstrous erection—and he almost forgot that he sat by a death bed. When he came to the end of an act and looked up, Lainie was staring at him, eyes blazing, holding out her cupped hands as if offering water. No words to explain the gesture, only an excruciating joy that filled them both. He leaned forward and laid his face in her hands.

That image begat *Galahad's Fool*. But sperm were unreliable collaborators. After the magic moment, there was the labor, the diapers, the teenage shit-fits, the student loans. What did that gesture say? The church steeple they'd sighted across the Tuscan hills spurred a rainy two hours' drive on broken hairpin roads toward a mystical chapel that proved to be a cypress tree piercing the mist. Much the same as the plodding on, dragging a mud-clogged bike home from Big Lake. Same as Galahad's half-baked Quest.

Sitting at his work table, he retouched Galahad's whiskery chin, giving the stubble a gray-flecked incoherence of age. As his hapless duo staggered toward the rising sun, Albert warned his brain to cease and desist. He might go for days with barely a glimmer, and then suddenly words and images ran in his head like bulls through the streets of Pamplona.

One notion kept returning: to lead the story close to its final breath, then stop. To speak as Albert the puppeteer. To tell of his wife, his grief, and the vast, indifferent wasteland that stretched ahead. To speak of his own quest, clear to him now, for just one pair of hands to cradle his face till the end of days. For one face that his hands might cradle.

And yet he'd still have to finish the show.

He and Jeanette had been together twice more. Both times, the gentle tact and taut silence and tentative touch had led to sharp passion, a flurry of tumult, a stab, a sweet ebb. And then afterward, through the next days, no change. They were simply colleagues on a project: Albert and Jeanette, not *Hon* or *Love*. Was there any way to cross the rickety bridge to intimacy? For that matter, did he want to cross it? Something in this woman was alien, unreachable, like one of the feral cats—Lainie called it the Skitty Kitty—who possessed a Buddhist serenity yet scooted at the slightest twitch. Might he himself flee from the risk of a deeper connection than *fuck-buddy*? And yet there had been two or three times when their eyes blinked open fully to one another, and for an instant they were mated.

§

He took the bus to the city to deliver flyers. He had hired a poster service, but they were never thorough. In the Mission, he left stacks in coffee shops down Valencia to 23rd, then trudged back up the other side, wearing a look of deep thought that hid a dead blank mind. Then across to The Garage, a little black-box theater on Sixth and Harrison where he'd be playing the three-week run of *Galahad's Fool*. The space was cheaper than others, and there were fewer horizontal denizens on the sidewalk.

He rang the buzzer, met Marty, a short, round soul with a haircut that cried *San Francisco!*—a fusion of mullet, Mohawk, and flirty ringlets. He needed to check the playing space again, the lighting positions and power sources for his dimmers. He'd be running cues onstage from his laptop as part of the one-man-band style, so he'd bring in his own equipment. Everything checked out, no problems. He thanked Marty, verified the time for the load-in, and started toward his lodging.

He was crashing overnight with old friends in the Haight, then catching the bus home in the morning. He didn't really want to see old friends, but Erin and Jesse had good wine and a comfortable couch. He decided to walk: it was only two or three miles, and even though his feet were giving out from the all-day tramp, it would give him more time to feel pleasantly morbid before revving up a smile for friends. And there were surprises along any street in San Francisco: the variegated architecture, a cascade of flowers down a wall, a shop whose name and window display gave no clue as to what they were selling, a poster in somebody's window depicting a possum with a protest sign. It almost made him happy to be alive.

His hero had been jerked off his ass and seemed to be moving forward, and Albert too. After the morning fog had cleared, the city was gemlike in radiance. And perhaps his relationship with Jeanette was ripening: they had quarreled.

She was coming regularly to the studio for evening rehearsals, helping to set props, operating the camcorder he employed to see how bad his performance was, and offering comments. He welcomed that. He rarely took a suggestion literally, but a comment would often pinpoint a symptom and spark a pell-mell fireworks of ideas. And he had a screaming urge for a sign from anyone that he could still be seen on the face of Planet Earth. Invisibility: the curse of being a geezer in the 21st century. Of course he had his daughter, friends he hoped at some point to stop avoiding, and the baristas who smiled across the counter. He could write pungent comments on websites ranging from puppetry to politics. But since high school, it had always been the work itself that gave him a bridge to the human race. Audiences might like it or loathe it, but ultimately, like the neighborhood flasher, he needed the seeing.

Jeanette saw him. And while her comments were tactful, her eyesight was merciless. She might start by praising the puppet designs, his writing or staging gimmicks, but those praises led inevitably to sharper verdicts, and the hounds dogged the fox relentlessly till they brought it to bay. It was a dance: now a tango, now a stomp. Eros fluttered between them like a baffled moth. They would greet and part with hugs, sometimes in passing, sometimes longer, their bodies saying *Hello, thanks, bless you, you're here.*

Then last week they'd quarreled. He couldn't quite remember what started it. She apologized for arriving an hour late: a phone call with her mother in Knoxville, she said, who was having medical problems. A relationship strong but painful, "like being in love with a cactus." He was pleased to pick up that shard of her past.

He had been obsessed by his Lost Boy problem: opening night loomed with poor Bobby still floating in limbo. Albert had faded out the kid, but it didn't feel quite right. He did a rough run-through. As they sat watching the video, he was feeling it wasn't bad. He'd managed to cut the show down to eighty-five minutes with no intermission. The style was intentionally crude: puppets and objects scattered over the stage, a laptop down-center, the puppeteer in coveralls and shoulder-length gray hair fumbling about the stage, sometimes drifting in a haze of senility, then suddenly bringing up a puppet with excruciating eyes. The show felt like a dismembered body with a fierce longing to join back together, and oddly that seemed right. Was the Quest not a fierce longing in his heart and in Galahad's?

But then, in the last ten minutes, it floundered into a muddle. As patriotism was the last refuge of the scoundrel, so they said, obscurity was the fig leaf of an artist who had not the foggiest idea what he believed, what he intended the audience to feel, or where the bathroom was. When Jeanette criticized the cameo appearance of the dragon, Albert didn't want to hear it. He made a dismissive comment, and then all hell broke loose.

"Look, Albert, if he really has to be there, just let him pop up, roar, and disappear, not make a big speech about dragons and quests."

"It's about—"

"It's about your thinking we need footnotes to get the meaning. Just tell the story."

"Don't tell me how to write a play—"

"It's like planting flowers and then pulling the stems to make them taller."

"It's funny, dammit! It's funny for a dragon to make a speech."

"Well then you're going to have to make the audience sign a pledge to laugh. There's nothing funny about—"

"What audience?" His back was to the wall. "There'll be a half-dozen people that can't figure what the fuck's going on!"

"Then what are we doing this for?"

"You're doing it because I hired you. I'm doing it to stay alive."

She took a deep breath and spoke in a near-whisper: the quieter her words, the more penetrating. "You know, my friend, I don't work at two-thirds my fee, plus help out with rehearsals, plus put up with your shit, Albert, just because it's a job."

He had a mad impulse to mutter something savage about her hair but checked himself.

"Your wife must have been a very patient woman," she added.

"Don't bring her into this, Jeanette, for godsake—"

"I've got a perfect right to bring her into it. You've called me Lainie three times this week."

It was the same dance, so familiar, as with his lost dancing partner. When puppeteer and costumer had both been thoroughly puréed in their trip through the Cuisinart, repeating everything half a dozen times, each time with greater exasperation, it ended pretty much the way as it had in earlier times: going back into rehearsal. The deadline forced you to stop flapping your mouth like a Muppet and get to work. But Jeanette stood in the doorway with cold, searching eyes.

"I'm sorry," Albert said quietly. "Please sit down. Don't stand in the door."

"I feel safer standing."

"I'd feel safer if you sat." He cleared the junk off the sofa—tools, pages of script, the problematic dragon—and she sat down. "Any other notes?"

"It just occurred to me," she said, "although this isn't wanting a whole other scene or something. But I wonder what's happening to the real Sammy. Back at the castle?"

"Disguised as the Lady? I guess running things and trying not to get caught naked by his lady's maids. That'd be kinda funny. If he's peeing in the chamber pot and they catch him."

"That could be a whole play."

"God help us."

In fact he had written the scene, then cut it. Though he grieved the loss of every line in the final honing, he actually loved to cut stuff: get rid of the fat as long as it didn't kill the fatso. Like his assaults on the storage closets, he wound up having more by having less. But he did miss losing the presence of Sammy the Fool, the actual fool, as the rest of the plot slouched forward.

"Okay, here's what happened." Albert lay back on a sofa cushion, staring at a bedraggled spiderweb in the rafters. Jeanette sat upright at the other end of the sofa. He felt her watching, so he spun his threads slowly, savoring the guilty pleasure of being seen.

§

Sammy was a quick study. He already knew the Lady's routines, and he was the perfect mimic. While servants noted that Lady Mara had become more private in personal matters, they put this down to loneliness for her husband. But Galahad held vast estates, commanded a private militia, and managed a network of alliances. At first the Lady tried to leave all matters to subordinates, but soon she . . . he . . . she became embroiled in the daily grind of politics, sanitation, taxation, law enforcement, church relations, road repair, the price of crops. The ultimate juggling act.

So the ersatz Lady played the role and by degrees, spring to summer to autumn, became the role. But the role demanded power, and power had its price. Sammy the Lady was playing a game of cards where the rules changed daily. She saw that with every judgment she uttered, every paper she signed, its consequence might echo for generations. At times she sat frozen, fearing the hidden claws of a single word. Even her religion could not declare the incontrovertible rightness of an action or offer a scrying glass to see its result.

But she was also the Fool, who knew the human comedy from the rectum on up. A society bred its people to certain assumptions, and if they were bred to mistrust, to steal and kill in order to survive, they would not take readily to liberation. Raise taxes on the rich and spend the revenues defending yourself against their cabals. Soften the sentence for crimes and feel the victim's bitter hatred and the offender's contempt. She seemed to be moving through a wilderness of fingers pointing willy-nilly. Around every corner came a fork in the road with no signpost, not even an impassable jut of rock to force her one way or the other. There was no straight path to virtuous rule, only the weary zigzag.

The day she was faced with a capital judgment, a crime that demanded the man be broken on the wheel, she sat as if paralyzed, then shuddered and spoke the words. She forced herself to watch with a face of stone. That night, she shoved her feather pillow to her mouth to muffle her sobs and prayed to become a servant again, a man, a freak, a fool.

Change came slowly, imperceptibly, yet it came. To alter the predisposition of a people to cheat, to fight, to angle for advantage—it seemed hopeless. Yet with patience, doubling back whenever the land, the light, or the riverflow gave her a clue to the terrain, she found a tortuous path toward justice, an unreachable destination, perhaps, but further than any had gone before.

God seemed to have become more tolerant in the raw enforcement of His will. There were heartaches, wrongs, privations, strife, but no more than were natural to humankind's daily grind. Compared with what people had known before, it was a golden age. In time, the minstrels made songs about its simple grace, and these songs intermixed with legends of a great warrior king, its blessings assigned to King Arthur, not to a noble lady who was in fact a man who was in fact a fool. Camelot was real, though misattributed.

In the Lady's last days, when she knew—when Sammy knew—that her master was lost to the wind, she felt her subjects' concern for the succession. There were no direct descendants but only a gaggle of cousins, nephews, great-uncles to claim the prize. If nothing could be done, she felt it was folly to do it, so she left it to be settled by time or the armies of the night. Her more urgent need was to ensure that at her demise, her secret and that of her other self would not be discovered as the body was prepared for dissolution. She feared the immodesty of death.

One moonless night, Sammy mounted the saddle and left, in a manservant's tunic and breeches, riding toward the sea cliffs.

§

"Yes, you're right," said Jeanette. "That's another play."

Albert sat sprawled on the rickety couch, still staring at the spiderweb, and she on the opposite end. She picked up her folded notes, gave him a few line corrections, mentioned a couple of times when the puppets went dead or when he took too long a pause. Then she moved closer beside him, reached out and touched his forehead. He heaved a sigh that might have been laughter or pain and held her hand in his. No expectation, just simple presence.

There was that time at the age of sixteen when he'd first kissed Karen, or *kissed with her* was a better way to say it. Leaving her house, running down to the bus stop, the silhouettes of branches and leaves and the yearning fingers of trees against the sky burned into him. The vision had never been so clear: life's unbearable intensity. As now, it shimmered, then passed.

"I don't know what's happening," he said.

"That's what's interesting."

Finally he looked at her. For a moment their eyes held fast. Then she was gone.

§

Crossing Market Street on the way to his overnight lodging, his mind gnawed on the problem of Bobby. The kid had to go back to his parental dolts. All parents, himself included, were dolts, and he had great empathy with dolts. Maybe Bobby could watch it all on TV. The boy needed to face up to the fact that we're all just a plot device. At the corner of Haight and Divisidero, Albert—very sore of foot—perched himself on a fireplug and scribbled Bobby homeward. He knew that the child would cry, and he knew that Mara the Fool would cry the way Lainie cried one day on the beach at Pescadero, looking out over the sea, hearing it wail for its dead ones and for the living who would be dead and for the pangs of birth, precursor to death. Lainie could hear the sea's grief, always. But that too was another play.

Albert arrived at his friends' apartment, hugged, had a light supper and very good wine, laughed about the bunch of them still being alive—though Erin and Jesse were only in their fifties—then sacked out on the sofa as his hosts stumbled off to bed. Yes, he'd get through it. He would open in three weeks, come hell or high water. In Lainie's twenty-eighth hour birthing Mara, riding another swell of pain that seemed the prank of some spiteful god, she'd muttered, "I'm not gonna fucking do this. I'm outta here!" Then she laughed, which made the pain worse. But of course she stayed and did it, and for the next thirty years, they would chant together on opening night, "I'm not gonna fucking do this! I'm outta here!" And then they'd do it.

He dozed off, blundering into a dream. In the cavernous waiting room of a railway station, he saw Bobby alone on a bench, like the sole survivor of shipwreck, watching the tiny black-and-white TV that Albert's mother had bought on credit when he was nine. The Lost Boy was watching a movie called *Galahad's Fool*.

§

Mommy and Daddy took a vacation. To England and a castle. I got lost. Half an hour and they found me. They were mad but I cried and they bought me a hot dog. Maybe I cried because they found me.

But I saw this movie about Sir Galahad, I think. He's looking for the Holy Grail. There's a fool and horses and dead men. I cried some more and they bought me ice cream.

I remember Sir Galahad made a big loud yell and hit Sammy and fell in a bush. It was all stickers and Sammy pulled him out. Sir Galahad was crying and Sammy had a bloody nose like I did when Lucas hit me.

Or maybe I saw a puppet show. It seemed like I was in it.

§

Albert reached through the TV screen to the drunken Galahad, grabbed his head, ripped it off, and threw it against the wall, spraying a burst of blood. "Stupid bastard!" he screamed. That woke him up.

Had he shouted out loud? He heard no stir from his friends' bedroom, so it didn't seem likely: the shout would have rousted the city. With a swell of despair, it struck him: he'd have to rebuild the head. Then slowly it dawned that he'd smashed it in a dream. Scant comfort: the adrenaline rush was real, and he'd lie awake for hours. *Somnum interruptum.* He sat up, heart pounding full tilt, staring into the night.

If he could only go back to the dream, he'd tell Bobby to switch to another channel, then reach into the screen, take Galahad by the shoulders, and speak to him man to man:

> *Get real. Stop chanting beatitudes and listen to what*
> *you mean. Drop the broken hilt and ditch the creaky*
> *armor. Smell the flowers. Look into those eyes you've*
> *seen ten thousand times and see who it really is.*

He adjusted the sleep mask that was hanging off one ear and settled back into the sofa pillow. It wasn't long before he dreamed himself gathering the shards of the Knight's shattered head, carrying them to his table, tuning the radio to gentle jazz, and starting the mend.

XXI

Of a Death under Hooves

Opening night. September 7th. Not ready, but not the shambles he'd expected. Thirty-odd people on the books, most of them friends or fellow puppeteers, but a few names he didn't recognize. Inevitably there would be a couple who brought their six-year-old: if you uttered the word *puppet*, people would bring kids, no matter if you were staging the Marquis de Sade. And they'd sit front row center, so that when they realized their appalling mistake and left in a rush they'd be the stars of the show. Oh well, it wasn't the Second Coming, it was just a play.

He drove down to the city early afternoon, stopping at Hard Core Espresso for a mocha and checking email via their Wi-Fi. A note from his daughter:

> *Well, so as always, break a leg. I feel like I should say something witty, but the only thing I can think of is that I love you.*
>
> *Right now we're camping on the floor of our hacienda. Alejandro is doing carpentry as we find the leaks and drafts. Glad I hooked up with a handyman & not an English major. I can't drive a nail straight, but I share the work by pestering him. Sometimes I think we're exactly like you & Mama, except in reverse. I'm the obsessive who gets lost inside my head & he's the one who knows how to keep things moving.*
>
> *Anyway: survive the opening & don't forget to do your freaking-the-demons dance.*

At the theater, two young guys helped with the afternoon set-up, and they were duly impressed by Albert's puppets. He had kept the lighting simple, so the cue-to-cue tech went rapidly. He walked up to a noodle shop on Sixth and Mission for an early dinner. Back at the theater, he set his cell phone's alarm for a half-hour nap on the funky, rump-sprung lobby sofa and drifted off. He was shaken awake by the timer's bleats.

Then the wait. He hated the waiting. His self-imposed call to be present at the theater was an hour and a half before curtain. He had to recheck the placement of puppets and props; to test that each lighting circuit was working, with no dead lamps, no instrument out of focus; to put on eyeliner and darken his brows; to stretch and do vocal warm-ups before the house opened at half hour. And then to retreat to the basement dressing room and wait and wait and wait.

He sat in a creaky yellow chair, painted over so many times it seemed to be held together by the paint. Sipping tepid coffee, he tried to blank his mind but kept wondering why he was sipping tepid coffee. At times he would stretch and yawn to loosen his voice between sips. How many times had he sat in these cold, bare dressing rooms, waiting for free-fall? Though he knew otherwise, it felt as if he'd been here before: the cracked white walls, the bald ceiling rafters, the curtained toilet cubicle, and the braided rug that formed a lumpy toupee on the concrete floor. Might be that his best service to the future of world drama would be to spend his last days sprucing up a few of the hundreds of shabby dressing rooms where, over the decades, he'd waited out his hours.

More than a few times, Lainie had asked, "Do you ever *like* performing?" True, he rarely gave evidence of taking pleasure in the craft he'd devoted his life to. *Pleasure* was a strange word for it. Sex or food, hearing the ocean's rumble, watching the solo turns of the hawks riding an updraft over the sea cliffs—those he could truly call pleasure. But performing? That was riding a drunken camel, juggling water balloons, dancing on the belly of a walrus. There was no pleasure in that. There was only the doing, and the doing was life itself.

There might be a touch of pathology to it. It might be that, as a storyteller, he organized life into beginnings, middles, and ends to give himself the illusion that it actually worked that way. Or it might be the adrenaline: to be flung, like the athlete or soldier, through a portal where every moment stretched taut as a banjo string awaiting the twang. Decades ago, Lainie riding behind him, their motorcycle blew a tire on the Autobahn, and he'd bulldogged it to the shoulder as cars shot past at ninety mph—a savage ten seconds of terror to a heaving, shivering halt. Best to cherish our tiny savageries, he mused: they keep us immune from the biggies.

But now he waited through an hour of minutes passing like funeral cars. With some shows, he liked to mingle with the audience as they came in, inviting them to the party. Maybe next weekend, but tonight he knew they'd see through his plastered smile to his shivering, plucked-chicken soul, so he sat in the basement, staring at a smudge on the mirror.

"Hi there."

He looked up. Jeanette stood at the foot of the stairs. Colorful long skirt, some sort of South American shawl, and her hair was fluffed up with a single elastic band atop the head, so her curls exploded upward like a ruddy geyser. She rapped on the door frame that lacked a door.

"Can I come in?"

"I think you're already in."

"The star's dressing room."

"Beyond my wildest dreams." Weird hair, he was going to say, but checked himself.

She approached and handed him a rose. "So break a leg."

Albert took the rose, smiled. "What do they say to costumers on opening night? Rip a seam?"

He had a sudden impulse to roar up and embrace her. Instead, in a moment of pure adolescent panic, he glanced away to the smudge on the mirror. He had thought the work pressure in the final days might blunt his attraction, and certainly it deflected it. Tech week was always like those war movies with the squad of Marines under fire, bonding like brothers, but you never saw them making love. Once he had met a high-stress bond trader, and he recognized his own working mindset: the machine-gun decisions, the flatness of affect, throttling every minute with the merciless precision of a serial killer. But Jeanette Wald had come along for the ride, had come all the way, and those words— "Let's talk after the show opens"—held promise. He held that promise close.

What to say, and when? Maybe straight out was best, a forthright "Hey, after the show, could we have that conversation?" Others flirted with eyes, with silence, with the tilt of the head, but he was driven to speech, and with an attractive woman his language emerged in epileptic word-balloons, monosyllabic sputters. When it came to courtship, he was still the tongue-tied scarecrow from high school. He'd written some credible let's-make-love dialogues—once even for Punch and Judy—but it always took three or four drafts, and real life didn't offer the privilege of rewrites.

He started to say, "How about after the show—" but couldn't hear his own voice.

Jeanette cut in. "Listen, I'll be seeing the show tonight, but then I have to get ready for a trip. I'm taking off on Sunday. Sorry, but it came up very suddenly, so if there's any repairs during the run, I'll give you the name of a friend, Jodie, and she'll do it for free. Is that okay? I mean I hope it's okay because I don't know what else to do."

End of sentence, slam of door. If this were a play, how would the guy respond? Maybe stick a finger in his eye? Maybe cry?

"Where to?"

"Knoxville."

"Knoxville?"

"Yeah, people live there, actually. Is that a problem?"

"No. No problem." What else could he say? "When are you back?"

"Not sure. Family stuff." Somehow he didn't believe it, but any questions would sound like cross-examination. Then, as if sensing a need to enhance credibility, she added, "My mom's having medical problems."

"Serious?"

"Not sure." There was a lot she wasn't sure of, it seemed, except the leaving: she seemed sure of that. The obvious thing was to ask if they might talk after the show, but her vague greenish eyes were distant, and her silence stood as firm as a nightclub bouncer. Again she said, "Not sure," as if in answer to a question he hadn't asked. "I'm sorry it's so sudden. I really wanted to see how the piece develops. I mean over the run."

"So do I."

"Anyway, I better get a seat. I'm sorry to break your concentration, I should have told you after the show, but—"

Make it a joke, Albert. "No problem. I don't do concentration."

"Five minutes," someone called down the stairs.

"Thank you, five," he called back.

Jeanette made a *Tally-ho!* gesture, then hurried up the

stairs. Albert felt his blood sugar drain. A sensation he dreaded: everything went dead. The thunderheads of depression were rolling in. He wanted to lie flat on the floor and get up after the final night of the show. *God dammit, yes! You should have told me afterward!*

But if Albert didn't do concentration, he did do survival. He rose abruptly, faced the mirror, swooped his hands into bizarre contortions, pulled lunatic faces with guttural grunts and trills, hopped about as if beset by fleas—a frantic ritual of clowning that Lainie called "the shaman freaking the demons." Then he stopped cold. He felt a swell of grief. So strange to be lonely alone: much better lonely together.

"Two minutes."

"Thank you, two."

He took the stairs three at a time, squeezed into the narrow stage-left wing space, and waited, rotating his wrists, stretching his fingers just to keep them alive. Through a rip in the flat, he could see about thirty in the house. A five-minute wait, then a girl came out on stage, attractive insofar as twenty-year-olds could be attractive to him. She went through her speech—*next show up, sign our mailing list, turn off devices, restrooms back-stage to the right, enjoy the show*—and at last, "Now we're really pleased to present . . . *Sir Galahad and His Fool.*" My God, it never failed.

But the crowd sounded energetic, primed to respond. He felt a lamp flicker: something wrong with Circuit 8, too late to fix. The houselights dimmed to half. He walked out onto the stage, down-center to the laptop on a stool, and punched the space bar. Stage lights bounced up, and the Quest was under way. In eighty-five minutes, the Fool would die.

In the guise of a crusty tour guide with a canvas flip chart of childlike drawings, he began the narrative, pretty much what he'd jotted ages ago:

> *Friends, what are you looking for? You're asking your-self, your significant other, asking any poor sucker you meet, WHAT AM I LOOKING FOR? But you know. You know already: you are chasing . . . the Holy Grail!*

He flipped the canvas pages, explaining the Grail, the Round Table, the knights riding off and crawling back bat-tered and scuffed. A wad of tourists were at his side: dolls with springs for necks and arms, so that one wiggle would start them all bobbing. The opening worked. Big laughs at the bobblehead tourists.

He brought up a sketch of Sir Galahad as a square-jawed hero, then raised a dumpy, pot-bellied doll in bathrobe and helmet as the middle-aged Knight. Another laugh. Others appeared as dolls: Lady Mara, the Priest, the Fool. Narrating Sammy's history as the puppet tried a one-handed juggle, he felt the attention wander. The danger of getting big laughs early in the show: nowhere to go but down.

He punched the space bar. A strobe unit flashed as he struck the flip chart, revealing Mom, Dad, and Bobby framed within a TV and illumining soldiers mounted on stands around the periphery. A soldier—just helmet, spear, and stuffed jockstrap—stood center stage. Then slowly, as if dragged up, came the Peasant, hands bound, glancing around confused. His body was naked foam rubber. Albert controlled him by rods in the head and shoulders—very simple responses—playing the scene almost as radio drama, supplying all the voices.

May God bring to you what you bring to me:
Let you go begging on bended knee!
Let you see your dearest creature die!
Drink your own tears!

Then, as tour guide, Albert fastened the puppet to a stake, flogged it, and peeled away the skin. It worked. He had experimented with liquid latex, letting it dry, then painting over it—a crude, sun-weathered texture that looked astonishingly real. Too real, almost. As the first gasp from the audience was about to become an audible *Ick!* he firmly held up his hand: "It's okay, it's a puppet." Held breath, thin laughter, then silence, and the figure's red nakedness hung suspended. In dead silence, he peeled off the face.

The best-written scenes were the weakest in the staging. The duets between Galahad and Mara, Mara and the Fool, or the Fool and Galahad were played simply by picking up their heads, wagging them to the dialogue. When one character became dominant—the Fool comforting the Lady or trying to amuse the Knight—Albert might pick up the puppet and bring it fully alive. Sometimes, indeed, the most minimal expression was the strongest, but he felt the absence of the partner. Cleverness disguised a crying need.

The audience liked the toy rocking-horses, butcher knives for swords, chopsticks for spears. They liked the breaks when the puppeteer scuttled around the stage from priest to bishop to cardinal or picked up the wrong puppet—intentionally, they thought—then played a comic confusion that mimicked the world's disorder. At the first battle, drawing out long strands of paper dolls cut from newspaper, taping them up across the stage, then descending like a banshee, shredding and wadding, he drew applause—all the while dreading to think how many strands he'd have to cut in the next three weeks.

The conquests went on: drawings of medieval castles, cathedrals, skyscrapers, the White House, each ripped to shreds, crushed in his fist and dripping stage blood. From time to time, perched at the side of the playboard, the Lost Boy cried out in terror or flicked his remote to change the channel or interrupted a heartfelt speech with a tiny snore. When the frantic scramble of the throwaway style settled into an extended scene, Albert's critical eye—which never slept or took a pee break—told him the rhythm was right: hurry up, slow down, let it breathe.

But in the first bonfire scene with the Fool and Galahad, again he felt the energy flag. Miles to go, to what purpose? He felt an overwhelming urge to cut to the chase, jump over forty minutes, play the final scene, walk off the stage, and die.

But he didn't. He trudged to the fork that led to a fork that led to a fork. The beggars were simply black hoods with hands wrought from cheap spoons and forks. Curly, Larry, and Moe were a single three-headed puppet toting a toddler's baseball bat. And when Albert brought forth the Angel of Death—a naked, winged female with a chicken's head—the audience perked up. Chickens were dependably freaky.

Then came the moment when Galahad struck Mara the Fool. Too much: one more rag ripped out of the cruelty bin. He felt the audience cringe as the blow came down with the rage of an old bitter man howling into the void.

Ten minutes left in the show. A few glitches: getting a light cue behind and blacking out a Galahad speech, picking up the long-dead Priest instead of the Fool. He wished he'd kept the bit where the Knight was ticketed for jaywalking: the audience needed a laugh. But Sammy's sidewalk busking was a hit: trios of objects attached to hoops that the puppet spun.

§

On the road again. The Fool carried the backpacks, water jug, scraps of Galahad's armor that had come unmoored, and the map of an alien land called California. The Knight still held the hilt of his broken sword. The day was hot and overcast with smog or a bitter curse in the air. They had taken a route called Frontage Road, though the map showed no city called Frontage. It ran beside a track where huge steel centaurs shot past at the speed of a crossbow bolt. The track stretched before them, a pulsing artery drained of blood.

Galahad's eyes were dead in the bleak afternoon. His tread was heavy, following the plod of the small, determined figure ahead of him. He had lost track of where he was, who he was, or any purpose to the march. But he felt vaguely that there was some lost meaning to it, something he had kindled, borne now by the creature who carried the packs. He strained to recall it.

They came to other cities, to vast landscapes seared by dragon breath, to rivers iridescent with sludge. Days and weeks peeled away like rabbit skin. The Knight hazily recollected the start of the journey: a nightmare's clutch, an evil that spurred him. But a dim spark that he had engendered was alight. *Peace . . . love . . . no fear . . . all free.* Words with a blurry meaning, yet he caught the whisper. Plodding before him, he saw the frail Fool, pregnant with light.

A late afternoon, sweltering but sunless. They heard the sound of hooves approaching, horsemen at a gallop. The riders came into view, all Knights of the Table Round: Sir Launcelot, Sir Tristram, Sir Lamorak, Sir Palomides, Sir Kay, and behind them Boris de Ganis, Gawain, Gaharis, Dodinas, Pellinore, Percival, and a gaggle of extras mounted on rampant nags, all impelled by a fierce mythic howl.

"Brothers," whispered Galahad. Men he knew, men he'd sat with at table, men who had braved the tournament, the crusades, the perilous dreams. But the stallions they rode were savage, unbroken, bits in their teeth, running mad. The knights— blinded by dust from the hooves, mere boys astride history's merciless steeds—groped to snag their lost reins.

"Brothers," whispered Galahad again. The horses were nearly upon them. With a frantic effort, the Fool pulled the Knight to the culvert, then scrambled up the bank, arms waving, into the road.

"Help! Help for your brother Galahad! As you love God! Help for Galahad!" And the hooves came hammering down.

§

Albert had staged this scene a dozen ways. Finally he'd settled on mounting a smaller Fool/Mara doll on a stand rigged with levers operated by a foot pedal to make her arms wave. He pounded the table with coconut shells on either side of the doll. Then he came to a sudden halt, grabbing the doll and slapping it down on its face. In the silence, he would speak.

> *So the Knights of the Table Round gallop into the night, the nightmares rising, the symphonies of butchery—Marathon, Carthage, Agincourt, Waterloo, Gettysburg, the Marne, the Somme, Stalingrad, Tet, Baghdad—and the Angel of Death is full.*

But he didn't say it tonight. Jeanette had called the speech redundant and preachy. Exactly what Lainie would have said. Jeanette had no right to be Lainie, even if Lainie was dead. But now the Fool was dead too, and all words were stillborn.

§

Galahad bent to pick up his broken jester. He slipped off the straps of the pack and raised the wisp of a body in his arms. He crossed the culvert and strode to an open field. He looked for a fitting place to lay down his burden, the shade of a tree or the bank of a stream, but there was only brown scrub and rubbish. He kept walking, thinking the landscape might change if he persisted.

The Fool's eyes came open. The Knight stopped. He stared into the eyes, saw a soul flickering, whispering love. A shudder passed through the body. The eyes dulled. The soul dissolved.

Let you see your dearest creature die.

He braced against a tide of grief. He knew it was coming. It would roll in slowly, an ocean swell, and slam the rocks. He had grieved the death of his mother, mourned his favorite hunting dog, the knights he had overcome, the countless dead, even the Peasant who cursed him—nightmares all. And he treasured this juggling freak, so delicate, so devoted, who could barely brighten a moment for more than a passing chuckle—and yet Sammy had kept him alive. This Fool deserved the deepest mourning.

But the grief never came. *What do I feel?* puzzled Galahad. Vast numbness, a dry lake bed, tears aborted, the glare of empty eyes. He felt nothing. He laid the body on an earth without fertility, a ground poisoned into submission. He heard the distant baying in the belly of the Beast. The wind died. He could hardly bear to breathe.

The Knight pulled back the hood of the motley cloak. The Fool's thin beard was gone, and the face resembled another face.

A curious headband of tiny bells seemed wrong somehow, unfit for a fool, and he pulled it away. The hair, the long flaxen hair of his wife flowed down. He stared without comprehension. Then up from his bowels, a cry, rising from bellow to shriek, ripped the sky like a battle-ax. The vultures that circled above could never be quit of the hearing.

§

In rehearsal, Albert had never been able to play this scene without breaking up somehow—a silence, a tightening of the face, a sudden intake of breath that verged on a sob but sounded like a hiccup. He was seeing Lainie's face at the splatter-point of death. Now, as he played it, he felt as Galahad did: appalled at his numbness, a scream without feeling the pain. He sensed a tremor in the audience but could hear only a distant breath that he thought might be his own.

He barely remembered the end of the play. He had put hours of work into the final moments—the crook-nosed hag, the drinking of tears, the reaching out—but by that point he was flying blind, slogging home from Big Lake. He made the final gesture, hit the foot pedal to fade the lights, then endured an endless silence. As the lights came up, there was scattered applause, then building, and people rising, exploding. *Yes!*

Triumph, it seemed. Curtain calls, curtain calls, and then he came out to the lobby as the audience emerged. There were the usual questions—*Who built the puppets? How do you do the eyes? Where did you get the idea?*—from people groping for something to say. An elderly woman, red-eyed, shook his hand while avoiding his gaze. A scrawny adolescent with a left ear full of rings made a swooping gesture, gleefully giggling, "Awesome! Awesome!" A Chinese woman about Mara's age stopped, reached out, touched his heart. A ventriloquist friend spoke in his goofy-marsupial voice: "I never seen nothing like that before!"

He smiled, shook hands, basked in the praise. "Thank you, thank you, wonderful audience, thank you." But the numbness held. He desperately wanted what they were giving him—communion, grace, gratitude—yet he could barely wait for them all to be gone. He knew what was coming. He had hopes that they'd start the buzz and he'd have full houses for the rest of the run. But his protective pessimism told him it didn't work that way any more. No reviewers tonight, none on the books, nothing to put the Sacred Quest at the top of the entertainment calendar or compete with a comedy club. "Thank you, thank you," and the dim lobby cleared.

Jeanette stood by the box-office table as the pretty young house manager rearranged the counter, stacked some discarded programs, then waved goodnight.

"Well, there it is," Albert said.

"Very good," said Jeanette. "Really, very good."

"Well, thank you. For everything. Really."

"It was a privilege." She held out her hand. He took it.

"Jeanette, I— It's really your show too, you realize? What you brought to it, and what you told me to get rid of. I mean, there was some fantastic writing in there that thank God I cut." He forced a laugh so she would know he was joking. This lobby scene, he felt, would need a rewrite.

"Thanks. Really, thanks." She nodded, smiled, but he sensed a reserve. "Listen," she said, finally withdrawing her hand, "I didn't drive, I just took the bus, but I have to get to San Rafael. Could you drop me there if you're driving back tonight?"

"San Rafael? Sure."

"I'm house-sitting for a friend till—" She hesitated. "Actually, I'm not leaving till Wednesday, but I have this pre-existing condition, so to speak. Packing, clean-up, that stuff."

He nodded. Reality was all relative.

He collected his shoulder bag, checked that the dimmers were off, and walked with her to the entrance, stopping to read the instructions for setting the alarm system. He punched buttons, then trusted to fate as he slammed the door.

Driving, there was a delicate formality between them, not a barrier exactly, just an instant of decision before each word or nod or smile. They talked about the show in technical terms— where it sagged, where the light levels were off, details that might be clarified, an accident that got a good laugh.

"You could take even more time when he sees the wife's face. The trembling is good, we just need a bit more time to absorb it."

"Right. Good." He hadn't noticed the trembling, but it seemed like a good idea.

He took the San Rafael exit, she directed him to the address, and they didn't speak until he pulled up in front of an old Victorian with the porch light on.

"That must be hard for you. That moment," she said.

"Actually, tonight I didn't feel a thing." He looked at her, and his first sob was like a sharp, silly snort. Then suddenly there were deep gasps and tears, unstoppable. Not embarrassing, just a fact. He had cried many times for fictional characters—for the hanging of Esmeralda, for David Copperfield's lost friend, for the resurrection of Hermione in *Winter's Tale*—but never since childhood for himself. Jeanette touched his shoulder, as if offering permission.

After a while the breath came back. It felt like forever, though not likely more than a minute. "Well, I guess maybe I did," he said.

She leaned to him and kissed his forehead. "G'night. I'll call to check on stuff."

"Thanks." He heard the flatness in his voice. It was obvious to him, and probably to her, that this was an unspoken goodbye. She reached to open the car door, then turned back to him. "Albert," she said, then looked away to stare at the glowing odometer. "I used to be a pathological liar, but now it only comes in little spasms."

He followed her gaze toward the mileage, looking to the numbers for a clue.

"Why am I saying this? What the hell is going on?" It was clear she didn't expect an answer.

"What, you mean like your hair is fake or something?" Dumb thing to say.

"Look—" She turned to face Albert directly. "There's nothing wrong with my mother except she's been dead for the last five years. I'm going to Knoxville because I've been offered a teaching job so I can stop just flopping from one thing to another. I don't know why I didn't just say that instead of coming out with some kind of stupid bullshit." She took a sharp inhale.

They sat in silence, except for the engine idling, as the California night wrapped its chill around them. Albert imagined huddling closer to a bonfire if there had been a bonfire, but there wasn't. He thought of asking why he was important enough to her to merit a lie, but he didn't. At last he said, "Well, congratulations. College theater? Costumes?" She nodded. Her eyes were wet. He was gripped by a yawning urge to touch her, embrace her, make love to this woman who was open to him for a moment, but he sat frozen, staring into the blackness.

"Funny thought," he said. "If the poor guy did find the Grail, would he ever reach out and grab it?"

And for a moment, it felt as if she were about to reach out her hand to him without his doing the reaching. But she didn't.

"Well, so," he said without knowing what he meant.

"So thanks for the ride."

"No problem. Let me know how things go."

"Will do."

She got out of the car, waved, and walked to the house up a path of stones bordered by primrose in shadowed blossom. Albert watched her disappear, then made his way back to the 101 and drove north.

XXII

The Grail

Lainie here. Me, always here in your head. Lainie of memory, Lainie of years, Lainie whose cardigans hang in the closet, Lainie stone dead. I run in your noggin like those ants that came every winter onto the kitchen counter. Still come, I guess.

Don't question my reality, Albert. I might be a figment. I might be a spirit. I might be a ringtone. Whatever, you hear me more balanced and whole than I ever felt in those days when I had sweat glands. Death has its perks.

Last day of the show. Final shot at the Holy Grail. Lifespan of the baby: three weeks, twelve showings, ten to thirty witnesses each. We made so many children together, Albert. I never doubted you'd birth this baby, but can you survive the postpartum? The dying-off? You went through it with every new show, especially the hits. I saw you mourn the going, gone. We made so many children, and you could see only their closing night.

Except for Mara. I'd been afraid that you could only love your work, that a child would be an afterthought. But you were there for her, and you let her breathe. You take joy in her now precisely because she's not yours, she's a creature running free. If you could only feel the same joy in your work or at least embrace its echoes.

Though our madness was kinda special, yes? Even the tsunamis: those late-night kitchen screaming fits or the haggle of collaboration? That last moment when you looked in my eyes? The last sight I ever had? That was good. I wonder if you're lighting beeswax candles now or those cheap things that burn down fast? I hope you're lighting beeswax.

They're calling places. Up the stairs to wait in the wings. Are you driven by lust for what's ahead or by demons biting your ass? You created Galahad, your shadow self, and flung him into a mapless world. I never had doubts you envisioned something sacred—the Grail of Laughter, the Grail of Absurdity, the Grail of Bitter Tears. Was I wrong? (Go on, enter, punch the first cue.) I'm asking as you condemn the Peasant, as the Fool begins to juggle. Do you believe in the Grail or only in the Quest?

Closing night and nothing to lose because it's all been lost. No doors will open, no sudden fame, only the taste on the fingertips now from the juicy touch. You might still touch it. It's going well tonight. You've got the timing down, getting the laughs and taking the slalom turns. It's more crafted, but you're not crafting it now, you're letting it breathe. You might still touch it.

You're at the fire watching the Fool. Who do you see now, me? Me, when we did the clown piece in red nose and fright wig? And after the show the night was crazy, the dark in deep colors, and we walked out to our shaggy back yard, leaves just coming onto the apple trees like feathers on the moon, and we spoke in whispers. We always lived in rivers.

Oops, wrong puppet, quick recovery. Your hero's perched in his tin-can tuxedo, crying sand, his army dying around him, and it's all come to rubble. Then he batters the Fool who loves him. In our life, you aimed the blows at yourself. "I'm sorry!" you cried as you flogged yourself raw, but you must have known that I felt it.

You weren't meant to live alone. What was it you said once? You needed to be alone, but you could be alone better with me? Sometimes you'd sit in loud places to write, go to parties just to feel bereft. (Pick up the beggar now.) My advice: go after the redhead or the barista or anything warm and fuzzy that votes progressive. Don't wait for the Grail, just order what's on the menu. Classical ballet or the hokey-pokey: it's all dance, and you need to dance. (Next beggar.) Divorce me. Divorce the dead. The closet full of my clothes: either wear'em or toss'em out. (Next.) Go to your new love bare-assed.

Galahad wore armor, you wore irony, and I loved your wry objectivity, except when it drove me nuts. But to give birth, you have to shed your armament. Breathe. Wait to push, then push. If you're torn, you're torn. Billions have done this, and this is you now, birthing a soul. Remember the line you wrote for my solo show? *You get naked to have a baby.*

You're coming up now to the miracle, which in half a year of writing it, rehearsing it, you've never believed. Nobody wants to see it, you think: we'd sooner have revenge on this bastard who's corkscrewed his madness into the world and yanked it raw. You think we can't believe in redemption because that would mean walking out to the stinky night at Sixth & Harrison with a heart at full tide. Only one more chance to make the miracle real. The miracle is the believing it.

§

The alarm did its thing, and he killed it. He heard the fleeting echo of Lainie's voice, and a poem she once gave him to read: *If that which you seek you find not within you, you will never find it anywhere.* He'd made a joke about swallowing his car keys, but the words stuck. He strained to hear them again. Instead, the bleat of the snooze alarm: 5:05 a.m. Today, the start of the trip.

Sunday had been the closing performance. Some nights during the run he had crashed with friends; on others he did the late drive home. The final night, he'd driven in for the show, then slept at a hostel on Post & Taylor to load out from the theater early Monday morning. Briefly he'd thought of springing for a decent hotel, but the simple fact was that he hated hotels. All those bucks just to sleep: you felt like you'd better stay awake all night just to get your money's worth. He opted for the hostel, managed to heave himself into the upper bunk of a six-bed dorm, and listened all night to a roommate snoring in French.

Next morning he went down to the theater, struck the set, packed puppets into the Honda, turned in his keys to Marty— with the haircut—who said, "Neat show," and drove the ninety minutes home. The rest of his day was limbo. He unloaded, stashed the puppet bins in the studio mausoleum, checked email, sat puzzling over a roadmap. He called for a pizza, drove out to pick it up, then grazed till mid-evening, scanning Google News to catch up with current disasters. Strange that the vodka held no attractions, not even to blunt the news.

The next two days straggled by. He wrestled the tax forms, paid some bills, sent a card to the post office to stop the mail, and pulled a few weeds in the backyard jungle. Late Wednesday, he threw stuff willy-nilly into a duffel. Finally, as if sealing an executive decision, he rose and set out the cat food.

"Okay, friends, that's all you get for a while. I'll be back, but I don't know when. Go eat the damned gophers."

He fell into bed and lay awake most of the night, it seemed, till blasted by the alarm. He crawled out of bed, hoping to get on the road by six. Struggling into clothes he'd laid out the night before, he realized he could walk out the door in ten minutes if he didn't shave. He brushed his hair and slipped on an elastic to hold his ponytail, picked up his shoulder bag and the duffel he'd set by the door, turned out the lights, and left.

Hard Core Espresso opened early for commuters, so after dropping the long-suffered tax returns in a mailbox, he stopped for a coffee and muffin. He had an urge to tell someone, anyone, about his journey, and the blond barista named Sandy was the closest thing available. But she wasn't there. Instead, it was a balding youngish guy with bushy sideburns and a musical-comedy jauntiness. Albert decided just to get the coffee.

"Off on a trip?" asked the kid.

"How'd you guess?" On the verge of doing the dumb-est thing of his life, he didn't need to confide in some mouthy young jerk, but if he said it out loud, it might start to seem real. "Knoxville, Tennessee."

"Girlfriend?" The kid was a stand-up comic trying to be waggish about an old guy chasing cross-country tail. "Hey, start-ing out early, it must be something special."

Albert wouldn't take the bait. He wasn't in the mood for humor at his own expense from anyone but himself. He stared into space, paid, picked up his coffee, and then surprised himself by replying, "Well, that's a possibility." Give the kid something to chew on. He got into the dog-eared Honda and wheeled onto the highway, chewing on it himself.

He hadn't expected Jeanette to follow through on her promise to email, but she did. A week after the opening weekend of the show, he had called late at night, not knowing why, and asked her some deep question like, "How are things going?"

"Well, it's after midnight here."

"Oh. Yeah. Time zones. Sorry."

"No, that's okay. Well, it's not okay, but it's okay." A hesi-tation. "Well, as you know, I'm a compulsive liar, so if I say it's okay . . ."

"I get it. Okay. I'm sorry. So, as I was saying?"

"Not bad. Kind of a mess. Last-minute thing, really sad. Their costumer got fired—arrested, in fact—for downloading kiddie porn. Lovable guy, supposedly, so it's a heavy scene, and I've got three weeks till opening night, which is, guess what, another round of nuns and Nazis, can you believe it? Ye gods. But the kids are great, and I found a good coffee shop." A long silence. "Albert, you know, I never said, but I got hired because they liked my designs for *Galahad*."

"What if I come for a visit?" He blurted it out and let it sit there. Not a fair question to spring on her after midnight. "After it closes? Week or so?"

"Are you serious?"

"Maybe, I dunno, whatever. Sometimes I just say stuff."

It was the silence he'd expected, and it seemed natural somehow. *Yes* and *No* were both hard to pronounce.

"I wonder." She chose her words carefully. "I wonder what our conversation would be if we didn't have Sir Galahad's issues to deal with."

And he chose his: "I guess we might tell our grueling life histories, hopefully in short bursts. Or we could just sit there looking mysterious as hell. You do a fairly good job of that, in fact, though I could probably match you with a bit of practice." Was the breath he heard a gentle laugh? "Might be interesting to investigate."

"You don't really know much about me," she said. "Not sure I do either."

"Well, true, I have questions in that regard. But I've always been drawn to stories I don't understand."

"I'm a story?"

"Sorry, but it's a fact."

They stuttered around for five or ten minutes. Somehow the long silences seemed right. It occurred to him that he should have had more silences in the show.

"Okay, tell you what," she said finally, "let me see what's going on, how things are going, and I'll email."

"That works."

"So, well hey, how's it going? How's the show? Another weekend?"

"Not big audiences, but they like it. Very responsive, actually. Think I haven't quite found it yet, but I'm looking."

"You will."

"Promise?"

"If you can trust a chronic liar."

They chatted a bit more and rang off. End of story: he could feel it.

The next few days before the final weekend of the show the weather turned chill. He ran through his lines a couple of times, took the car in for a tire rotation and an MRI, made a stab at weeding the garden, and calculated the mileage to Knoxville, all the while imagining her struggle to tell him no with tactful finality. Thursday morning, her message came—*Sure, why not?*—and he had to think if he'd meant it.

There were several more emails about timing and logistics, and another phone call where it seemed that neither he nor Jeanette said more than a half dozen words. But that's all it took to launch this improbable trip to Knoxville. Forty hours' drive, according to Google, and what awaited him there? A woman who, as far as he could tell, was ten or fifteen years younger, cute in a hard-edged way, fumbling to find herself, pushy, and sporadically dishonest. Would he get there to find the portcullis closed and then drive back across Missouri, Nebraska, Colorado, and on, tasting the bitters every mile? Or would lightning strike, they'd dive into bed, and he'd wake to measure out life's tablespoons in Knoxville, Tennessee? Was Knoxville a fertile ground for *Galahad's Fool*? What would he do with the house and the bins of puppets and the feral cats? What about Lainie's ashes?

And what would he tell Mara—his daughter Mara—when she asked, "Wow, Papa, is that a jump or what?" He wondered if she and Alejandro would stay together. He wondered if they'd marry. He wondered—startling thought—if she'd bear a child. It was out of his hands. He could only wait for her news, and she could only wait for his.

For a journey that made no sense, he might as well take a route that made no sense. Northern I-80 he'd traveled too many times, and the southern I-40 trip kept him too long in California. Something drove him to cross the border fast. So it was across to the south of Lake Tahoe, US-50 through Nevada, hook up with I-70, and then drop south when he felt like it, if he ever did.

Crossing the rutted plains of Nevada felt like Galahad's stagger over the potholed asphalt stretch of a deserted shopping mall, though transmuted by the grand vision of crags and thunderheads, basin and range. Late at night in central Utah, he pulled off the highway to tilt the seat back and catch a few hours' nap. *They rode till evensong*, a phrase he remembered from somewhere. He rolled down the window to feel the desert chill, then closed it. Nothing to see but a thin crescent moon over a sea of blackness. He imagined, far out beyond the reach of sodium vapor lights, a webwork of dark arroyos flooded with dreams.

The absurdity of it. Six months spent on the fruitless search for a gilt-plated loving cup you could snag at Goodwill for a buck and a half. Did he ever believe in the Grail or even in the Quest? Yes, in fact. In the final performance, he felt he had touched it. But then there was the applause, the curtain calls, packing up, loading out, the long drive home. The memory trickled away.

Still, the image persisted, like a maddening itch in the epiglottis that no amount of swallowing could ease. Now, in the cavernous night, enclosed in the Honda's drafty womb, he heard the rising wind: the rush of a mother's inmost blood. A wisp of cloud drifted over the sliver of moon, and again he saw Galahad's eyes.

§

The Knight looks into the dead wife's waxen face. The onlookers see the puppet turn to the puppeteer, the two on either side of a razor-edged question mark. They stand like that. (Albert had never planned that moment.)

The hero turns back to his own raw world. The sun bears down on a cartoon waste, a jagged horizon, some scribbles that might be gawky trees or circling buzzards. He walks stiffly, bearing his wife's ragged corpse like a cast-off shirt.

He treks over a moonscape of craters. He stares at distant shapes that might be the silhouettes of history—Stonehenge, the Pyramids, the Parthenon—or only sandstone sculpted by wind and war. He grows older by the hour, mid-forties, fifties, sixties, and he feels his teeth crumble like shantytowns.

He sees flashes across the sky and the glare of a shadowless hell. Before him looms a castle. The buzzards are angels now, filling the sky, and he knows that here must reside the vessel holding a nectar of hope for humankind. He staggers toward its portal.

But it grows more distant as he nears it, and what he saw as a castle is only a peasant's shack. He tightens his grip on his beloved's remains, but he's holding only cobwebs dissolving in the wind. Figures surround him, dark against the sun. He halts. The scraps of his armor melt like candle wax and his skin pulls away. The fierce wind that he feels must be the pain and he the one who screams those impressive screams.

His filmy eyes go wider. A woman, her face a blur, steps out of the sun. The bone-thin silhouette of a peasant wife speaks in a gravelly whisper:

No food in the house, good sir, but here's a cup.

Her hand is outstretched, offering water to the haggard puppet, now only the shell of a head and a ragged tabard. Her lips never move.

> *Take it. I'm in mind of my own man, laid out bloody. He*
> *that gave me children and no one to give him water.*
> *Take it.*

Galahad clutches the cup. A plain tin cup, tinker's ware, empty. He looks up to the woman's hook nose, sunken cheeks, the wen on her lip, and into eternal eyes.

Drink your own tears.

His tears come then, flowing like flaxen hair. The battered cup brims. He drinks from the Grail.

§

That final night Albert let the cup and the puppet fall to the floor. He faced the thirty-odd people, reached out with Lainie's cupped hands—the gesture he'd known from the start—and offered drink.

In those few seconds, final audience, final show, he knew it was all illusion—his fingers to their hearts and theirs to his with the shock of epiphany—but an illusion deeply felt. He had touched belief. Belief wasn't a constant thing. It wasn't a state of bliss or the rock star surfing backward over his fans like seaweed on the breakers. It was a night mosquito buzzing in your ear. However you tried to slap and kill it, the damnable thing returned. You had to depend on that.

The desert cold stirred him from his nap. He stretched, jerked the seat upright, and dug into a sack on the passenger seat for a handful of almonds. Then he rousted the weary Honda and rumbled into Utah's darkness. Unseen terrain. A quest.

—Afterword—

We've worked together for fifty-seven years and slept in the same bed. We've written sixty-odd shows for ourselves and for other theatres. We've done thousands of tour performances all over the country. We've created thirteen puppet plays, from *Alice in Wonder* to *King Lear*. We're not Albert & Lainie Fisher—for the moment, neither of us is dead—but there are obvious commonalities. And now we're writing prose fiction.

While partnerships are common in scientific papers and filmscripts, they're infrequent in playwriting, rare in fiction. Supposedly, the novel is a vehicle for personal expression. Yet we feel that full-bodied individuality can manifest from close collaboration. No different than love-making: you can do it alone, or two people can do their own little rehearsed acts in tandem, but at its best it's a dialogue of perpetual discovery.

At any rate, co-creation has been our practice since our first interaction as theatre undergrads, translating a scene of *Woyzeck* from the German for a stage directing class. We're often asked how collaboration is possible in writing, and it's difficult to answer: try describing in detail how you breathe. No, it doesn't involve him typing on the left side of the keyboard, her on the right. Often it's a burst at the keyboard, followed by demon editing. Sometimes it involves taped improvisation, followed by radical rewrites. Sometimes it's writing separately, followed by selective cut-and-paste. Every project has its own *how*, but it always involves endless dialogue ranging from vast existential labyrinths to the placement of a comma.

For us, the heart of any writing isn't in the phrasings, the metaphors, or even the moments of epiphany. It's in the acuity and the gnarl of the questions that spur the journey—the prods that impel the surly mule to scramble up the mountain. What starts the journey? What sustains it? What guides it at the fork in the road?

Who can say what was happening in Heraclitus' life when he wrote, "The only constant is change"? For us, major changes—in work, goal, geography, love life, family, money—have loomed about every seven years. Loss of a mate hasn't happened, but it will, inevitably, and that question is part of what sparked *Galahad's Fool*. Albert is quite perceptive in sensing that, as he's authoring his characters, someone is authoring him. So it's possible that, as we chart Arthur's journey, some novelist on the astral plane—hopefully not a hack—is manipulating us. If so, that writer seems never quite satisfied, revises constantly, keeps dreaming up new twists to the plot, and revels in paradox.

—Conrad Bishop & Elizabeth Fuller

www.ingramcontent.com/pod-product-compliance
Lightning Source LLC
Chambersburg PA
CBHW061505050726

47593CB00002B/460